THE MYSTERY OF THE
BOULE CABINET

BURTON E. STEVENSON

(1872 ——)

A NOTE ON THE AUTHOR OF "THE MYSTERY OF THE BOULE CABINET"

BURTON Stevenson is one of the leading librarians in the United States, and surrounded constantly as he is by hundreds of thousands of books, it is understandable that he be best known for two formidable anthologies that are treasured the world over: "The Home Book of Verse" and "The Home Book of Familiar Quotations." Luckily for mystery fans, however, Mr. Stevenson gets tired every now and so often of the cloistered life, and by way of relaxation, dashes off detective stories that rate "triple A" every shot out of the bag. By far the best of them is "The Mystery of the Boule Cabinet."

Mr. Stevenson was born in Chillicothe, Ohio, and still makes his home there. He is a graduate of Princeton. His most recent literary labor is a new and amazingly complete edition of the "Home Book of Quotations."

The Ferret Library

BENNETT A. CERF, EDITOR

THE MYSTERY OF
THE BOULE CABINET

BY

BURTON E. STEVENSON

A. L. BURT COMPANY · PUBLISHERS · NEW YORK

To

𝔄. 𝔅. 𝔐.

Fellow-Sherlockian

CONTENTS

CONTENTS

THE MYSTERY OF THE
BOULE CABINET

CHAPTER I

"HELLO!" I said, as I took down the receiver of my desk 'phone in answer to the call.

"Mr. Vantine wishes to speak to you, sir," said the office-boy.

"All right," and I heard the snap of the connection.

"Is that you, Lester?" asked Philip Vantine's voice.

"Yes. So you're back again?"

"Got in yesterday. Can you come up to the house and lunch with me to-day?"

"I'll be glad to," I said, and meant it, for I liked Philip Vantine.

"I'll look for you, then, about one-thirty."

And that is how it happened that, an hour later, I was walking over toward Washington Square, just above which on the Avenue the old Vantine mansion stood. It was almost the last survival of the old régime, for the tide of business had long since overflowed from the neighbouring streets into the Avenue and swept its fashionable folk far uptown. Tall office and loft buildings had replaced the brownstone houses; only here and there did some old family hold on, like a sullen and desperate rear-guard defying the advancing enemy.

Philip Vantine was one of these.   He had been born in the house where he still lived, and declared that he would die there.   He had no one but himself to please in the matter, since he was unmarried and lived alone, and he mitigated the increasing roar and dust of the neighbourhood by long absences abroad.   It was from one of these that he had just returned.

I may as well complete this pencil-sketch. Vantine was about fifty years of age, the possessor of a comfortable fortune, something of a connoisseur in art matters, a collector of old furniture, a little eccentric — though now that I have written the word, I find that I must qualify it, for his only eccentricity was that he persisted, in spite of many temptations, in remaining a bachelor. Marriageable women had long since ceased to consider him; mothers with maturing daughters dismissed him with a despairing shake of the head. It was from them that he got the reputation of being an eccentric. But his reasons for remaining single in no way concerned his lawyers — a position which our firm had held for many years, and the active work of which had come gradually into my hands.

It was not very arduous work, consisting for the most part of the drawing of leases, the collecting of rents, the reinvestment of funds, and the adjustment of minor differences with tenants — all of which were left to our discretion. But occasionally it was necessary to consult our client on some matter of unusual importance, or to get his signature to some paper, and at such times I always enjoyed the talk which followed the completion of the business; for Vantine was a good talker, with a knowledge of men and of the world gained by much travel and by a detached, humourous and penetrating habit of mind.

He came forward to meet me, as I gave his man my hat and stick, and we shook hands heartily. I was glad to see him, and I think he was glad to see me. He was looking in excellent health, and brown from the voyage over.

" It's plain to see that the trip did you good," I said.

" Yes," he agreed; " I never felt more fit. But come along; we can talk at table. There's a little difficulty I want you to untangle for me."

I followed him upstairs to his study, where a table laid for two had been placed near a low window.

"I had lunch served up here," Vantine explained, as we sat down, "because this is the only really pleasant room left in the house. If I didn't own that plot of ground next door, this place would be impossible. As it is, I can keep the sky-scrapers far enough away to get a little sunshine now and then. I've had to put in an air filter, too, and double windows in the bedrooms to keep out the noise, but I dare say I can manage to hang on."

"I can understand how you'd hate to move into a new house," I said.

Vantine made a grimace.

"I couldn't endure a new house. I'm used to this one — I can find my way about in it; I know where things are. I've grown up here, you know, and as a man gets older, he values such associations more and more. Besides, a new house would mean new fittings. . ."

He paused and glanced about the room. Every piece of furniture in it was the work of a master.

" I suppose you found some new things while you were away?" I said. "You always do. Your luck's proverbial."

"Yes — and it's that I want to talk to you about. I brought back six or eight pieces; I'll show them to you presently. They are all pretty good, and one is a thing of beauty. It's more than that — it's an absolutely unique work of art. Only, unfortunately, it isn't mine."

" It isn't yours? "

" No, and I don't know whose it is. If I did, I'd go buy it. That's what I want you to do for me. It's a Boule cabinet — the most exquisite I ever saw."

"Where did it come from?" I questioned, more and more surprised.

" It came from Paris, and it was addressed to me. The only explanation I can think of is that my shippers in Paris made a mistake, sent me a cabinet belonging to some one else, and sent mine to the other person."

" You had bought one, then? "

"Yes, and it hasn't turned up. But beside this one, it's a mere daub. My man Parks got it through the customs yesterday. As there was a Boule cabinet on my manifest, the mistake wasn't discovered until the whole lot was brought up here and uncrated this morning."

"Weren't they uncrated in the customs?"

"No; I've been bringing things in for a good many years, and the customs people know I'm not a thief."

"That's quite a compliment," I pointed out. "They've been tearing things wide open lately."

"They've had a tip of some sort, I suppose. Come in," he added, answering a tap at the door.

The door opened and Vantine's man came in.

"A gentleman to see you, sir," he said, and handed Vantine a card.

Vantine looked at it a little blankly.

"I don't know him," he said. "What does he want?"

"He wants to see you, sir; very bad, I should say."

"What about?"

"Well, I couldn't just make out, sir; but it seems to be important."

"Couldn't make out? What do you mean, Parks?"

"I think he's a Frenchman, sir; anyway, he doesn't know much English He's not much of a looker, sir — I've seen hundreds like him sitting out in front of the cafés along the boulevards, taking all afternoon to drink a bock."

Vantine seemed struck by a sudden idea, and he looked at the card again. Then he tapped it meditatively on the table.

"Shall I show him out, sir?" asked Parks at last.

"No," said Vantine, after an instant's hesitation. "Tell him to wait," and he dropped the card on the table beside his plate.

"I tell you, Lester," he went on as Parks withdrew, "when I went downstairs this morning and saw that cabinet, I could hardly believe my eyes. I thought I knew furniture, but I hadn't any idea such a cabinet existed. The most beautiful I had ever seen is at the Louvre. It stands in the Salle Louis Fourteenth, to the left as you enter. It belonged to Louis himself. Of course I can't be certain without a careful examination, but I believe that cabinet, beautiful as it is, is merely the counterpart of this one."

He paused and looked at me, his eyes bright with the enthusiasm of the connoisseur.

"I'm not sure I understand your jargon," I said. "What do you mean by 'counterpart?'"

"Boule furniture," he explained, "is usually

of ebony inlaid with tortoise-shell, and incrusted
with arabesques in metals of various kinds. The
execution had to be very exact, and to get it
so, the artist clamped together two plates of equal
size and thickness, one of metal, the other of tortoise-shell, traced his design on the top one, and
then cut them both out together. The result was
two combinations, the original, with a tortoise-
shell ground and metal applications; and the
counterpart, a metal ground with tortoise-shell
applications. The original was really the one
which the artist designed and whose effects he
studied; the counterpart was merely a resultant
accident with which he was not especially concerned. Understand?"

"Yes, I think so," I said. "It's a good deal
as though Michael Angelo, when he made one of
his sketches, white on black, put a sheet of carbon
under his paper and made a copy at the same
time, black on white."

"Precisely. And it's the original which has
the real artistic value. Of course, the counterpart is often beautiful too, but in a much lower
degree."

"I can understand that," I said.

"And now, Lester," Vantine went on, his eyes

shining more and more, " if my supposition is correct — if the Grand Louis was content with the
counterpart of this cabinet for the long gallery
at Versailles, who do you suppose owned the original? "

I saw what he was driving at.

" You mean one of his mistresses? "

" Yes, and I think I know which one — it belonged to Madame de Montespan."

I stared at him in astonishment as he sat back
in his chair, smiling across at me.

" But," I objected, " you can't be sure —"

" Of course I'm not sure," he agreed quickly.
" That is to say, I couldn't prove it.   But there is
some — ah — contributory evidence, I think you
lawyers call it.   Boule and the Montespan were
in their glory at the same time, and I can imagine
that flamboyant creature commissioning the flamboyant artist to build her just such a cabinet."

" Really, Vantine," I exclaimed, " I didn't
know you were so romantic.   You quite take my
breath away."

He flushed a little at the words, and I saw how
deeply in earnest he was.

" The craze of the collector takes him a long
way sometimes," he said.   " But I believe I know

what I'm talking about. I am going to make a careful examination of the cabinet as soon as I can. Perhaps I'll find something — there ought to be a monogram on it somewhere. What I want you to do is to cable my shippers, Armand et Fils, 62 Rue du Temple, find out who owns this cabinet, and buy it for me."

"Perhaps the owner won't sell," I suggested.

"Oh yes, he will. Anything can be bought — for a price."

"You mean you're going to have this cabinet, whatever the cost?"

"I mean just that."

"But, surely, there's a limit.

"No, there isn't."

"At least you'll tell me where to begin," I said. "I don't know anything of the value of such things."

"Well," said Vantine, "suppose you begin at fifty thousand francs. We mustn't seem too eager. It's because I'm so eager, I want you to carry it through for me. I can't trust myself."

"And the other end?"

"There isn't any other end. Of course, strictly speaking, there is, because my money isn't unlimited; but I don't believe you will have to go over a million francs."

I gasped.

"You mean you're willing to give forty thousand dollars for this cabinet?"

Vantine nodded.

"Maybe a little more. If the owner won't accept that, you must let me know before you break off negotiations. I'm a little mad about it, I fancy — all collectors are a little mad. But I want that cabinet, and I'm going to have it."

I did not reply. I only looked at him. And he laughed as he caught my glance.

"I can see you share that opinion, Lester," he said. "You fear for me. I don't blame you — but come and see it."

He led the way out of the room and down the stairs; but when we reached the lower hall, he paused.

"Perhaps I'd better see my visitor first," he said. "You'll find a new picture or two over there in the music-room — I'll be with you in a minute."

I started on, and he turned through a doorway at the left.

An instant later, I heard a sharp exclamation; then his voice calling me.

" Lester! Come here! " he cried.

I ran back along the hall, into the room which he had entered. He was standing just inside the door.

" Look there," he said, with a queer catch in his voice, and pointed with a trembling hand to a dark object on the floor.

I moved aside to see it better. Then my heart gave a sickening throb, for the object on the floor was the body of a man.

CHAPTER II

IT needed but a glance to tell me that the man was dead. There could be no life in that livid face, in those glassy eyes.

"Don't touch him," I said, for Vantine had started forward. "It's too late."

I drew him back, and we stood for a moment shaken as one always is by sudden and unexpected contact with death.

"Who is he?" I asked, at last.

"I don't know," answered Vantine hoarsely. "I never saw him before." Then he strode to the bell and rang it violently. "Parks," he went on sternly, as that worthy appeared at the door, "what has been going on in here?"

"Going on, sir?" repeated Parks, with a look of amazement not only at the words but at the tone in which they were uttered. "I'm sure I don't know, sir. . ."

Then his glance fell upon the huddled body and he stopped short, his eyes staring, his mouth open.

"Well," said his master sharply. "Who is he? What is he doing here?"

"Why — why," stammered Parks thickly, "that's the man who was waiting to see you, sir."

"You mean he has been killed in this house?" demanded Vantine.

"He was certainly alive when he came in, sir," said Parks, recovering something of his self-possession. "Maybe he was just looking for a quiet place where he could kill himself. He seemed kind of excited."

"Of course," agreed Vantine, with a sigh of relief, "that's the explanation. Only I wish he had chosen some other place. I suppose we shall have to call the police, Lester?"

"Yes," I said, "and at once. Suppose you leave it to me. We'll lock up this room, and nobody must leave the house until the police arrive."

"Very well," assented Vantine, visibly relieved. "I'll see to that," and he hastened away, while I went to the 'phone, called up police headquarters, and told briefly what had happened.

Twenty minutes later, there was a ring at the bell, and Parks opened the door and admitted four men.

"Why, hello, Simmonds," I said, recognising

in the first one the detective-sergeant who had assisted in clearing up the Marathon mystery. And back of him was Coroner Goldberger, whom I had met in two previous cases, while the third countenance, looking at me with a quizzical smile, was that of Jim Godfrey, the *Record's* star reporter. The fourth man was a policeman in uniform, who, at a word from Simmonds, took his station at the door.

"Yes," said Godfrey, as we shook hands, "I happened to be talking to Simmonds when the call came in, and I thought I might as well come along. What is it?"

"Just a suicide, I think," and I unlocked the door into the room where the dead man lay.

Simmonds, Goldberger and Godfrey stepped inside. I followed and closed the door.

"Nothing has been disturbed," I said. "No one has touched the body."

Simmonds nodded, and glanced inquiringly about the room, but Godfrey's eyes, I noticed, were on the face of the dead man. Goldberger dropped to his knees beside the body, looked into the eyes and touched his fingers to the left wrist. Then he stood erect again and looked down at the body, and as I followed his gaze, I noted its attitude more accurately than I had done in the first shock of discovering it.

It was lying on its right side, half on its stomach, with its right arm doubled under it and its left hand clutching at the floor above its head. The knees were drawn up as though in a convulsion and the face was horribly contorted, with a sort of purple tinge under the skin, as though the blood had been suddenly congealed. The eyes were wide open, and their glassy stare added not a little to the apparent terror and suffering of the face. It was not a pleasant sight, and after a moment I turned my eyes away with a shiver of repugnance.

The coroner glanced at Simmonds.

"Not much question as to the cause," he said. "Poison of course."

"Of course," nodded Simmonds.

"But what kind?" asked Godfrey.

"It will take a post-mortem to tell that," and Goldberger bent for another close look at the distorted face. "I'm free to admit the symptoms aren't the usual ones."

Godfrey shrugged his shoulders.

"I should say not," he agreed, and turned away to an inspection of the room.

" What can you tell us about it, Mr. Lester? "
Goldberger questioned.

I told all I knew — how Parks had announced a
man's arrival, how Vantine and I had come downstairs together, how Vantine had called me, and
finally how Parks had identified the body as that
of the strange caller.

" Have you any theory about it? " Goldberger
asked.

" Only that the call was merely a pretext —
that what the man was really looking for was a
place where he could kill himself unobserved."

" How long a time elapsed after Parks announced the man before you and Mr. Vantine
came downstairs? "

" Half an hour, perhaps."

Goldberger nodded.

" Let's have Parks in," he said.

I opened the door and called to Parks, who was
sitting on the bottom step of the stair.

Goldberger looked him over carefully as he
stepped into the room, but there could be no two
opinions about Parks. He had been with Vantine
for eight or ten years, and the earmarks of the
competent and faithful servant were apparent all
over him.

" Do you know this man? " Goldberger asked, with a gesture toward the body.

" No, sir," said Parks.   " I never saw him till about an hour ago, when Rogers called me downstairs and said there was a man to see Mr. Vantine."

" Who is Rogers? "

" He's the footman, sir.   He answered the door when the man rang."

" Well, and then what happened? "

" I took his card up to Mr. Vantine, sir."

" Did Mr. Vantine know him? "

" No, sir; he wanted to know what he wanted."

" What *did* he want? "

" I don't know, sir; he couldn't speak English hardly at all — he was French, I think."

Goldberger looked down at the body again and nodded.

" Go ahead," he said.

"And he was so excited," Parks added, " that he couldn't remember what little English he did know."

" What made you think he was excited? "

" The way he stuttered, and the way his eyes glinted.   That's what makes me think he just came in here to kill himself quiet like—I shouldn't be surprised if you found that he'd escaped from somewhere. I had a notion to put him out without bothering Mr. Vantine — I wish now I had — but I took his card up, and Mr. Vantine said for him to wait; so I came downstairs again and showed the man in here and said Mr. Vantine would see him presently, and then Rogers and me went back to our lunch and we sat there eating till the bell rang, and I came in and found Mr. Vantine here."

" Do you mean to say that you and Rogers went away and left this stranger here by himself ? "

" The servants' dining-room is right at the end of the hall, sir. We left the door open so that we could see right along the hall, clear to the front door. If he'd come out into the hall, we'd have seen him."

" And he didn't come out into the hall while you were there ? "

" No, sir."

" Did anybody come in ? "

" Oh no, sir; the front door has a snap-lock. It can't be opened from the outside without a key."

" So you are perfectly sure that no one either

entered or left the house by the front door while you and Rogers were sitting there?"

"Nor by the back door either, sir; to get out the back way, you have to pass through the room where we were."

"Where were the other servants?"

"The cook was in the kitchen, sir. This is the housemaid's afternoon out."

The coroner paused. Godfrey and Simmonds had both listened to this interrogation, but neither had been idle. They had walked softly about the room, had looked through a door opening into another room beyond, had examined the fastenings of the windows, and had ended by looking minutely over the carpet.

"What is the room yonder used for?" asked Godfrey, pointing to the connecting door.

"It's a sort of store-room just now, sir," said Parks. "Mr. Vantine is just back from Europe, and we've been unpacking in there some of the things he bought while abroad."

"I guess that's all," said Goldberger, after a moment. "Send in Mr. Vantine, please."

Parks went out, and Vantine came in a moment later. He corroborated exactly the story told by Parks and myself, but he added one detail.

"Here is the man's card," he said, and held out a square of pasteboard.

Goldberger took the card, glanced at it, and passed it on to Simmonds.

"That don't tell us much," said the latter, and gave the card to Godfrey. I looked over his shoulder and saw that it contained a single engraved line:

M. Théophile d'Aurelle

"Except that he's French, as Parks suggested," said Godfrey. "That's evident, too, from the cut of his clothes."

"Yes, and from the cut of his hair," added Goldberger. "You say you didn't know him, Mr. Vantine?"

"I never before saw him, to my knowledge," answered Vantine. "The name is wholly unknown to me."

"Well," said Goldberger, taking possession of the card again and slipping it into his pocket, "suppose we lift him onto that couch by the window and take a look through his clothes."

The man was slightly built, so that Simmonds and Goldberger raised the body between them without difficulty and placed it on the couch. I saw Godfrey's eyes searching the carpet.

"What I should like to know," he said, after a moment, "is this: if this fellow took poison, what did he take it out of? Where's the paper, or bottle, or whatever it was?"

"Maybe it's in his hand," suggested Simmonds, and lifted the right hand, which hung trailing over the side of the couch.

Then, as he raised it into the light, a sharp cry burst from him.

"Look here," he said, and held the hand so that we all could see.

It was swollen and darkly discoloured.

"See there," said Simmonds, "something bit him," and he pointed to two deep incisions on the back of the hand, just below the knuckles, from which a few drops of blood had oozed and dried.

With a little exclamation of surprise and excitement, Godfrey bent for an instant above the injured hand. Then he turned and looked at us.

"This man didn't take poison," he said, in a low voice. "He was murdered!"

CHAPTER III

THE WOUNDED HAND

" HE was murdered!" repeated Godfrey, with conviction; and, at the words, we drew together a little, with a shiver of repulsion. Death is awesome enough at any time; suicide adds to its horror; murder gives it the final touch.

So we all stood silent, staring as though fascinated at the hand which Simmonds held up to us; at those tiny wounds encircled by discoloured flesh and with a sinister dash of clotted blood running away from them. Then Goldberger, taking a deep breath, voiced the thought which had sprung into my own brain.

" Why, it looks like a snake-bite!" he said, his voice sharp with astonishment.

And, indeed, it did. Those two tiny incisions, scarcely half an inch apart, might well have been made by a serpent's fangs.

The quick glance which all of us cast about the room was, of course, as involuntary as the chill which ran up our spines; yet Godfrey and I —

yes, and Simmonds — had the excuse that, once upon a time, we had had an encounter with a deadly snake which none of us was likely ever to forget. We all smiled a little sheepishly as we caught each other's eyes.

" No, I don't think it was a snake," said Godfrey, and again bent close above the hand. " Smell it, Mr. Goldberger," he added.

The coroner put his nose close to the hand and sniffed.

" Bitter almonds ! " he said.

" Which means prussic acid," said Godfrey, " and not snake poison." He fell silent a moment, his eyes on the swollen hand. The rest of us stared at it too; and I suppose all the others were labouring as I was with the effort to find some thread of theory amid this chaos. " It might, of course, have been self-inflicted," Godfrey added, quite to himself.

Goldberger sneered a little. No doubt he found the incomprehensibility of the problem rather trying to his temper.

" A man doesn't usually commit suicide by sticking himself in the hand with a fork," he said.

" No," agreed Godfrey blandly; " but I would point out that we don't know as yet that it *is* a case of suicide; and I'm quite sure that, whatever it may be, it isn't usual."

Goldberger's sneer deepened.

" Did any reporter for the *Record* ever find a case that *was* usual? " he queried.

It was a shrewd thrust, and one that Godfrey might well have winced under. For the *Record* theory was that nothing was news unless it was strange and startling, with the inevitable result that the *Record* reporters endeavoured to make everything strange and startling, to play up the outré details at the expense of the rest of the story, and even, I fear, to invent such details when none existed.

Godfrey himself had been accused more than once of a too-luxuriant imagination. It was, perhaps, a realisation of this which had persuaded him, years before, to quit the detective force and take service with the *Record*. What might have been a weakness in the first position, was a mighty asset in the latter one, and he had won an immense success.

Please understand that I set this down in no spirit of criticism. I had known Godfrey rather intimately ever since the days when we were thrown together in solving the Holladay case, and

I admired sincerely his ready wit, his quick insight, and his unshakable aplomb. He used his imagination in a way which often caused me to reflect that the police would be far more efficient if they possessed a dash of the same quality; and I had noticed that they were usually glad of his assistance, while his former connection with the force and his careful maintenance of the friendships formed at that time gave him an entrée to places denied to less-fortunate reporters. I had never known him to do a dishonourable thing — to fight for a cause he thought unjust, to print a fact given to him in confidence, or to make a statement which he knew to be untrue. Moreover, a lively sense of humour made him an admirable companion, and it was this quality, perhaps, which enabled him to receive Goldberger's thrust with a good-natured smile.

"We've got our living to make, you know," he said. "We make it as honestly as we can. What do *you* think, Simmonds?"

"I think," said Simmonds, who, if he possessed an imagination, never permitted it to be suspected, "that those little cuts on the hand are merely an accident. They might have been caused in half a dozen ways. Maybe he hit his hand on something when he fell; maybe he jabbed it on a buckle; maybe he had a boil on his hand and lanced it with his knife."

" What killed him, then? " Godfrey demanded.

" Poison — and it's in his stomach.   We'll find it there."

" How about the odour? " Godfrey persisted.

" He spilled some of the poison on his hand as he lifted it to his mouth.   Maybe he had those cuts on his hand and the poison inflamed them. Or maybe he's got some kind of blood disease."

Goldberger nodded his approval, and Godfrey smiled as he looked at him.

" It's easy to find explanations, isn't it? " he queried.

" It's a damned sight easier to find a natural and simple explanation," retorted Goldberger hotly, " than it is to find an unnatural and far-fetched one — such as how one man could kill another by scratching him on the hand.   I suppose you think this fellow was murdered?   That's what you said a minute ago."

" Perhaps I was a little hasty," Godfrey admitted, and I suspected that, whatever his thoughts, he had made up his mind to keep them to himself.   " I'm not going to theorise until I've got something to start with. The facts seem to point to suicide; but if he swallowed prussic acid, where's the bottle? He didn't swallow that too, did he?"

" Maybe we'll find it in his clothes," suggested Simmonds.

Thus reminded, Goldberger fell to work looking through the dead man's pockets. The clothes were of a cheap material and not very new, so that, in life, he must have presented an appearance somewhat shabby. There was a purse in the inside coat pocket containing two bills, one for ten dollars and one for five, and there were two or three dollars in silver and four five-centime pieces in a small coin purse which he carried in his trousers' pocket. The larger purse had four or five calling cards in one of its compartments, each bearing a different name, none of them his. On the back of one of them, Vantine's address was written in pencil.

There were no letters, no papers, no written documents of any kind in the pockets, the remainder of whose contents consisted of such odds and ends as any man might carry about with him — a cheap watch, a pen-knife, a half-empty packet of French tobacco, a sheaf of cigarette paper, four or five keys on a ring, a silk handkerchief, and perhaps some other articles which I have forgotten — but not a thing to assist in establishing his identity.

" We'll have to cable over to Paris," remarked Simmonds. " He's French, all right — that silk handkerchief proves it."

" Yes — and his best girl proves it, too," put in Godfrey.

" His best girl? "

For answer, Godfrey held up the watch, which he had been examining. He had opened the case, and inside it was a photograph — the photograph of a woman with bold, dark eyes and full lips and oval face — a face so typically French that it was not to be mistaken.

" A lady's maid, I should say," added Godfrey, looking at it again. " Rather good-looking at one time, but past her first youth, and so compelled perhaps to bestow her affections on a man a little beneath her — no doubt compelled also to contribute to his support in order to retain him. A woman with many pasts and no future —"

" Oh, come," broke in Goldberger impatiently, " keep your second-hand epigrams for the *Record*. What we want are facts."

Godfrey flushed a little at the words and laid down the watch.

"There is one fact which you have apparently overlooked," he said quietly, "but it proves beyond the shadow of a doubt that this fellow didn't drift in here by accident. He came here of intention, and the intention wasn't to kill himself, either."

"How do you know that?" demanded Goldberger incredulously.

Godfrey picked up the purse, opened it, and took out one of the cards.

"By this," he said, and held it up. "You have already seen what is written on the back of it — Mr. Vantine's name and the number of this house. That proves, doesn't it, that this fellow came to New York expressly to see Mr. Vantine?"

"Perhaps you think Mr. Vantine killed him," suggested Goldberger sarcastically.

"No," said Godfrey; "he didn't have time. You understand, Mr. Vantine," he added, smiling at that gentleman, who was listening to all this with perplexed countenance, "we are simply talking now about possibilities. You couldn't possibly have killed this fellow because Lester has testified that he was with you constantly from the moment this man entered the house until his body was found, with the exception of the few seconds which elapsed between the time you entered this room and the time he joined you here, summoned by your cry. So you are out of the running."

"Thanks," said Vantine drily.

"I suppose, then, you think it was Parks," said Goldberger.

"It may quite possibly have been Parks," agreed Godfrey gravely.

"Nonsense!" broke in Vantine impatiently. "Parks is as straight as a string — he's been with me for eight years."

"Of course it's nonsense," assented Goldberger. "It's nonsense to say that he was killed by anybody. He killed himself. We'll learn the cause when we identify him — jealousy maybe, or maybe just hard luck — he doesn't look affluent."

"I'll cable to Paris," said Simmonds. "If he belongs there, we'll soon find out who he is."

"You'd better call an ambulance and have him taken to the morgue," went on Goldberger. "Somebody may identify him there. There'll be

a crowd to-morrow, for of course the papers will
be full of this affair —"

"The *Record,* at least, will have a very full
account," Godfrey assured him.

"And I'll call the inquest for the day after,"
Goldberger continued. "I'll send my physician
down to make a post-mortem right away. If
there's any poison in this fellow's stomach, we'll
find it."

Godfrey did not speak, but I knew what was
in his mind. He was thinking that, if such poison
existed, the vessel which had contained it had not
yet been found. The same thought, no doubt, occurred to Simmonds, for after ordering the
policeman in the hall to call the ambulance, he
returned and began a careful search of the room,
using his electric torch to illumine every shadowed
corner. Godfrey devoted himself to a similar
search, but both were without result. Then Godfrey made a minute inspection of the injured hand,
while Goldberger looked on with ill-concealed
impatience, and finally he moved toward the
door.

"I think I'll be going," he said. "But I'm
interested in what your physician will find, Mr.
Coroner."

"He'll find poison, all right," asserted Goldberger, with decision.

"Perhaps he will," admitted Godfrey.
"Strange things happen in this world. Will you
be at home to-night, Lester?"

"Yes, I expect to be," I answered.

"You're still at the Marathon?"

"Yes," I said; "suite fourteen."

"Perhaps I'll drop around to see you," he said,
and a moment later we heard the door close behind him as Parks let him out.

"Godfrey's a good man," said Goldberger,
"but he's too romantic. He looks for a mystery
in every crime, whereas most crimes are merely
plain, downright brutalities. Take this case.
Here's a man kills himself, and Godfrey wants us
to believe that death resulted from a scratch on
the hand. Why, there's no poison on earth would
kill a man as quick as that — for he must have
dropped dead before he could get out of the room
to summon help. If it was prussic acid, he swallowed it. Remember, he wasn't in this room
more than fifteen or twenty minutes, and he was
quite dead when Mr. Vantine found him. Men
don't die as easily as all that — not from a scratch
on the hand. They don't die easily at all. It's

astonishing how much it takes to kill a man —
how the spirit, or whatever you choose to call it,
clings to the body."

"How do you explain the address on the card,
Mr. Goldberger?" I asked.

"My theory is that this fellow really had some
business with Mr. Vantine; probably he wanted
to borrow some money, or ask for help; and then,
while he was waiting, he suddenly gave the thing
up and killed himself. The address has no bearing whatever that I can see on the question of
suicide. And I'll say this, Mr. Lester, if this
isn't suicide, it's the strangest case I ever had
anything to do with."

"Yes," I agreed, "if it isn't suicide, we come
to a blank wall right away."

"That's it," and Goldberger nodded emphatically. "Here's the ambulance," he added,
as the bell rang.

The bearers entered with the stretcher, placed
the body on it, and carried it away. Goldberger
paused to gather up the articles he had taken from
the dead man's pockets.

"You gentlemen will have to give your testi-
mony at the inquest," he said. "So will Parks
and Rogers. It will be day after to-morrow,

probably at ten o'clock, but I'll notify you of the hour."

"Very well," I said; "we'll be there," and Goldberger bade us good-bye and left the house. "And now," I added to Vantine, "I must be getting back to the office. They'll be asking the police to look for me next. Man alive!" and I glanced at my watch, "it's after four o'clock."

"Too late for the office," said Vantine. "Better come upstairs and have a drink. Besides, I want to talk with you."

"At least I'll let them know I'm still alive," I said, and I called up the office and allayed any anxiety that may have been felt there concerning me. I must admit that it did not seem acute.

"I feel the need of a bracer after all this excitement," Vantine remarked as he opened the cellarette. "Help yourself. I dare say you're used to this sort of thing —"

"Finding dead men lying around?" I queried with a smile. "No — it's not so common as you seem to think."

"Tell me, Lester," and he looked at me earnestly, "do you think that poor devil came in here just to get a chance to kill himself quietly?"

"No, I don't," I said.

" Then what did he come in for? "

" I think Goldberger's theory a pretty good one — that he had heard of you as a generous fellow and came in here to ask help; and while he was waiting, suddenly gave it up —"

" And killed himself? " Vantine completed.

I hesitated. I was astonished to find, at the back of my mind, a growing doubt.

" See here, Lester," Vantine demanded, " if he didn't kill himself, what happened to him? "

" Heaven only knows," I answered in despair. " I've been asking myself the same question, without finding a reasonable answer to it. As I said to Goldberger, it's a blank wall. But if anybody can see through it, Jim Godfrey can."

Vantine seemed deeply perturbed. He took a turn or two up and down the room, then stopped in front of me and looked me earnestly in the eye.

" Tell me, Lester," he said, " do you believe that theory of Godfrey's — that that insignificant wound on the hand caused death? "

" It seems absurd, doesn't it? But Godfrey is a sort of genius at divining such things."

" Then you *do* believe it? "

I asked myself the same question before I answered.

"Yes, I do," I said finally.

Vantine walked up and down the room again, his eyes on the floor, his brows contracted.

"Lester," he said at last, "I have a queer feeling that the business which brought this man here in some way concerned the Boule cabinet I was telling you about. Perhaps it belonged to him."

"Hardly," I protested, recalling his shabby appearance.

"At any rate, I remember, as I was looking at his card, that some such thought occurred to me. It was for that reason I told Parks to ask him to wait."

"It's possible, of course," I admitted. "But that wouldn't explain his excitement. And that reminds me," I added, "I haven't sent off that cable."

"Any time to-night will do. It will be delivered in the morning. But you haven't seen the cabinet yet. Come down and look at it."

He led the way down the stair. Parks met us in the lower hall.

"There's a delegation of reporters outside, sir," he said. "They say they've got to see you."

Vantine made a movement of impatience.

"Tell them," he said, "that I positively refuse to see them or to allow my servants to see
them. Let them get their information from the
police."

"Very well, sir," said Parks, and turned away
grinning.

Vantine passed on through the ante-room in
which we had found the body of the unfortunate
Frenchman, and into the room beyond. Five or
six pieces of furniture, evidently just unpacked,
stood there, but, ignorant as I am of such things,
he did not have to point out to me the Boule cabinet. It dominated the room, much as Madame
de Montespan, no doubt, dominated the court at
Versailles.

I looked at it for some moments, for it was certainly a beautiful piece of work, with a wealth
of inlay and incrustation little short of marvellous. But I may as well say here that I never
really appreciated it. The florid styles of the
Fourteenth and Fifteenth Louis are not at all to
my taste, and I am too little of a connoisseur to
admire a beauty which has no personal appeal for
me. So I am afraid that Vantine found me a
little cold.

Certainly there was nothing cold about the way

he regarded it. His eyes gleamed with a strange fire as he looked at it; he ran his fingers over the inlay with a touch almost reverent; he pulled out for me the little drawers with much the same air that another friend of mine takes down his Kilmarnock Burns from his bookshelves; he pointed out to me the grace of its curves in the same tone that one uses to discuss the masterpiece of a great artist. And then, finding no echo to his enthusiasm, he suddenly stopped.

"You don't seem to care for it," he said, looking at me.

"That's my fault and not the fault of the cabinet," I pointed out. "I'm not educated up to it; I'm too little of an artist, perhaps."

He was flushed, as a man would be should another make a disparaging remark about his wife, and he led the way from the room at once.

"Remember, Lester," he said a little sternly, pausing with his hand on the front door, "there is to be no foolishness about securing that cabinet for me. Don't you let it get away. I'm in deadly earnest."

"I won't let it get away," I promised. "Perhaps it's just as well I'm not over-enthusiastic about it."

"Let me know as soon as you have any news," he said, and opened the door for me.

I had intended walking home, but as I turned up the Avenue, I met sweeping down it a flood of girls just released from the workshops of the neighbourhood. I struggled against it for a few moments, then gave it up, hailed a taxi, and settled back against the cushions with a sigh of relief. I was glad to be out of Vantine's house; something there oppressed me. Was Vantine quite normal, I wondered? Could any man be normal who was willing to pay forty thousand dollars for a piece of furniture? Especially a man who could not afford such extravagance? I knew the size of Vantine's fortune; it was large, but forty thousand dollars represented a considerable fraction of a year's income. And then I smiled to myself. Of course Vantine had been jesting when he named that limit. The cabinet could be bought for a tenth of it at the most. And still smiling, I left the taxi, paid the driver, and mounted to my rooms.

CHAPTER IV

THE THUNDERBOLT

IT was about eight o'clock that evening that Godfrey tapped at my door, and when I let him in I could tell by the way his eyes were shining that he had some news.

" I can't stay long," he said. " I've got to get down to the office and put the finishing touches on that story;" but nevertheless he filled his pipe from the tobacco jar I pushed toward him and sank into the chair opposite my own.

I knew Godfrey, so I waited patiently until the pipe was going nicely, then —

Well? " I asked.

' It's like old times, isn't it, Lester? " and he smiled across at me. " How many conferences have we had in this room? How many pounds of your tobacco have I made away with? "

" Not half enough recently," I said. " You haven't been here for months."

" I'm sure to drift back sooner or later, because you seem to have a knack of getting in on the interesting cases. And I want to say this, Lester, that of all I ever had, not one has promised better than this one does. If it only keeps up — but one mustn't expect too much! "

" You've been working on it, of course? "

" I haven't been idle, and just now I'm feeling rather pleased with myself. The coroner's physician finished his post-mortem half an hour or so ago."

" Well? " I said again.

" The stomach was absolutely normal. It showed no trace of poison of any kind."

He stretched himself, lay back in his chair, sent a smoke-ring circling toward the ceiling, and watched it, smiling absently.

" Rather a facer for our friend Goldberger," he added, after a minute.

" What's the matter with Goldberger? He seemed rather peeved with you this afternoon."

" No wonder. He's Grady's man and we're after Grady. Grady isn't fit to head the detective bureau — he got the job through his pull with Tammany — he's stupid and I suspect he's crooked. The *Record* says he has got to go."

" So of course he *will* go," I commented smiling.

" He certainly will," assented Godfrey seriously, " and that before long. But meanwhile it's a little difficult for me, because his people don't know which way to jump. Once he's out, everything will be serene again."

I wasn't interested in Grady, so I came back to the case in hand.

"Look here, Godfrey," I said, "if it wasn't poison, what was it?"

"But it *was* poison."

"Inserted at the hand?"

He nodded.

"Goldberger says there's no poison known which could be used that way and which would act so quickly."

"Goldberger is right in that," agreed Godfrey; "but there's a poison unknown that will — because it did."

"It wasn't a snake bite?"

"Oh, no; snake poison wouldn't kill a man that quickly — not even a fer-de-lance. That fellow practically dropped where he was struck."

"Then what was it?"

Godfrey was sitting erect again. He was not smiling now. His face was very stern.

"That is what I am going to find out, Lester," he said; "that is the problem I've set myself to solve — and it's a pretty one. There is one thing certain — that fellow was killed by some agency outside himself.   In some way, a drop or two of poison was introduced into his blood by an instrument something like a hypodermic needle; and that poison was so powerful that almost instantly it caused paralysis of the heart.   After all, that isn't so remarkable as it might seem.   The blood in the veins of the hand would be carried back to the heart in four or five seconds."

" But you've already said there's no poison so powerful as all that."

" I said we didn't know of any.   I wouldn't be so sure that Catherine de Medici didn't."

" What has Catherine de Medici to do with it ? "

" Nothing — except that what has been done may always be done again.   Those old stories are, no doubt, exaggerated; but it seems fairly certain that the Queen of Navarre was killed with a pair of poisoned gloves, the Duc d'Anjou with the scent of a poisoned rose, and the Prince de Porcian with the smoke of a poisoned lamp.   This case isn't as extraordinary as those."

" No," I agreed, and fell silent, shivering a little, for there is something horrible and revolting about the poisoner.

" After all," went on Godfrey at last, " there
is one thing that neither you nor I nor any reasonable man can believe, and that is that this Frenchman came from heaven knows where — from
Paris, perhaps — with Vantine's address in his
pocket, and hunted up the house and made his
way into it simply to kill himself there.   He had
some other object, and he met his death while
trying to accomplish it."

" Have you found out who he is ? "

" No; he's not registered at any of the hotels;
the French consul never heard of him; he belongs
to none of the French societies; he's not known
in the French quarter.   He seems to have
dropped from the clouds.   We've cabled our
Paris office to look him up; we may hear from
there to-night.   But even if we discover the identity of Théophile d'Aurelle, it won't help us any."

" Why not? " I demanded.

" Because it is evident that that isn't his name."

" Go ahead and tell me, Godfrey," I said, as
he looked at me, smiling.   " I don't see it."

" Why, it's plain enough.   He had five cards
in his pocket, no two alike.   The sixth, selected
probably at random, he had sent up to Vantine."

I saw it then of course; and I felt a good deal

as the Spanish savants must have felt when Co-
lumbus stood the egg on end. Godfrey smiled
again at my expression.

"The real d'Aurelle, whoever he may turn out
to be, may be able to help us," he added. "If
he can't, we may learn something from the Paris
police. The dead man's Bertillon measurements
have been cabled over to them. Even that won't
help if he has never been arrested. And of
course we can't get at motives until we find out
something about him."

"But Godfrey," I said, "suppose you knew
who he was and what he wanted with Vantine —
suppose you could make a guess at who killed him
and why — how was it done? That is what
stumps me. How was it done?"

"Ah!" agreed Godfrey. "That's it! How
was it done? I told you it was a pretty case,
Lester. But wait till we hear from Paris."

"That reminds me," I said, sitting up suddenly,
"I've got to cable to Paris myself on some business for Mr. Vantine."

"Not connected with this affair?"

"Oh, no; his shippers over there sent him a
piece of furniture that doesn't belong to him. He
asked me to straighten the matter out."

I rang for the hall-boy, asked for a cable-blank, and sent off a message to Armand & Son, telling them of the mistake and asking them to cable the name of the owner of the cabinet now in Mr. Vantine's possession. Godfrey sat smoking reflectively while I was thus engaged, staring straight before him with eyes that saw nothing; but as I sat down again and took up my pipe, ready to continue the conversation, he gave himself a sort of shake, put on his hat, and got to his feet.

" I must be moving along," he said. " There's no use sitting here theorising until we have some sort of foundation to build on."

" Goldberger was right in one thing," I remarked. " He pointed out, after you left, that most crimes are not romances, but mere brutalities. Perhaps this one — "

The ringing of my telephone stopped me.

" Hello," I said, taking down the receiver.

" Is that you, Mr. Lester? " asked a voice.

" Yes."

" This is Parks," and I suddenly realised that his voice was unfamiliar because it was hoarse and quivering with emotion. " Could you come down to the house right away, sir? "

"Why, yes," I said wonderingly, "if it's important. Does Mr. Vantine need me?"

"We all need you!" said the voice, and broke into a dry sob. "For God's sake, come quick, Mr. Lester!"

"All right," I said without further parley, for evidently he had lost his self-control. "Something has happened down at Vantine's," I added to Godfrey, as I hung up the receiver. "Parks seems to be scared to death. He wants me to come down right away," and I reached for my hat and coat.

"Shall I come, too?" asked Godfrey.

Even under the stress of the moment, I could not but smile at the question and at the tone in which it was uttered.

"Perhaps you'd better," I agreed. "It sounded pretty serious."

We went down together in the elevator, and three minutes later we had hailed a taxi and were speeding eastward toward the Avenue. It had started to drizzle and the asphalt shone like a black mirror, dancing with the lights along either side. The streets were almost empty, for the theatre-crowd had passed, and as we reached the Avenue and turned down-town, the driver pushed

up his spark and we hurtled along toward
Fourteenth street at a speed which made me think
of the traffic regulations. But no policeman interfered, and five minutes later we drew up before
the Vantine place.

Parks must have been on the front steps looking for me, for he came running down them almost before the car had stopped. I caught a
glimpse of his face under the street lights, as I
turned from paying the driver, and it fairly
startled me.

" Is it you, Mr. Lester? " he gasped. " Good
God, but I'm glad you're here —"

I caught him by the arm.

" Steady, man," I said. " Don't let yourself
go to pieces. Now — what has happened? "

He seemed to take a sort of desperate grip of
himself.

" I'll show you, sir," he said, and ran up the
steps and along the hall to the door of the ante-
room where we had found the Frenchman's body.
" In there, sir! " he sobbed. " In there! " and
clung to the wall as I opened the door and stepped
inside.

The room was ablaze with light and for an
instant my eyes were so dazzled that I could dis-

tinguish nothing.   Dimly I saw Godfrey spring
forward and drop to his knees.

Then my eyes cleared, and I saw, on the very
spot where d'Aurelle had died, another body —
or was it the same, brought back that the tragedy
of the afternoon might, in some mysterious way,
be re-enacted?

I remember bending over and peering into the
face —

It was the face of Philip Vantine.

A minute must have passed as I stood there
dazed and shaken.   I was conscious, in a way,
that Godfrey was examining him.   Then I heard
his voice.

"He's dead," he said.

Then there was an instant's silence.

"Lester, look here!" cried Godfrey's voice,
sharp, insistent.   "For God's sake, look here!"

Godfrey was kneeling there holding something
toward me.

"Look here!" he cried again.

It was the dead man's hand he was holding;
the right hand; a swollen and discoloured hand.
And on the back of it, just below the knuckles,
were two tiny wounds from which a few drops of
blood had trickled.

And as I stared at this ghastly sight, unable to believe my eyes, I heard a choking voice behind me saying over and over again:

"It was that woman done it! It was that woman done it! Damn her! It was that woman done it!"

CHAPTER V

GRADY TAKES A HAND

I HAVE no very clear remembrance of what happened after that. The shock was so great that I had just strength enough to totter to a chair and drop into it, and sit there staring vaguely at that dark splotch on the carpet. I told myself that I was the victim of a dreadful nightmare; that all this was the result of over-wrought nerves and that I should wake presently. No doubt I had been working too hard. I needed a vacation — well, I would take it . . .

And all the time I knew that it was not a nightmare, but grim reality; that Philip Vantine was dead — killed by a woman. Who had told me that? And then I remembered the sobbing voice . . .

Two or three persons came into the room — Parks and the other servants, I suppose; I heard Godfrey's voice giving orders; and finally someone held a glass to my lips and commanded me to drink. I did so mechanically; coughed, spluttered, was conscious of a grateful warmth, and drank

eagerly again. And then I saw Godfrey standing over me.

"Feel better?" he asked.

I nodded.

"I don't wonder it knocked you out," he went
on. "I'm feeling shaky myself. I had them call
Vantine's physician — but he can't do anything."

"He's dead, then?" I murmured, my eyes on
that dark and crumpled object which had been
Philip Vantine.

"Yes — just like the other."

Then I remembered, and I caught his arm and
drew him down to me.

"Godfrey," I whispered, "whose voice was it
— or did I dream it — something about a
woman?"

"You didn't dream it — it was Rogers — he's
almost hysterical. We'll get the story as soon as
he quiets down."

Someone called him from the door and he
turned away, leaving me staring blankly at nothing. So there had been a woman in Vantine's life!
Perhaps that was why he had never married.
What ugly skeleton was to be dragged from its
closet?

But if a woman killed Vantine, the same woman

also killed d'Aurelle. Where was her hiding-place? From what ambush did she strike?

I glanced about the room, as a tremor of horror seized me. I arose, shaking, from the chair and groped my way toward the door. Godfrey heard me coming, swung around, and with one glance at my face, came to me and caught me by the arms.

"What is it, Lester?" he asked.

"I can't stand it here," I gasped. "It's too horrible!"

"Don't think about it. Come out here and have another drink."

He led me into the hall, and a second glass of brandy gave me back something of my self-control. I was ashamed of my weakness, but when I glanced at Godfrey, I saw how white his face was.

"Better take a drink yourself," I said.

I heard the decanter rattle on the glass.

"I don't know when I have been so shaken," he said, setting the glass down empty. "It was so gruesome — so unexpected — and then Rogers carrying on like a madman. Ah, here's the doctor," he added, as the front door opened and Parks showed a man in.

I knew Dr. Hughes, of course, returned his nod.

and followed him and Godfrey into the ante-room. But I had not yet sufficiently recovered to do more than sit and stare at him as he knelt beside the body and assured himself that life had fled. Then I heard Godfrey telling him all we knew, while Hughes listened with incredulous face.

"But it's absurd, you know!" he protested, when Godfrey had finished. "Things like this don't happen here in New York. In Florence, perhaps, in the Middle Ages; but not here in the twentieth century!"

"I can scarcely believe my own senses," Godfrey agreed. "But I saw the Frenchman lying here this afternoon; and now here's Vantine."

"On the same spot?"

"As nearly as I can tell."

"And killed in the same way?"

"Killed in precisely the same way."

Hughes turned back to the body again, and looked long and earnestly at the injured hand.

"What sort of instrument made this wound, would you say, Mr. Godfrey?" he questioned at last.

"A sharp instrument, with two prongs. My theory is that the prongs are hollow, like a hypo-dermic needle, and leave a drop or two of poison

at the bottom of the wound.   You see a vein has
been cut."

"Yes," Hughes assented.   "It would scarcely
be possible to pierce the hand here without striking a vein.   One of the prongs would be sure to
do it."

"That's the reason there are two of them, I
fancy."

"But you are, of course, aware that no poison
exists which would act so quickly?" Hughes inquired.

Godfrey looked at him strangely.

"You yourself mentioned Florence a moment
ago," he said.   "You meant, I suppose, that such
a poison did, at one time, exist there?"

"Something of the sort, perhaps," agreed
Hughes.   "The words were purely instinctive,
but I suppose some such thought was running
through my head."

"Well, the poison that existed in Florence five
centuries ago, exists here to-day.   There's the
proof of it," and Godfrey pointed to the body.

Hughes drew a deep breath of wonder and
horror.

"But what sort of devilish instrument is it?"
he cried, his nerves giving way for an instant, his

voice mounting shrilly. "Above all, who wields it?"

He stared about the room as though half-expecting to see some mighty and remorseless arm poised, ready to strike. Then he shook himself together.

"I beg pardon," he said, mopping the sweat from his face; "but I'm not used to this sort of thing; and I'm frightened — yes, I really believe I'm frightened," and he laughed a little unsteady laugh.

"So am I," said Godfrey; "so is Lester; so is everybody. You needn't be ashamed of it."

"What frightens me," went on Hughes, evidently studying his own symptoms, "is the mystery of it — there is something supernatural about it — something I can't understand. How does it happen that each of the victims is struck on the right hand? Why not the left hand? Why the hand at all?"

Godfrey answered with a despairing shrug.

"That is what we've got to find out," he said.

"We shall have to call in the police," suggested Hughes. "Maybe they can solve it."

Godfrey smiled a little sceptical smile, quickly suppressed.

"At least they will have to be given the chance," he agreed. "Shall I attend to it?"

"Yes," said Hughes; "and you would better do it right away. The sooner they get here the better."

"Very well," assented Godfrey, and left the room.

Hughes sat down heavily on the couch near the window, and mopped his face again with a shaking hand. Death he was accustomed to — but death met decently in bed and resulting from some understood cause. Death in this horrible and mysterious form shook him; he could not understand it, and his failure to understand appalled him. He was a physician; it was his business to understand; and yet here was death in a form as mysterious to him as to the veriest layman. It compelled him to pause and take stock of himself — always a disconcerting process to the best of us!

That was a trying half hour. Hughes sat on the couch breathing heavily, staring at the floor, perhaps passing his own ignorance in review, perhaps wondering if he had always been right in prescribing this or that. As for me, I was thinking of my dead friend. I remembered Philip

Vantine as I had always known him — a kindly, witty, cultured gentleman. I could see his pleasant eyes looking at me in friendship, as they had looked a few hours before; I could hear his voice, could feel the clasp of his hand. That such a man should be killed like this, struck down by a mysterious assassin, armed with a poisoned weapon . . . ´

A woman! Always my mind came back to that. A woman! Poison was a woman's weapon. But who was she? How had she escaped? Where had she concealed herself? How was she able to strike so surely? Above all, why should she have chosen Philip Vantine, of all men, for her victim — Philip Vantine, who had never injured any woman — and then I paused. For I realised that I knew nothing of Vantine except what he had chosen to tell me. Parks would know. And then I shrank from the thought. Must we probe that secret? Must we compel a man to betray his master?

My face was burning. No, we could not do that — that would be abominable . . .

The door opened and Godfrey came in. This time, he was not alone. Simmonds and Goldberger followed him, and their faces showed that they were as shaken and nonplussed as I. There was a third man with them whom I did not know; but I soon found out that it was Freylinghuisen, the coroner's physician.

They all looked at the body, and Freylinghuisen knelt beside it and examined the injured hand; then he sat down by Dr. Hughes, and they were soon deep in a low-toned conversation whose subject I could guess. I could also guess what Simmonds and Godfrey were talking about in the farther corner; but I could not guess why Goldberger, instead of getting to work, should be walking up and down, pulling impatiently at his moustache and glancing at his watch now and then. He seemed to be waiting for some one, but not until twenty minutes later did I suspect who it was. Then the door opened again to admit a short, heavy-set man, with florid face, stubbly black moustache, and little, close-set eyes, preternaturally bright. He glanced about the room, nodded to Goldberger, and then looked inquiringly at me.

" This is Mr. Lester, Commissioner Grady," said Goldberger, and I realised that the chief of the detective bureau had come up from headquarters to take personal charge of the case.

"Mr. Lester is Mr. Vantine's attorney," the coroner added.

"Glad to know you, Mr. Lester," said Grady shortly.

"And now I guess we're ready to begin," went on the coroner.

"Not quite," said Grady grimly. "We'll excuse all reporters first," and he looked across at Godfrey, his face darkening.

I felt my own face flushing and started to protest, but Godfrey silenced me with a little gesture.

"It's all right, Lester," he said. "Mr. Grady is quite within his rights. I'll withdraw — until he sends for me."

"You'll have a long wait, then!" retorted Grady, with a sarcastic laugh.

"The longer I wait, the worse it will be for you, Mr. Grady," said Godfrey quietly, opened the door and closed it behind him.

Grady stared after him for a moment in crimson amazement. Then, mastering himself with an effort, he turned to the coroner.

"All right, Goldberger," he said, and sat down to watch the proceedings.

A very few minutes sufficed for Hughes and Freylinghuisen and me to tell all we knew of this

tragedy and of the one which had preceded it.
Grady seemed already acquainted with the details of d'Aurelle's death, for he listened without
interrupting, only nodding from time to time.

" You've got a list of the servants here, of
course, Simmonds," he said, when we had finished the story.

" Yes, sir," and Simmonds handed it to him.

" H-m," said Grady, as he glanced it over.
" Five of 'em.   Know anything about 'em? "

" They've all been with Mr. Vantine a long
time, sir," replied Simmonds.   " So far as I've
been able to judge, they're all right."

" Which one of 'em found Vantine's body? "

" Parks, I think," I said.   " It was he who
called me."

" Better have him in," said Grady, and doubled
up the list and slipped it into his pocket.

Parks came in looking decidedly shaky, but
answered Grady's questions clearly and concisely.
He told first of the events of the afternoon, and
then passed on to the evening.

" Mr. Vantine had dinner at home, sir," he
said. " It was served, I think, about seven o'clock.
He must have finished a little before eight.
I didn't see him, for I was straightening things

around up in his room and putting his clothes away. But he told Rogers —"

"Never mind what he told Rogers," broke in Grady. "Just tell us what you know."

"Very well, sir," said Parks submissively. "I had a lot of work to do — we just got back from Europe yesterday, you know — and I kept on, putting things in their places and straightening around, and it must have been half-past eight when I heard Rogers yelling for me. I thought the house was on fire, and I came down in a hurry. Rogers was standing out there in the hall, looking like he'd seen a ghost. He kind of gasped and pointed to this room, and I looked in and saw Mr. Vantine lying there —"

His voice choked at the words, but he managed to go on after a moment.

"Then I telephoned for Mr. Lester," he added, "and that's all I know."

"Very well," said Grady. "That's all for the present. Send Rogers in."

Rogers's face, as he entered the room, gave me a kind of shock, for it was that of a man on the verge of hysteria. He was a man of about fifty, with iron-grey hair and a smooth-shaven face, ordinarily ruddy with health. But now his face was livid, his cheeks lined and shrunken, his eyes blood-shot and staring. He reeled rather than walked into the room, one hand clutching at his throat as though he were choking.

"Get him a chair," said Grady, and Simmonds brought one forward and remained standing beside it. "Now, my man," Grady continued, "you'll have to brace up. What's the matter with you, anyhow? Didn't you ever see a dead man before?"

"It ain't that," gasped Rogers. "It ain't that — though I never saw a murdered man before."

"What?" demanded Grady, sharply. "Didn't you see that fellow this afternoon?"

"That was different," Rogers moaned. "I didn't know him. Besides, I thought he'd killed himself. We all thought so."

"And you don't think Vantine did?"

"I know he didn't," and Rogers's voice rose to a shrill scream. "It was that woman done it! Damn her! She done it! I knowed she was up to some crooked work when I let her in!"

CHAPTER VI

THE WOMAN IN THE CASE

IT was coming now; the secret, however sordid, however ugly, was to be unveiled. I saw Grady's face set in hard lines; I could hear the stir of interest with which the others leaned forward . . .

Grady took a flask from his pocket and opened it.

"Take a drink of this," he said, and placed it in Rogers's hand.

I could hear the mouth of the flask clattering against his teeth, as he put it eagerly to his mouth and took three or four long swallows.

"Thank you, sir," he said more steadily, and handed the flask back to its owner. A little colour crept into his face; but I fancied there was a new look in his eyes — for, as the horror faded, fear took its place.

Grady screwed the cap on the flask with great deliberation, and returned it to his pocket. And all the time Rogers was watching him furtively, wiping his mouth mechanically with a trembling hand.

"Now, Rogers," Grady began, "I want you to take your time and tell us in detail everything that happened here to-night. You say a woman did it. Well, we want to hear all about that woman. Now go ahead; and remember there's no hurry."

"Well, sir," began Rogers slowly, as though carefully considering his words, "Mr. Vantine came out from dinner about seven forty-five — maybe a little later than that — and told me to light all the lights in here and in the next room. You see there are gas and electrics both, sir, and I lighted them all. He had gone into the music-room on the other side of the hall, so I went over there and told him the lights were all lit. He was looking at a new picture he'd bought, but he left it right away and came out into the hall.

" 'I don't want to be disturbed, Rogers,' he said, and came in here and shut the door after him.

" It was ten or fifteen minutes after that that the door-bell rang, and when I opened the door, there was a woman standing on the steps."

He stopped and swallowed once or twice as

though his throat were dry, and I saw that his fingers were twitching nervously.

" Did you know her? " questioned Grady.

Rogers loosened his collar with a convulsive movement.

" No, sir, I'd never seen her before," he answered hoarsely.

" Describe her."

Rogers closed his eyes as though in an effort of recollection.

" She wore a heavy veil, sir, so that I couldn't see her very well; but the first thing I noticed was her eyes — they were so bright they seemed to burn right through me. Her face looked white behind her veil, and I could see how red her lips were — I didn't like her looks, sir, from the first."

" How was she dressed? "

" In a dark gown, sir, cut so skimpy that I knowed she was French before she spoke."

" Ah! " said Grady. " She was French, was she? "

" Yes, sir; though she could speak some English. She asked for Mr. Vantine. I told her Mr. Vantine was busy. And then she said something very fast about how she must see him, and all the time she kept edging in and in, till the first thing I knowed she was inside the door, and then she just pulled the door out of my hand and shut it. I ask you, sir, is that the way a lady would behave?"

"No," said Grady, "I dare say not. But go ahead,— and take your time."

Rogers had regained his self-confidence and he went ahead almost glibly.

"'See here, madam,' says I, 'we've had enough trouble here to-day with Frenchies, and if you don't get out quietly, why I'll have to put you out.'

"'I must see Mistaire Vangtine,' she says, very fast. 'I must see Mistaire Vangtine. It is most necessaire that I see Mistaire Vangtine.'

"'Then I'll have to put you out,' says I, and took hold of her arm. And at that she screamed and jerked herself away; and I grabbed her again, and just then Mr. Vantine opened the door there and came out into the hall.

"'What's all this, Rogers?' he says. 'Who is this party?'

"But before I could answer, that wild cat had rushed over to him and begun to reel off a string of French so fast I wondered how she got her breath. And Mr. Vantine looked at her kind of surprised at first, and then he got more interested, and finally he asked her in here and shut the door, and that was the last I saw of them."

"You mean you didn't let the woman out?" demanded Grady.

"Yes, sir, that's just what I mean. I thought if Mr. Vantine wanted to talk with her, well and good; that was his business, not mine; so I went back to the pantry to help the cook with the silver, expecting to hear the bell every minute. But the bell didn't ring, and after maybe half an hour, I came out into the hall again to see if the woman had gone; and I walked past the door of this room but didn't hear nothing; and then I went on to the front door, and was surprised to find it wasn't latched."

"Maybe you hadn't latched it," suggested Grady.

"It has a snap-lock, sir; when that woman slammed it shut, I heard it catch."

"You're sure of that?"

"Quite sure, sir."

"What did you do then?"

"I closed the door, sir, and then came back along the hall. I felt uneasy, some way; and I stood outside the door there listening; but I couldn't hear nothing; and then I tapped, but there wasn't no answer; so I tapped louder, with my heart somehow working right up into my mouth. And still there wasn't no answer, so I just opened the door and looked in — and the first thing I see was him —"

Rogers stopped suddenly, and caught at his throat again.

" I'll be all right in a minute, sir," he gasped. " It takes me this way sometimes."

" No hurry," Grady assured him, and then, when his breath was coming easier, " What did you do then? "

" I was so scared I couldn't scarcely stand, sir; but I managed to get to the foot of the stairs and yell for Parks, and he came running down — and that's all I remember, sir."

" The woman wasn't here? "

" No, sir."

" Did you look through the rooms? "

" No, sir; when I found the front door open, I knowed she'd gone out. She hadn't shut the door because she was afraid I'd hear her."

" That sounds probable," agreed Grady. " But what makes you think she killed Vantine? "

" Well, sir," answered Rogers, slowly, " I

guess I oughtn't to have said that; but finding the door open that way, and then coming on Mr. Vantine sort of upset me — I didn't know just what I was saying."

" You don't think so now, then?" questioned Grady sharply.

" I don't know what to think, sir."

" You say you never saw the woman before?"

" Never, sir."

" Had she ever been here before?"

" I don't think so, sir. The first thing she asked was if this was where Mr. Vantine lived."

Grady nodded.

" Very good, Rogers," he said. " I'll be offering you a place on the force next. Would you know this woman if you saw her again?"

Rogers hesitated.

" I wouldn't like to say sure, sir," he answered, at last. " I might and I might not."

" Red lips and a white face and bright eyes aren't much to go on," Grady pointed out. " Can't you give us a closer description?"

" I'm afraid not, sir. I just got a general impression, like, of her face through her veil."

" You say you didn't search these rooms?"

" No, sir, I didn't come inside the door."

" Why not? "

" I was afraid to, sir."

" Afraid to? "

" Yes, sir; I'm afraid to be here now."

" Did Parks come in? "

" No, sir; I guess he felt the same way I did."

" Then how did you know Vantine was dead?
Why didn't you try to help him? "

" One look was enough to tell me that wasn't
no use," said Rogers, and glanced with visible
horror at the crumpled form on the floor.

Grady looked at him keenly for a moment, but
there seemed to be no reason to doubt his story.
Then the detective looked about the room.

" There's one thing I don't understand," he
said, " and that is why Vantine should want
all these lights. What was he doing in here? "

" I couldn't be sure, sir; but I suppose he was
looking at the furniture he brought over from
Europe. He was a collector, you know, sir.
There are five or six pieces in the next room."

Without a word, Grady arose and passed into
the room adjoining, we after him; only Rogers
remained seated where he was. I remember
glancing back over my shoulder and noting how
he huddled forward in his chair, as though

crushed by a great weight, the instant our backs were turned.

But I forgot Rogers in contemplation of the scene before me.

The inner room was ablaze with light and the furniture stood hap-hazard about it, just as I had seen it earlier in the day. Only one thing had been moved. That was the Boule cabinet.

It had been carried to the centre of the room and placed in the full glare of the light from the chandelier. It stood there blazing with arrogant beauty, a thing apart.

Who had helped Vantine place it there, I wondered? Neither Rogers nor Parks had mentioned doing so. I turned back to the outer room.

Rogers was sitting crouched forward in his chair, his hands over his eyes, and I could feel him jerk with nervousness as I touched him on the shoulder.

" Oh, is it you, Mr. Lester? " he gasped. " Pardon me, sir; I'm not at all myself, sir."

" I can see that," I said soothingly, " and no wonder. I just wanted to ask you — did you help move any of the furniture in the room yonder? "

" Help move it, sir? "

" Yes — help change the position of any of it since this afternoon? "

" No, sir; I haven't touched any of it, sir."

" That's all right, then," I said, and turned back into the inner room.

Vantine had said that he intended examining the cabinet in detail at the first opportunity; I remembered how his eyes had gleamed as he looked at it; how his hand had trembled as he caressed the arabesques. No doubt he was making that examination when he had heard a woman's cry and had gone out into the hall to see what the matter was.

Then he and the woman had entered the ante-room together; he had closed the door; and then . . .

Like a lightning-flash a thought leaped into my brain — a reason — an explanation — wild, improbable, absurd, but still an explanation!

I choked back the cry which rose to my lips; I gripped my hands behind me in a desperate attempt to hold myself in check; and fascinated as by a deadly serpent, I stood staring at the cabinet.

For there, I felt certain, lay the clue to the mystery!

CHAPTER VII

GRADY, Simmonds and Goldberger examined the
room minutely, for they seemed to feel that the
secret of the tragedy lay somewhere within its four
walls; but I watched them only absently, for I had
lost interest in the proceedings. I was perfectly
sure that they would find nothing in any way bearing upon the mystery. I heard Grady comment
upon the fact that there was no door except the
one opening into the ante-room, and saw them
examine the window-catches.

"Nobody could raise these windows without
alarming the house," Grady said, and pointed to
a tiny wire running along the woodwork.
"There's a burglar alarm."

Simmonds assented, and finally the trio returned
to the ante-room.

"We'd like to look over the rest of the house,"
Grady said to Rogers, who was sitting erect again,
looking more like himself, and the four men went
out into the hall together. I remained behind
with Hughes and Freylinghuisen. They had

lifted the body to the couch and were making a careful examination of it. Heavy at heart, I sat down near by and watched them.

That Philip Vantine should have been killed by enthusiasm for the hobby which had given him so much pleasure seemed the very irony of fate, yet such I believed to be the case. To be sure, there were various incidents which seemed to conflict with such a theory, and the theory itself seemed wild to the point of lunacy; but at least it was a ray of light in what had been utter darkness. I turned it over and over in my mind, trying to fit into it the happenings of the day — I must confess with very poor success. Freylinghuisen's voice brought me out of my reverie.

"The two cases are precisely alike," he was saying. "The symptoms are identical. And I'm certain we shall find paralysis of the heart and spinal cord in this case, just as I did in the other. Both men were killed by the same poison."

"Can you make a guess as to the nature of the poison?" Hughes inquired.

"Some variant of hydrocyanic acid, I fancy — the odour indicates that; but it must be about fifty times as deadly as hydrocyanic acid is."

They wandered away into a discussion of possible variants, so technical and be-sprinkled with abstruse words and formulæ that I could not follow them. Freylinghuisen, of course, had all this sort of thing at his fingers' ends — post-mortems were his every-day occupation, and no doubt he had been furbishing himself up since this last one, in preparation for the inquest, where he would naturally wish to shine. I could see that he enjoyed displaying his knowledge before Hughes, who, although a practitioner of the highest standing, with an income greater than Freylinghuisen's many times over, had no such expert knowledge of toxicology as a coroner's physician would naturally possess.

The two detectives and the coroner came back while the discussion was still in progress and listened in silence to Freylinghuisen's statement of the case. Grady's mahogany face told absolutely nothing of what was passing in his brain, but Simmonds was plainly bewildered. It was evident from his look that nothing had been found to shed any light on the mystery; and now that his suicide theory had fallen to pieces, he was completely at sea. So, I suspected, was Grady, but he was too self-composed to betray it.

The coroner drew the two physicians aside and talked to them for a few moments in a low tone. Then he turned to Grady.

"Freylinghuisen thinks there is no necessity for a post-mortem," he said. "The symptoms are in every way identical with those of the other man who was killed here this afternoon. There can be no question that both of them died from the same cause. He is ready to make his return to that effect."

"Very well," assented Grady. "The body can be turned over to the relatives, then."

"There aren't any relatives," I said; "at least, no near ones. Vantine was the last of this branch of the family. I happen to know that our firm has been named as his executors in his will, so if there is no objection, I'll take charge of things."

"Very well, Mr. Lester," said Grady again; and then he looked at me. "Do you know the provisions of the will?" he asked.

"I do."

"In the light of those provisions, do you know of any one who would have an interest in Vantine's death?"

"I think I may tell you the provisions," I said, after a moment. "With the exception of a few legacies to his servants, his whole fortune is left to the Metropolitan Museum of Art."

" You have been his attorney for some time? "

" We have been his legal advisers for many years."

" Have you ever learned that he had an enemy? "   ·

" No," I answered instantly; " so far as I know, he had not an enemy on earth."

" He was never married, I believe? "

" No."

" Was he ever, to your knowledge, involved with a woman? "

" No," I said again.   " I was astounded when I heard Rogers's story."

" So you can give us no hint as to this woman's identity? "

" I only wish I could! " I said, with fervour.

" Thank you, Mr. Lester," and Grady turned to Simmonds. " I don't see that there is anything more we can do here," he added. " There's one thing, though, Mr. Lester, I will have to ask you to do. That is to keep all the servants here until after the inquest. If you think there is any doubt of your ability to do that, we can, of course, put them under arrest —"

" Oh, that isn't necessary," I broke in. " I will be responsible for their appearance at the inquest."

" I'll have to postpone it a day," said Goldberger. " I want Freylinghuisen to make some tests to-morrow. Besides, we've got to identify d'Aurelle, and these gentlemen seem to have their work cut out for them in finding this woman —"

Grady looked at Goldberger in a way which indicated that he thought he was talking too much, and the coroner stopped abruptly. A moment later, all four men left the house.

Dr. Hughes lingered for a last word.

" The undertaker had better be called at once," he said.

I knew what he meant. Already the face of the dead man was showing certain ugly discolourations.

" I can send him around on my way home," he added, and I thanked him for assuming this unpleasant duty.

As the door closed behind him, I heard a step on the stair, and turned to see Godfrey calmly descending.

" I came in a few minutes ago," he explained, in answer to my look, " and have been glancing

around upstairs. Nothing there. How did our
friend Grady get along? "

" Fairly well; but if he guesses anything, his
face didn't show it."

" His face never shows anything, because
there's nothing to show. He has cultivated that
sibylline look until people think he's a wonder.
But he's simply a stupid ignoramus."

" Oh, come, Godfrey," I protested, " you're
prejudiced. He went right to the point. Do you
know Rogers's story? "

" About the woman? Certainly. Rogers told
it to me before Grady arrived."

" Well," I commented, " you didn't lose any
time."

" I never do," he assented blandly. " And
now I'm going to prove to you that Grady is
merely a stupid ignoramus. He has heard all
the evidence, but does he know who that woman
was? "

" Of course not," I said, and then I looked at
him. " Do you mean that you do? Then I'm an
ignoramus, too! "

" My dear Lester," protested Godfrey, " you
are not a detective — that's not your business; but
it *is* Grady's. At least it is supposed to be, and the

safety of this city as a place of residence depends more or less upon the truth of that assumption. On the strength of it, he has been made deputy police commissioner, in charge of the detective bureau."

"Then you mean that you *do* know who she was?"

"I'm pretty sure I do — that is what I came back to prove. Where's Rogers?"

"I'll ring for him," I said, and did so, and presently he appeared.

"Did you ring, sir?" he asked.

He was still miserably nervous, but much more self-controlled than he had been earlier in the evening.

"Yes," I said. "Mr. Godfrey wishes to speak to you."

It seemed to me that Rogers turned visibly paler; there was certainly fear in the glance he turned upon my companion. But Godfrey smiled reassuringly.

"We'd better give him his instructions about the reporters, first thing, hadn't we, Lester?" he inquired.

"Which reporters?" I queried.

"All the others, of course. They will be

storming this house, Rogers, before long. You will meet them at the door, you will refuse to admit one of them; you will tell them that there is nothing to be learned here, and that they must go to the police. Tell them that Commissioner Grady himself is in charge of the case and will no doubt be glad to talk to them. Is that right, Lester?"

"Yes, Ulysses," I agreed, smiling.

"And now," continued Godfrey, watching Rogers keenly, "I have a photograph here that I want you to look at. Did you ever see that person before?" and he handed a print to Rogers.

The latter hesitated an instant, and then took the print with a trembling hand. Stark fear was in his eyes again; then slowly he raised the print to the light, glanced at it . . .

"Catch him, Lester!" Godfrey cried, and, sprang forward.

For Rogers, clutching wildly at his collar, spun half around and fell with a crash. Godfrey's arm broke the fall somewhat, but as for me, I was too dazed to move.

"Get some water, quick!" Godfrey commanded sharply, as Parks came running up. "Rogers has been taken ill."

And then, as Parks sped down the hall again, I saw Godfrey loosen the collar of the unconscious man and begin to chafe his temples fiercely.

"I hope it isn't apoplexy," he muttered. "I oughtn't to have shocked him like that."

At the words, I remembered; and, stooping, picked up the photograph which had fluttered from Rogers's nerveless fingers. And then I, too, uttered a smothered exclamation as I gazed at the dark eyes, the full lips, the oval face — the face which d'Aurelle had carried in his watch!

CHAPTER VIII

BUT it wasn't apoplexy. It was Parks who re-
assured us, when he came hurrying back a minute
later with a glass of water in one hand and a
small phial in the other.

"He has these spells," he said. "It's a kind
of vertigo. Give him a whiff of this."

He uncorked the phial and handed it to Godfrey, and I caught the penetrating fumes of ammonia. A moment later, Rogers gasped convul-
sively.

"He'll be all right pretty soon," remarked
Parks, with ready optimism. "Though I
never saw him quite so bad."

"We can't leave him lying here on the floor,"
said Godfrey.

"There's a couch-seat in the music-room,"
Parks suggested, and the three of us bore the still
unconscious man to it.

Then Godfrey and I sat down and waited, while
he gasped his way back to life.

"Though he can't really tell us much," God-

frey observed. "In fact, I doubt if he'll be willing to tell anything. But his face, when he looked
at the picture, told us all we need to know."

Thus reminded, I took the photograph out of
the pocket into which I had slipped it, and looked
at it again.

"Where did you get it?" I asked.

"The police photographer made some copies.
This is one of them."

"But what made you suspect that the two
women were the same?"

"I don't just know," answered Godfrey reflectively. "They were both French — and
Rogers spoke of the red lips; somehow it seemed
probable. Mr. Grady will find some things he
doesn't know in to-morrow's *Record*. But then
he usually does. This time, I'm going to rub it
in. Hello," he added, "our friend is coming
around."

I looked at Rogers and saw that his eyes were
open. They were staring at us as though wondering who we were. Godfrey passed an arm under
his head and held the glass of water to his lips.

"Take a swallow of this," he said, and Rogers
obeyed mechanically, still staring at him over the
rim of the glass. "How do you feel?"

"Pretty weak," Rogers answered, almost in a whisper. "Did I have a fit?"

"Something like that," said Godfrey cheerfully; "but don't worry. You'll soon be all right again."

"What sent me off?" asked Rogers, and stared up at him. Then his face turned purple and I thought he was going off again. But after a moment's heavy breathing, he lay quiet. "I remember now," he said. "Let me see that picture again."

I passed it to him. His hand was trembling so he could hardly take it, but I saw he was struggling desperately to control himself, and he managed to hold the picture up before his eyes and look at it with apparent unconcern.

"Do you know her?" Godfrey asked.

To my infinite amazement, Rogers shook his head.

"Never saw her before," he muttered. "When I first looked at her, I thought I knew her; but it ain't the same woman."

"Do you mean to say," Godfrey demanded sternly, "that that is not the woman who called on Mr. Vantine to-night?"

Again Rogers shook his head.

"Oh, no," he protested; "it's not the same woman at all. This one is younger."

Godfrey made no reply, but he sat down and looked at Rogers, and Rogers lay and gazed at the picture, and gradually his face softened, as though at some tender memory.

"Come, Rogers," I urged at last. "You'd better tell us all you know. If this is the woman, don't hesitate to say so."

"I've told you all I know, Mr. Lester," said Rogers, but he did not meet my eyes. "And I'm feeling pretty bad. I think I'd better be getting to bed."

"Yes, that's best," agreed Godfrey promptly. "Parks will help you," and he held out his hand for the photograph.

Rogers relinquished it with evident reluctance. He opened his lips as though to ask a question, then closed them again and got slowly to his feet, Parks aiding him.

"Good-night, gentlemen," he said weakly, and shuffled away, leaning heavily on Parks's shoulder.

"Well!" said I, looking at Godfrey. "What do you think of that?"

"He's lying, of course. We've got to find out why he's lying and bring it home to him. But

it's getting late — I must get down to the office.
One word, Lester — be sure Rogers doesn't give
you the slip."

" I'll have him looked after," I promised.
" But I fancy he'll be afraid to run away. Besides, it is possible he's telling the truth. I don't
believe any woman had anything to do with either
death."

Godfrey turned, as he was starting away, and
stopped to look at me.

" Who did then? " he asked.

" Nobody."

" You mean they both suicided in that abnormal
way? "

" No, it wasn't suicide — they were killed —
but not by a human being — at least, not directly."
I felt that I was floundering hopelessly, and
stopped. " I can't tell you now, Godfrey," I
pleaded. " I haven't had time to think it out.
You've got enough for one day."

" Yes," he smiled; " I've got enough for one
day. And now good-bye. Perhaps I'll look in on
you about midnight on my way home, if I get
through by then."

I sighed. Godfrey's energy became a little
wearing sometimes. I was already longing for

bed, and there remained so much to be done. But he, after a day which I knew had been a hard one and with a many-column story still to write, was apparently as fresh and eager as ever.

"All right," I agreed. "If you see a light, come up. If there isn't any light, I'll be in bed and I'll kill you if you wake me."

"Conditions accepted," he laughed, as I opened the door for him.

Parks joined me as I turned back into the house.

"I got Rogers to bed, sir," he said. "He'll be all right in the morning. But he's a queer duck."

"How long have you known him, Parks?"

"He's been with Mr. Vantine about five years. I don't know much about him; he's a silent kind of fellow, keeping to himself a good deal and sort of brooding over things. But he did his work all right, except once in a while when he keeled over like he did to-night."

"Parks," I said suddenly, "I'm going to ask you a question. You know that Mr. Vantine was a friend of mine, and I thought a great deal of him. Now, what with this story Rogers tells, and one or two other things, there is talk of a woman. Is there any foundation for talk of that kind?"

"No, sir," said Parks emphatically. "I've been Mr. Vantine's valet for eight years and more, and in all that time he has never been mixed up with a woman in any shape or form. I always fancied he'd loved a lady who died — I don't know what made me think so; but anyhow, since I've known him, he never looked at a woman — not in that way."

"Thank you, Parks," I said with a sigh of relief. "I've been through so much to-day, that I felt I couldn't endure that; and now — "

"Beg pardon, sir," said a voice at my elbow; "we have everything ready, sir."

I turned with a start to see a little, clean-shaven man standing there, rubbing his hands softly together and gazing blandly up at me.

"The undertaker's assistant, sir," explained Parks, seeing my look of astonishment. "He came while you and Mr. Godfrey were in the music-room. Dr. Hughes sent him."

"Yes, sir," added the little man; "and we have the corpse ready for the coffin. Very nice it looks, too; though it was a hard job. Was it poison killed him, sir?"

"Yes," I answered, with a feeling of nausea, "it was poison."

"Very powerful poison, too, I should say, sir; we didn't get here none too soon. Where shall we put the body, sir?"

"Why not leave it where it is?" I asked impatiently.

"Very good, sir," said the man, and presently he and his assistant took themselves off, to my intense relief.

"And now, Parks," I began, "there is something I want to say to you. Let us go somewhere and sit down."

"Suppose we go up to the study, sir. You're looking regularly done up, if you'll permit me to say so, sir. Shall I get you something?"

"A brandy-and-soda," I assented; "and bring one for yourself."

"Very good, sir," and a few minutes later we were sitting opposite each other in the room where Vantine had offered me similar refreshment not many hours before. I looked at Parks as he sat there and turned over in my mind what I had to say to him. I liked the man and I felt he could be trusted. At any rate, I had to take the risk.

"Now, Parks," I began again, setting down my glass, "what I have to say to you is very serious, and I want you to keep it to yourself: I know that you were devoted to Mr. Vantine — I may as well tell you that he has remembered you in his will — and I am sure you are willing to do anything in your power to help solve the mystery of his death."

"That I am, sir," Parks agreed warmly. "I was very fond of him, sir; nobody will miss him more than I will."

I realised that the tragedy meant far more to Parks than it did even to me, for he had lost not only a friend but a means of livelihood, and I looked at him with heightened sympathy.

"I know how you feel," I said, "and I am counting on you to help me. I have a sort of idea how his death came about. Only the vaguest possible idea," I added hastily, as his eyes widened with interest; "altogether too vague to be put into words. But I can say this much — the mystery, whatever it is, is in the ante-room where the bodies were found or in the room next to it where the furniture is. Now, I am going to lock up those rooms, and I want you to see that nobody enters them without your knowledge."

"Not very likely that anybody will want to enter them, sir," and Parks laughed a grim little laugh.

"I am not so sure of that," I dissented, speaking very seriously. "In fact, I am of the opinion that there *is* somebody who wants to enter those rooms very badly. I don't know who he is and I don't know what he is after, but I am going to make it your business to keep him out, and to capture him if you catch him trying to get in."

"Trust me for that, sir," said Parks promptly. "What is it you want me to do?"

"I want you to put a cot in the hallway outside the door of the ante-room and sleep there to-night. To-morrow I will decide what further precautions are necessary."

"Very good, sir," said Parks. "I'll get the cot up at once."

"There is one thing more," I went on. "I have given the coroner my personal assurance that none of the servants will leave the house until after the inquest. I suppose I can rely on them?"

"Oh yes, sir. I'll see they understand how important it is."

"Rogers especially," I added, looking at him.

"I understand, sir," said Parks quietly.

" Very well. And now let us go down and lock up those rooms."

They were still ablaze with light, but both of us faltered a little, I think, on the threshold of the ante-room. For in the middle of the floor stood a stretcher, and on it was an object covered with a sheet, its outlines horribly suggestive. But I took myself in hand and entered. Parks followed me and closed the door.

The ante-room had two windows, and the room beyond, which was a corner one, had three. All of them were locked, but a pane of glass seemed to me an absurdly fragile barrier against any one who really wished to enter.

" Aren't there some wooden shutters for these windows?" I asked.

" Yes, sir; they were taken down yesterday and put in the basement. Shall I get them?"

" I think you'd better," I said. " Will you need any help?"

" No, sir; they're not heavy. If you'll wait here, you can snap the bolts into place when I lift them up from the outside."

" Very well," I agreed, and Parks hurried away.

I entered the inner room and stopped before

the Boule cabinet. There was a certain air of
arrogance about it as it stood there in that blaze
of light, its inlay aglow with a thousand subtle
reflections; a flaunting air, the air of a courtesan
conscious of her beauty and pleased to attract attention — just the air with which Madame de
Montespan must have sauntered down the mirror
gallery at Versailles, ablaze with jewels, her skirts
rustling, her figure swaying suggestively. Something threatening, too; something sinister and
deadly —

There was a rattle at the window, and I saw
Parks lifting one of the shutters into place. I
threw up the sash and pressed the heavy bolts
carefully into their sockets, then closed the sash
and locked it. The two other windows were
secured in their turn, and with a last look about
the room, I turned out the lights. The ante-
room windows were soon shuttered in the same
way, and with a sigh of relief I told myself that
no entrance to the house could be had from that
direction. With Parks outside the only door, the
rooms ought to be safe from invasion.

Then, before extinguishing the lights, I ap-
proached that silent figure on the stretcher, lifted
the sheet and looked for the last time upon the

face of my dead friend. It was no longer staring and terrible, but calm and peaceful as in sleep — almost smiling. With wet eyes and contracted throat, I covered the face again, turned out the lights, and left the room. Parks met me in the hall, carrying a cot which he placed close across the doorway.

" There," he said; " nobody will get into that room without my knowing it."

" No," I agreed; and then a sudden thought occurred to me. " Parks," I said, " is it true that there is a burglar-alarm on all the windows? "

" Yes, sir. It rings a bell in Mr. Vantine's bedroom and another in mine, and sends in a call to the police."

" Is it working? "

" Yes, sir; Mr. Vantine himself tested it this evening just before dinner."

" Then why didn't it work when I opened those windows just now? " I demanded.

Parks laughed.

" Because I threw off the switch, sir," he explained, " when I came out to get the shutters. The switch is in a little iron box on the wall just back of the stairs, sir. It's one of my duties to turn it on every night before I go to bed."

I breathed a sigh of relief.

" Is it on again now? "

" It certainly is, sir.   After what you told me, I'd not be likely to forget it."

" You'd better have a weapon handy, too," I suggested.

" I have a revolver, sir."

" That's good.   And don't hesitate to use it. I'm going home — I'm dead tired."

" Shall I call a taxi, sir? "

" No, the walk will do me good.   I'll see you to-morrow."

Parks helped me into my coat and opened the door for me.   Glancing back after a moment, I saw that he was standing on the steps gazing after me.   I could understand his reluctance to go back into that death-haunted house, and I found my-self breathing deeply with the relief of getting out of it.

CHAPTER IX

GUESSES AT THE RIDDLE

THE walk uptown did me good. The rain·had ceased and the air felt clean and fresh as though it had been washed. I took deep breaths of it, and the feeling of fatigue and depression which had weighed upon me gradually vanished. I was in no hurry — went out of my way a little, indeed, to walk out into Madison Square and look back at the towering mass of the Flatiron building, creamy and delicate as carved ivory under the rays of the moon — and it was long past midnight when I finally turned in at the Marathon. Higgins, the janitor, was just closing the outer doors, and he joined me in the elevator a moment later.

" There's a gentleman waiting to see you, sir," he said, as the car started upward. " Mr. Godfrey, sir. He came in about ten minutes ago. He said you were expecting him, so I let him into your rooms."

" That was right," I said, and reflected again upon Godfrey's exhaustless energy.

I found him lolling in an easy chair, and he looked up with a smile at my entrance.

"Higgins said you hadn't come in yet," he explained, "so I thought I'd wait a few minutes on the off chance that you mightn't be too tired to talk. If you are, say so, and I'll be moving along."

"I'm not too tired," I said, hanging up my coat. "I feel a good deal better than I did an hour ago."

"I saw that you were about all in."

"How do you keep it up, Godfrey?" I asked, sitting down opposite him. "You don't seem tired at all."

"I *am* tired, though," he said, "a little. But I've got a fool brain that won't let my body go to sleep so long as there is work to be done. Then as soon as everything is finished, the brain lets go and the body sleeps like a log. Now I knew I couldn't go to sleep properly to-night until I had heard the very interesting theory you are going to confide to me. Besides, I have a thing or two to tell you."

"Go ahead," I said.

"We had a cable from our Paris office just before I left. It seems that Théophile d'Aurelle

plays first fiddle in the orchestra of the Casino
de Paris. He played as usual to-night, so that
it is manifestly impossible that he should also
be lying in the New York morgue. Moreover,
none of his friends, so far as he knows, is in
America. No doubt he may be able to identify
the photograph of the dead man, and we've
already started one on the way, but we can't hear
from it for six or eight days. But my guess was
right — the fellow's name isn't d'Aurelle."

"You say you have a photograph?"

"Yes, I had some taken of the body this afternoon. Here's one of them. Keep it; you may
have a use for it."

I took the print, and as I gazed at the face de-
picted upon it, I realised that the distorted countenance I had seen in the afternoon had given
me no idea of the man's appearance. Now the
eyes were closed and the features composed and
peaceful, but even death failed to give them any
dignity. It was a weak and dissipated face, the
face of a hanger-on of cafés, as Parks had said
— of a loiterer along the boulevards, of a man
without ambition and capable of any depth of
meanness and deceit. At least that is how I
read it.

"He's evidently low-class," said Godfrey, watching me. "One of those parasites without work and without income, so common in Paris. Shop-girls and ladies' maids have a weakness for them."

"I think you are right," I agreed; "but at the same time, if he was of that type, I don't see what business he could have had with Philip Vantine."

"Neither do I; but there are a lot of other things I don't see, either. We're all in the dark, Lester; have you thought of that? Absolutely in the dark."

"Yes, I have thought of it," I said slowly.

"No doubt we can establish this fellow's identity in time — sooner than we think, perhaps, for most of the morning papers will run his picture, and if he is known here in New York at all, it will be recognised by some one. When we find out who he is, we can probably guess at the nature of his business with Vantine. We can find out who the woman was who called to see Vantine to-night — that is just a case of grilling Rogers; then we can run her down and get her secret out of her. We can find why Rogers is trying to shield her. All that is comparatively simple.

But when we have done it all, when we have all these facts in hand, I am afraid we shall find that they are utterly unimportant."

"Unimportant?" I echoed. "But surely—"

"Unimportant because we don't want to know these things. What we want to know is how Philip Vantine and this unknown Frenchman were killed. And that is just the one thing which, I am convinced, neither the man nor the woman nor Rogers nor anybody else we have come across in this case can tell us. There's a personality behind all this that we haven't even suspected yet and which, I am free to confess, I don't know how to get at. It puzzles me; it rather frightens me; it's like a threatening shadow which one can't get hold of."

There was a moment's silence; then I decided the time had come for me to speak.

"Godfrey," I said, "what I am about to tell you is told in confidence and must be held in confidence until I give you permission to use it. Do you agree?"

"Go on," he said, his eyes on my face.

"Well, I believe I know how these two men were killed. Listen."

And I told him in detail the story of the Boule cabinet; I repeated Vantine's theory of its first ownership; I named the price which he was ready to pay for it; I described the difference between an original and a counterpart, and dwelt upon Vantine's assertion that this was an original of unique and unquestionable artistry.   Long before I had finished, Godfrey was out of his chair and pacing up and down the room, his face flushed, his eyes glowing.

" Beautiful ! " he murmured from time to time. " Immense !   What a case it will make, Lester ! " he cried, stopping before my chair and beaming down upon me as I finished the story.   " Unique, too; that's the beauty of it !   As unique as this adorable Boule cabinet ! "

" Then you see it, too ? " I questioned, a little disappointed that my theory should seem so evident.

" See it ? " and he dropped into his chair again. " A man would be blind not to see it.   But all the same, Lester, I give you credit for putting the facts together.   So many of us — Grady, for instance ! — aren't able to do that, or to see which facts are essential and which are negligible.   Now the fact that Vantine had accidentally come into possession of a Boule cabinet would probably seem negligible to Grady, whereas it is the one big essential fact in this whole case.   And it was you who saw it."

"You saw it too," I pointed out, " as soon as I mentioned it."

"Yes; but you mentioned it in a way which made its importance manifest.   I couldn't help seeing it.   And I believe that we have both arrived at practically the same conclusions.   Here they are," and he checked them off on his fingers. " The cabinet contains a secret drawer.   This is inevitable, if it really belonged to Madame de Montespan.   Any cabinet made for her would be certain to have a secret drawer — she would require it, just as she would require lace on her underwear or jewelled buttons on her gloves. That drawer, since it was, perhaps, to contain such priceless documents as the love letters of a king — even more so, if the love letters were from another man ! — must be adequately guarded, and therefore a mechanism was devised to stab the person attempting to open it and to inject into the wound a poison so powerful as to cause instant death.   Am I right so far? "

"Wonderfully right," I nodded.   " I had not

put it so clearly, even to myself. Go ahead."

"We come to the conclusion, then," continued Godfrey, "that the business of this unknown Frenchman with Vantine in some way concerned this cabinet."

"Vantine himself thought so," I broke in. "He told me afterwards that it was because he thought so he consented to see him."

"Good! That would seem to indicate that we are on the right track. The Frenchman's business, then, had something to do with this cabinet, and with this secret drawer. Left to himself, he discovered the cabinet in the room adjoining the ante-room, attempted to open the drawer and was killed."

"Yes," I agreed; "and now how about Vantine?"

"Vantine's death isn't so simply explained. Presumably the unknown woman also called on business relating to the cabinet. She also wanted to open the secret drawer in order to secure its contents — that seems fairly certain from her connection with the first caller."

"You still think it was her photograph he carried in his watch?"

"I am sure of it. But how did it happen that

it was Vantine who was killed? Did the woman, warned by the fate of the man, deliberately set Vantine to open the drawer in order that she might run no risk? Or was she also ignorant of the mechanism? Above all, did she succeed in get-ting away with the contents of the drawer?"

"What *was* the contents of the drawer?" I demanded.

"Ah, if we only knew!"

"Perhaps the woman had nothing to do with it. Vantine himself told me that he was going to make a careful examination of the cabinet. No doubt that is exactly what he was doing when the woman's arrival interrupted him. He might have let her out of the house himself, and then, returning to the cabinet, stumbled upon the secret drawer after she had gone."

"Yes; that is quite possible, too. At any rate, you agree with me that both men were killed in some such way as I have described?"

"Absolutely. I think there can be no doubt of it."

"There are objections — and rather weighty ones. The theory explains the two deaths, it ex-plains the similarity of the wounds, it explains how both should be on the right hand just below the knuckles, it explains why both bodies were found in the same place since both men started to summon help. But in the first place, if the Frenchman got the drawer open, who closed it?"

"Perhaps it closed itself when he let go of it."

"And closed again after Vantine opened it?"

"Yes."

"It would take a very clever mechanism to do that."

"But at least it's possible."

"Oh yes, it's possible. And we must remember that the poisoners of those days were very ingenious. That was the heydey of La Voisin and the Marquise de Brinvilliers, of Elixi, and heaven knows how many other experts who had followed Catherine de Medici to France. So that's all quite possible. But there is one thing that isn't possible and that is that a poison which, if it is administered as we think it is, must be a liquid, could remain in that cabinet fresh and ready for use for more than three hundred years. It would have dried up centuries ago. Nor would the mechanism stay in order so long. It must be both complicated and delicate. Therefore it would have to be oiled and overhauled from time to time. If it is worked by a spring — and I

don't see how else it can be worked — the spring
would have to be renewed and wound up."

" Well? " I asked, as he paused.

" Well, it is evident that the drawer contains
something more modern than the love letters of
Louis Fourteenth. It must have been put in
working order quite recently. But by whom and
for what purpose? That is the mystery we have
to solve — and it is a mighty pretty one. And
here's another objection," he added. " That
Frenchman knew about the secret drawer because,
according to our theory, he opened it and got
killed. Why didn't he also know about the
poison? "

That was an objection, truly, and the more I
thought of it, the more serious it seemed.

" It may be," said Godfrey at last, " that d'Aurelle was going it alone — that he had broken
with the gang — "

" The gang? "

" Of course there is a gang. This thing has
taken careful planning and concerted effort. And
the leader of the gang is a genius! I wonder if
you understand how great a genius? Think: he
knows the secret of the drawer of Madame de
Montespan's cabinet; but above all he knows the

secret of the poison — the poison of the Medici!
Do you know what that means, Lester?"

"What *does* it mean?" I asked, for Godfrey
was getting ahead of me.

"It means he is a great criminal — a really
great criminal — one of the elect from whom
crime has no secrets. Observe. He alone knows
the secret of the poison; one of his men breaks
away from him and pays for his mutiny with his
life. He is the brain; the others are merely the
instruments!"

"Then you don't believe it was by accident that
cabinet was sent to Vantine?"

"By accident? Not for an instant! It was
part of a plot — and a splendid plot!"

"Can you explain that to me too?" I queried
a little ironically, for I confess it seemed to me
that Godfrey was permitting his imagination to
run away with him.

He smiled good-naturedly at my tone.

"Of course this is all mere romancing," he admitted. "I am the first to acknowledge that. I
was merely following out our theory to what
seemed its logical conclusion. But perhaps we
are on the wrong track altogether. Perhaps
d'Aurelle, or whatever his name is, just blundered

in, like a moth into a candle-flame. As for the plot — well, I can only guess at it. But suppose you and I had pulled off some big robbery — "

He stopped suddenly, and his face went white and then red.

"What is it, Godfrey?" I cried, for his look frightened me.

He lay back in his chair, his hands pressed over his eyes. I could see how they were trembling — how his whole body was trembling.

"Wait!" he said hoarsely. "Wait!" Then he sat upright, his face tense with anxiety. "Lester!" he cried, "the cabinet — it isn't guarded!"

"Yes it is," I said. "At least I thought of that!"

And I told him of the precautions I had taken to keep it safe. He heard me out with a sigh of relief.

"That's better," he said. "Parks wouldn't stand much show, I'm afraid, if worst came to worst, but I think the cabinet is safe — for to-night. And before another night, Lester, we will have a look for ourselves."

"A look?"

" Yes; for the secret drawer ! "

I stared at him fascinated.

" And we shall find it ! " he added.

" D'Aurelle and Vantine found it," I muttered thickly.

" Well ? "

" And they're both dead ! "

" It won't kill us. We will go about it armoured, Lester. That poisoned fang may strike — "

" Don't ! " I cried, and cowered back into my chair. " I — I can't do it, Godfrey. God knows, I'm no coward — but not that ! "

" You shall watch me do it ! " he said.

" That would be even worse ! "

" But I'll be ready, Lester. There will be no danger. Come, man ! Why, it's the chance of a lifetime — to rifle the secret drawer of Madame de Montespan ! Yes ! " he added, his eyes glowing, " and to match ourselves against the greatest criminal of modern times ! "

His shrill laugh told how excited he was.

" And do you know what we shall find in that drawer, Lester ? But no — it is only a guess — the wildest sort of a guess — but if it is right — if it is right ! "

He sprang from his chair, biting his lips, his whole frame quivering. But he was calmer in a moment.

"Anyway, you will help me, Lester? You will come?"

There was a wizardry in his manner not to be resisted. Besides — to rifle the secret drawer of Madame de Montespan! To match oneself against the greatest criminal of modern times! What an adventure!

"Yes," I answered, with a quick intaking of the breath; "I'll come!"

He clapped me on the shoulder, his face beaming.

"I knew you would! To-morrow night, then — I'll call for you here at seven o'clock. We'll have dinner together — and then hey for the great secret! Agreed?"

"Agreed!" I said.

He caught up coat and hat and started for the door.

"There are things to do," he said; "that armour to prepare — the plan of campaign to consider, you know. Good-night then, till — this evening!"

The door closed behind him and his footsteps

died away down the hall.   I looked at my watch
— it was nearly two o'clock.

Dizzily I went to bed. But my sleep was
broken by a fearful dream — a dream of a serpent with blazing eyes and dripping fangs, poised
to strike!

CHAPTER X

PREPARATIONS

My first thought when I awoke next morning was for Parks, for Godfrey's manner had impressed me with the feeling that Parks was in much more serious danger than either he or I suspected. It was with a lively sense of relief, therefore, that I heard Parks's voice answer my call on the 'phone.

"This is Mr. Lester," I said. "Is everything all right?"

"Everything serene, sir," he answered. "It would take a mighty smooth burglar to get in here now, sir."

"How is that?" I asked.

"Reporters are camped all around the house, sir. They seem to think somebody else will be killed here to-day."

He laughed as he spoke the words, but I was far from thinking the idea an amusing one.

"I hope not," I said quickly. "And don't let any of the reporters in, nor talk to them. Tell them they must go to the police for their informa-

tion.   If they get too annoying, let me know and
I'll have an officer sent around."

" Very good, sir."

" And, Parks."

" Yes, sir? "

" Don't let anybody in the house — no matter
what he wants — unless Mr. Grady or Mr. Simmonds or Mr. Goldberger accompanies him.
Don't let anybody in you don't know.   If there is
any trouble, call me up.   I want you to be careful about this."

" I understand, sir."

" How is Rogers? " I asked.

" Much better, sir.   He wanted to get up, but I
told him he might as well stay in bed and I'd
look after things.   I thought that was the best
place for him, sir."

" It is," I agreed.   " Keep him there as long
as you can.   I'll come in during the day, if possible; in any event, Mr. Godfrey and I will be
there this evening.   Call me at the office if you
need me for anything."

" Very good, sir," said Parks again, and I hung
up.

I glanced through Godfrey's account of the
affair while I ate my breakfast, and noted with

amusement the sly digs taken at Commissioner Grady. Under the photograph of the unknown woman was the legend:

MR. VANTINE'S MYSTERIOUS CALLER
(Grady Please Notice)

And it was intimated that when Grady wanted any real information about an especially puzzling case, he had to go to the *Record* to get it.

This, however, was merely by the way, for the story of the double tragedy, fully illustrated, was flung across many columns and was plainly considered the great news feature of the day.

I glanced at two or three other papers on my way downtown. All of them featured the tragedy with a riot of pictures — pictures of d'Aurelle and Vantine, of Grady (very large), of Simmonds, of Goldberger, of Freylinghuisen, of the Vantine house, diagrams of the ante-room showing the position in which the bodies were found, anatomical charts showing the exact nature of the wounds, pictures of the noted poisoners of history with a highly-coloured description of their achievements — but when it came to the story of the tragedy itself, their accounts were far less detailed and informed than that in the *Record*.

They were indeed, for the most part, mere far-ragos of theories, guesses, blood-curdling sugges-tions, and mysterious hints of important informa-tion confided to the reporters but withheld from the public until the criminal had been run to earth. That this would soon be accomplished not a single paper doubted, for had not Grady, the mighty Grady, taken personal charge of the case? (Here followed a glowing history of Grady's career.)

It was evident enough that all these reporters had been compelled to go to Grady for their in-formation, and I could fancy them damning him between their teeth as they penned these panegy-rics. I could also fancy their city editors damn-ing as they compared these incoherent imagin-ings with the admirable and closely-written story in the *Record,* and I suspected that it was the realisation of the *Record's* triumph which had caused the descent of the phalanx of reporters upon the Vantine place.

I went over the whole affair with Mr. Royce, as soon as he reached the office, and spent the rest of the day arranging the papers relating to Van-tine's affairs and getting them ready to probate. Parks called me up once or twice for instructions as to various details, and Vantine's nearest relative, a third or fourth cousin, wired from somewhere in the west that he was starting for New York at once. And then, toward the middle of the afternoon, came the cablegram from Paris which I had almost forgotten to expect:

" Royce & Lester, New York.
" Regret mistake in shipment exceedingly. Our representative will call to explain.
" Armand et Fils."

So there was an end of the romance Godfrey had woven and which I had been almost ready to believe — the romance of design, of a carefully-laid plot, and all that. It had been merely accident after all. And I smiled a little sarcastically at myself for my credulity. No doubt my own romance of a secret drawer and a poisoned mechanism would prove equally fabulous. In my over-wrought state of the night before, it had seemed reasonable enough; but here, in the cold light of day, it seemed preposterous. How Grady and Goldberger would have laughed at it!

I put the whole thing impatiently away from me and turned to other work, but I found I could not conquer a certain deep-seated nervousness; so at last I locked my desk, told the boy I would not be back, and took a taxi for a long drive through the park. The fresh air, the smell of the trees, the sight of the children playing along the paths, did me good, and I was able to greet Godfrey with a smile when he called for me at seven o'clock.

"I've engaged a table at a little place around the corner," he said. "It is managed by a friend of mine and I think you'll like it."

I did. Indeed the dinner was so good that it demanded undivided attention, and not until the coffee was on the table and the cigars lighted did we speak of the business which had brought us together.

"Anything new?" I asked, as we pushed back our chairs.

"No, nothing of any importance. The man at the morgue has not been identified. In the first place, the Paris police have never taken his Bertillon measurements."

"Then he's not a criminal?"

"He has never been arrested," Godfrey qualified. "More peculiar is the fact that he hasn't been recognised here. Two million people, probably, saw his photograph in the papers this morning. Some of them thought they knew him and went around to the morgue to see his body, but nothing came of it. The police have no report of any such man missing."

"That *is* peculiar, isn't it!" I commented.

"It's very peculiar. It means one of two things — either the fellow's friends are keeping dark purposely, or he didn't have any friends, here in New York at least. But even then, one would think that whoever rented him a room would wonder what had become of him and would make some inquiries."

"Perhaps he hadn't rented a room," I suggested. "Perhaps he had just reached New York, and went direct to Vantine's."

Godfrey's face lighted up.

"From the steamer, of course! I ought to have guessed as much from the cut of his hair. He hasn't been out of France more than ten days or so. Excuse me a moment."

He hurried away and five minutes passed before he came back.

"I 'phoned the office to send some men around to the boats which came in yesterday. If he was a passenger, some one of the stewards will recog-

nise his photograph.   There were three boats
he might have come on — the *Arabic* and *Ascania*
from Cherbourg, and the *France* from Havre.
There is nothing else that I know of," he added
thoughtfully, " except that Freylinghuisen thinks
he has discovered the nature of the poison.   He
says it is some very powerful variant of prussic
acid."

" Yes," I said, " I heard him say something
of the sort last night."

" I had a talk with him this afternoon about it,
and he was quite learned," Godfrey went on.
" This is a great chance for him to get before the
public and he's making the most of it.   I gathered
from what he said that ordinary prussic acid,
which is deadly enough, heaven knows, contains
only two per cent. of the poison, while the strongest solution yet obtained contains only four per
cent.   Freylinghuisen says that whoever con-
cocted this particular poison has evidently discovered a new way of doing it — or re-discovered
an old way — so that it is at least fifty per cent.
effective.   In other words, if you can get a fraction of a drop of it in a man's blood, you kill him
by paralysis quicker than if you put a bullet
through his heart."

" Nothing could save him, then? " I questioned.

" Nothing on earth. Oh, I don't say that if somebody had an axe handy and chopped your arm off at the shoulder an instant after you were struck on the hand, you mightn't have a chance to live; but it would take mighty quick work, and even then it would be nip and tuck. Freyling-huisen thinks it is a new discovery. I don't. I think some one has dug up one of the old Medici formulæ. Maybe it was placed in the secret drawer, so that there would never be any lack of ammunition for the mechanism."

" Godfrey," I said, " are you still bent on fool-ing with that thing? "

" More than ever; I'm going to find that secret drawer. And if the fangs strike — well, I'm ready for them. See here what I had made to-day."

He drew from his pocket something that looked like a steel gauntlet, such as one sees on suits of old armour. He slipped it over his right hand.

" You see it covers the back of the hand com-pletely," he said, " half way down the first joint of the fingers. It is made of the toughest steel and would turn a bullet. And do you see how it is depressed in the middle, Lester? "

"Yes," I said, "I was wondering why you had it made in that shape."

"I want to get a sample of that poison. My theory is that when the fangs strike the hand, the shock drives out a drop or two of the poison. I don't want those drops to get away; I want them to roll into this depression, and I shall very carefully bottle them. Think what they are, Lester — the poison of the Medici!"

I sat for a moment looking at him, half in amusement, half in sorrow. It seemed a pity that his theory must come tumbling down, it was so picturesque and he was so interested and enthusiastic over it. And it would make such a good story! He caught my glance and put the gauntlet back into his pocket.

"Well, what is it?" he asked quietly.

For answer I got out the cablegram and passed it across to him. He read it with brows contracted.

"That seems to put a puncture in our little romance, doesn't it?" I asked at last.

He nodded thoughtfully.

"Yes, it does," and he read the message again word by word. "Armand's man hasn't called yet?"

"No, I didn't get the message till about three o'clock. I suppose he'll be around to-morrow."

"You will have to turn the cabinet over to him, of course?"

"Why yes, it belongs to him. At least it doesn't belong to Vantine."

He slipped the message into its envelope and handed it back to me. I could see that he was perplexed and upset.

"Well, in spite of this," he said finally, "I am still interested in that cabinet, Lester, and I wish you would keep possession of it as long as you can. At least I wouldn't give it up until he delivered to you the other cabinet which Vantine really bought."

"Oh, I'll make him do that," I agreed quickly. "That will no doubt take a few days — longer than that if Vantine's cabinet is in Paris."

Godfrey raised a finger to the waiter, asked for the check and paid it.

"And now let us go down and have a look at this one," he said, "as we intended doing. You will think me foolish, Lester, but even that cablegram hasn't shaken my belief in the existence of that secret drawer."

"And all the rest?" I asked.

"Yes," he answered slowly, "and all the rest." He said nothing more until we stopped before the Vantine house, but I could see from his puckered brows how desperately he was trying to untangle this quirk in the mystery.

"The siege seems to have been lifted," I remarked, as we alighted.

"The siege?"

"Parks telephoned me that your esteemed contemporaries had the place surrounded. I told him to hold the fort!"

"Poor boys!" he commented smiling. "To think that all they know is what Grady is able to tell them!" Then he stopped before the house and made a careful survey of it.

"Which room is the cabinet in?" he asked.

"The ante-room is there at the left where those two shuttered windows are. The cabinet is in the corner room — there is one window on this side and two on the other."

"Wait till I take a look at them," he said, and vaulting the low railing, he walked quickly along the front of the house and around the corner. He was gone only a minute. "They're all right," he said, in a tone of relief.

" Of course they're all right.   You didn't suppose —"

" If that cabinet contains what I thought it did,
Lester — yes," he added a little savagely, as he
saw my look, " and what I still think it does — it
wouldn't be safe in the strongest vault of the
National City Bank," and he motioned for me to
ring the bell.

I did so in silence.

Parks answered it almost instantly and I could
tell from the way his face changed how glad he
was to see me.

" Well, Parks," I said, as we stepped inside,
" everything is all right, I hope? "

" Yes, sir," he answered.   " But — but it gets
on the nerves a little, sir."

I heard a movement behind me as I gave Parks
my coat, and turned to see Rogers sitting on the
cot.

" Hello," I said, " so you're able to be up, are
you? "

" Yes, sir," he answered, without looking at
me.   " I thought I'd come down and keep Parks
company."

Parks smiled a little sheepishly.

" I asked him to, Mr. Lester," he said.   " I

got so lonesome and jumpy here by myself that I
just had to have somebody to talk to.   Especially,
after the burglar-alarm rang."

"The   burglar-alarm?"   repeated   Godfrey
quickly.   "What do you mean?"

"We've got a burglar-alarm on the windows,
sir.   It's usually turned off in the day-time, but
I thought I'd better leave it on to-day, and it rang
about half-past five this afternoon.   I thought at
first that one of the other servants had raised a
window, but none of them had.   Something went
wrong with it, I guess."

"Did I take a look at the windows?"   I
asked.

"Yes, sir; a policeman came to see what was
the matter and we went around and examined the
windows, but they were all locked.   It made me
feel kind of scary for a while."

"Does the alarm work now?"

"No, sir; the policeman said there must be
a short circuit somewhere and that he'd notify
the people who put it in, but nobody has come
around yet to fix it."

"We'd better take a look at the windows ourselves," said Godfrey.   "You stay here, Parks.
We can find them all right; and I don't want

you to leave that door unguarded for a single instant."

We went from window to window and Godfrey examined each of them with a minuteness that astonished me, for I had no idea what he expected to find. But we completed the circuit of the ground floor without his apparently discovering anything out of the way.

"Let's take a look at the basement," he said, and led the way downstairs with a readiness which told me that he had been over the house before.

In the kitchen, we came upon the cook and housemaid sitting close together and talking in frightened whispers. They watched us apprehensively and I stopped to reassure them, while Godfrey proceeded with his search. Then I heard him calling me.

I found him in a kind of lumber-room, standing before its single small window, his electric torch in his hand.

"Look there," he said, his voice quivering with excitement, and threw a circle of light on the jamb of the window at the spot where the upper and lower sashes met.

"What is it?" I asked after a moment. "I don't see anything wrong."

"You don't? You don't see that this house was to be entered to-night? Then what does this mean?"

With his finger-nail, he turned up the end of a tiny insulated wire. And then I saw that the wire had been cut.

CHAPTER XI

THE BURNING EYES

FOR an instant I did not grasp the full significance of that severed wire. Then I understood.

"Yes," said Godfrey drily, "that romance of
mine is looking up again. Somebody was pre-
paring for a quiet invasion of the house to-night
— somebody, of course, interested in that cabinet."

"He wasn't losing any time," I ventured.

"He knew he hadn't any to lose. When you
put those wooden shutters up, you warned him
that you suspected his game. He knew, if the
alarm was on, it would ring when he cut the wire,
but he also knew that the chances were a hundred
to one against the cut being discovered, or the
alarm put in working order, before to-morrow."

"Why can't we ambush him?" I suggested.

"We might try, but it will be a mighty risky
undertaking, Lester."

"One risky undertaking is enough for to-
night," I said with a sigh, for my belief in the existence of the secret drawer and the poison and
all the rest of it had come back with a rush. I

felt almost apologetic toward Godfrey for ever doubting him. "We'd better wait and see if we survive the first one before we arrange for any more."

"All right," Godfrey laughed. "But I'll fix this break."

He got out his pen-knife, loosened two or three of the staples which held the wire in place, drew it out, scraped back the insulation, and twisted the ends tightly together.

"There," he added, "that's done. If the invader tampers with the window again, he will set off the alarm. But I don't believe he'll touch it. I fancy he already knows his little game is discovered."

"How would he know it?" I demanded incredulously.

"If he is keeping an eye on this window, as he naturally would do, he has seen my light. Perhaps he is watching us now."

I glanced at the dark square of the window with a little shiver. This business was getting on my nerves again. But Godfrey turned away with a shrug of the shoulders.

"Now for the cabinet," he said, and led the way back up-stairs.

Rogers was still sitting dejectedly on the cot,
and looking at him more closely, I could see
that he was white and shaken. His trouble,
whatever its nature, plainly lay heavy on his
mind.

"Have you anything to tell us this evening,
Rogers?" I asked kindly, but he only shook his
head.

"I've told you everything I know, sir," he answered in a low voice.

"I'm not going to worry you, Rogers," I went
on, "but I want you to think it over. You can
rely upon me to help you, if I can."

He looked up quickly, but caught himself and
turned his eyes away.

"Thank you, sir," was all he said.

"And now," I added briskly, "I'll have to
ask you to get up. Move the cot away from the
door, Parks."

Parks obeyed me with astonished face.

"You're not going in there, sir!" he protested,
as I turned the knob.

"Yes, we are," I said, and opened the door.
"Is — is . . ."

"No, sir," broke in Parks, understanding.
"The undertakers brought the coffin and put him

in it and moved him over to the drawing-room this afternoon, sir."

"I'm glad of that. I want all the lights lit, Parks, just as they were last night."

Parks reached inside the door and switched on the electrics. Then he went away, came back in a moment with a taper, and proceeded to light the gas-lights. A moment later, the lights in the inner room were also blazing.

"There you are, sir," said Parks, and retreated to the door. "Will you need me?"

"Not now. But wait in the hall outside. We may need you." I had an impulse to tell him to have an axe handy, but I saw Godfrey smiling.

"Very good, sir," said Parks, evidently re-lieved, and went out and closed the door.

I led the way into the inner room.

"Well, there it is," I said, and nodded toward the Boule cabinet, standing in the full glare of the light, every inlay and incrustation glittering like the eyes of a basilisk. "It isn't too late to give it up, Godfrey."

"Oh yes, it is," he said coolly, as he removed his coat. "It was too late the moment you told me that story. Why, Lester, if I gave it up, I should never sleep again!"

"And if you don't, you may never wake again,"
I pointed out.

He laughed lightly.

"What a dismal prophet you are! Draw up a
chair and watch me."

He pulled back his shirt-sleeves and placed
his electric torch on the floor beside the cabinet.
Then he paused with folded arms to contemplate
this masterpiece of Monsieur Boule.

"It *is* a beauty," he said at last, and then drew
out the little drawers, one after another, looked
them over, and placed them carefully on a chair.
"Now," he added, "let us see if there is any
space that isn't accounted for."

He took from his pocket a folding rule of ivory,
opened it, and began a series of measurements
so searching and intricate that half an hour
passed without a word being spoken. Then he
pulled up another chair and sat down beside me.

"I seem to be pretty much up against it," he
said, "no doubt just as the designer of the cabinet
would wish me to be. The whole bottom of the
table is inclosed, and those three little drawers
take up only a small part of the space. Then the
back of the cabinet seems to be double — at least,
there's a space of three inches I can't account for.

So there's room for a dozen secret drawers, if the Montespan required so many. And now to find the combination."

He adjusted the steel gauntlet carefully to his right hand and sat down on the floor before the cabinet.

"I'll begin at the bottom," he said. "If there is any spot I miss, tell me of it."

He ran his fingers up and down the tapering legs, carefully feeling every inequality of the elaborate bronze ornamentation. Particularly did his fingers linger on every boss and point, striving to push it in or move it up or down; but they were all immovable. Then he examined the bottom of the cabinet minutely, using his torch to illumine every crevice; but again without result.

Another half hour passed so, and when at last he rose stiffly to his feet, his forehead was beaded with perspiration.

"It's trying work," he said, sitting down again and mopping his face. "But isn't it a beauty, Lester? The more I look at it, the more wonderful it seems."

"I told Philip Vantine I wasn't up to it, and I'm not," I said.

"Nor am I, but I can appreciate it to the extent

of my capacity. It's the Louis Fourteenth ideal
of beauty — splendour carried to the nth degree.
Look at that garland across the front — can you
imagine anything more graceful? And the en-
graving — nothing cut-and-dried about that. It
was done by a burin in the hand of a master —
no doubt by Boule himself. I don't wonder Vantine was rather mad about it. But we haven't
found that drawer yet," and he drew his chair
close to the cabinet.

"I'd point out one thing to you, Godfrey," I
said: "if you go on poking about with the fingers
of both hands as you've been doing, you are just
as apt to get struck on the left hand as on the
right."

"That's true," he agreed. "Stop me if I forget."

There were three drawers across the lower
part of the cabinet, and these Godfrey removed.
He inserted his hand into the space from which
he had taken them, and examined it carefully.
Then, inch by inch, he ran his fingers over the
bosses and arabesques with which the sides and
front of the table were incrusted. It seemed to me
that, if the secret drawer were anywhere, it must
be somewhere in this part of the cabinet, and I

watched him with breathless interest. Once I
thought he had found the drawer, for a piece of
inlay at the side of the table seemed to give a
little under the pressure of his fingers; but no
hidden spring was touched; no drawer sprang
open; no poisoned fangs descended.

"Well," said Godfrey, sitting back in his chair
at last, and wiping his face again, "there's so
much done. If there is any secret drawer
in the lower part of the cabinet, it is mighty
cleverly concealed. Now we'll try the upper
part."

The upper part of the cabinet consisted of a
series of drawers rising one above the other, and
terminated by a triangular pediment, its tympanum ornamented with some beautiful little
bronzes. The drawers themselves were concealed
by two doors opening in the centre, and covered
with a most intricate design of arabesqued in-
crustations.

"If there is a secret drawer here," said Godfrey, "it is somewhere in the back, where there
seems to be a hollow space. But to discover the
combination . . ."

He ran his fingers over the inlay, and then,
struck by a sudden thought, tested each of the

little figures along the tympanum, but they were all set solidly in place.

"There's one thing sure," he said, " the combination, whatever it is, is of such a nature that it could not be discovered accidentally — by a person leaning on the cabinet, for instance.   It isn't a question of merely touching a spring; it is probably a question of releasing a series of levers, which must be worked in a certain order or the drawer won't open.   I'm afraid we are up against it."

" I can't pretend I'm sorry," I said, with a sigh of relief.   " As far as I am concerned, I'm perfectly willing that the drawer should go undiscovered."

" Well, I am not! " retorted Godfrey curtly, and he sat regarding the cabinet with puckered brows.   Then he rose and began tapping at the back.

I don't know what it was — for I was conscious of no noise — but some mysterious attraction drew my eyes to the window at the farther side of the room.   Near the top of the wooden shutter which Parks and I had put in place, was a small semi-circular opening to allow the passage of a little light, perhaps, and peering through this opening were two eyes — two burning eyes . . .

They were fixed upon Godfrey with such fever-
ish intentness that they did not see my glance, and
I lowered my head instantly.

"Godfrey," I said, in a shaking voice, "don't
look up; don't move your head; but there is some
one peering through the hole in the shutter opposite us."

Godfrey did not answer for quite a minute, but
kept calmly on with his examination of the cabinet.

"Did he see you look at him?" he asked, at
last.

"No, he was looking at you, with his eyes almost starting out of his head. I never saw such
eyes!"

"Did you see anything of his face?"

"No, the hole is too small. I fancy I saw the
fingers of one hand which he had thrust through
to steady himself."

"How high is the hole?"

"Near the top of the window."   •

Godfrey came back to his chair a moment later,
sat down in it, and passed his handkerchief slowly
over his face. Then he leaned forward, apparently to examine the legs of the cabinet.

"I saw him," he said. "Or rather, I saw his eyes. Rather fierce, aren't they?"

"They're a tiger's eyes," I said with conviction.

"Well, there is no use going ahead with this while he is out there. Even if we found the drawer, we'd both be dead an instant later."

"You mean he'd kill us?"

"He would shoot us instantly. Imagine what a sensation that would make, Lester. Parks hears two pistol shots, rushes in and finds us lying here dead. Grady would have a convulsion — and we should both be famous for a few days."

"I'll seek fame in some other way," I said drily. "What are you going to do about it?"

"We've got to try to capture him; and if we do — well, we shall have the fame all right! But it's a good deal like trying to pick up a scorpion — we're pretty sure to get hurt. If that fellow out there is who I think he is, he's about the most dangerous man on earth."

He went on tapping the surface of the cabinet. As for me, I would have given anything for another look at those gleaming eyes. They seemed to be burning into me; hot flashes were shooting up and down my back.

"Why can't I go out as though I were going
after something," I suggested. "Then Parks
and I could charge around the corner and get
him."

"You wouldn't get him, he'd get you. You
wouldn't have a chance on earth. If there is a
window upstairs over that one, you might drop
something out on him, or borrow Parks's pistol
and shoot him —"

"That would be pretty cowardly, wouldn't it?"
I suggested mildly.

"My dear Lester," Godfrey protested, "when
you attack a poisonous snake, you don't do it
with bare hands, do you?"

I couldn't help it — I glanced again at the
window . . .

"He's gone!" I cried.

Godfrey was at the window in two steps.

"Look at that," he said, "and then tell me
he isn't a genius!"

I followed the direction of his pointing finger
and saw that, just opposite the opening in the
shutter, a little hole had been cut in the window-
pane.

"That fellow foresees everything," said Godfrey, with enthusiasm. "He probably cut that

hole as soon as it was dark. He must have guessed we were going to examine the cabinet to-night — and he wanted not only to see, but to hear. He heard everything we said, Lester!"

"Let's go after him!" I cried, and without waiting for an answer, I sprang across the ante-room and snatched open the door which led into the hall.

Parks and Rogers were sitting cn the couch just outside and I never saw two men more thoroughly frightened.

"For God's sake, Mr. Lester!" gasped Rogers, and stopped, his hand at his throat.

"Is it Mr. Godfrey?" cried Parks.

"There's a man outside. Got your pistol, Parks?"

"Yes, sir," and he took it from his pocket.

I snatched it from him, opened the front door, leaped the railing, and stole along the house to the corner.

Then, taking my courage in both hands, I charged around it.

There was no one in sight, but from some-where near at hand came a burst of mocking laughter.

CHAPTER XII

GODFREY IS FRIGHTENED

I WAS still staring about me, that mocking laughter in my ears, when Godfrey joined me.

"He got away, of course," he said coolly.

"Yes, and I heard him laugh!" I cried.

Godfrey looked at me quickly.

"Come, Lester," he said soothingly, "don't let your nerves run away with you."

"It wasn't my nerves," I protested, a little hotly. "I heard it quite plainly. He can't be far away."

"Too far for us to catch him," Godfrey retorted, and torch in hand, proceeded to examine the window-sill and the ground beneath it. "There is where he stood," he added, and the marks on the sill were evident enough. "Of course he had his line of retreat blocked out," and he flashed his torch back and forth across the grass, but the turf was so close that no trace of footsteps was visible.

We went slowly back to the house, and Godfrey sat down again to a contemplation of the cabinet.

"It's too much for me," he said, at last. "The only way I can find that drawer, I'm afraid, is with an axe. But I don't want to smash the thing to pieces —"

"I should say not! It would be like smashing the Venus de Milo."

"Hardly so bad as that. But we won't smash it yet awhile. I'm going to look up the subject of secret drawers — perhaps I'll stumble upon something that will help me."

"And then, of course," I said, disconsolately, "it is quite possible that there isn't any such drawer at all."

But Godfrey shook his head decidedly.

"I don't agree with you there, Lester. I'll wager that fellow who was looking in at us could find it in a minute."

"He seemed mighty frightened lest you should."

"He had reason to be," Godfrey rejoined grimly. "I'll have another try at it to-morrow. One thing we've got to take care of, and that is that our friend of the burning eyes doesn't get a chance at it first."

" Those shutters are pretty strong," I pointed out. " And Parks is no fool."

" Yes," agreed Godfrey, " the shutters are pretty strong — they might keep him out for ten minutes — scarcely longer than that. As for Parks, he wouldn't last ten seconds. You don't seem to understand the extraordinary character of this fellow."

" During your period of exaltation last night," I reminded him, " you referred to him as the greatest criminal of modern times."

" Well," smiled Godfrey, " perhaps that *was* a little exaggerated. Suppose we say one of the greatest — great enough, surely, to walk all around us, if we aren't on guard. I think I would better drop a word to Simmonds and get him to send down a couple of men to watch the house. With them outside, and Parks on the inside, it ought to be fairly safe."

" I should think so! " I said. " One would imagine you were getting ready to repel an army. Who is this fellow, anyway, Godfrey? You seem to be half afraid of him! "

" I'm wholly afraid of him, if he's who I think he is — but it's a mere guess as yet, Lester. Wait a day or two. I'll call up Simmonds."

He went to the 'phone, while I sat down again
and looked at the cabinet in a kind of stupefaction.
What was the intrigue of which it seemed to be
the centre? Who was this man, that Godfrey
should consider him so formidable? Why should
he have chosen Philip Vantine for a victim?

Godfrey came back while I was still groping
blindly amid this maze.

"It's all right," he said. "Simmonds is sending two of his best men to watch the house." He
stood for a moment gazing down at the cabinet.
"I'm coming back to-morrow to have another try
at it," he added. "I have left the gauntlet there
on the chair, so if you feel like having a try yourself, Lester . . ."

"Heaven forbid!" I protested. "But perhaps I would better tell Parks to let you in. I
hope I won't find you a corpse here, Godfrey!"

"So do I! But I don't believe you will. Yes,
tell Parks to let me in whenever I come around.
And now about Rogers."

"What about him?"

"I rather thought I might want to grill him to-
night. But perhaps I would better wait till I get
a little more to go on." He paused for a moment's thought. "Yes; I'll wait," he said,

finally.   " I don't want to run any risk of failing."

We went out into the hall together, and I told Parks to admit Godfrey whenever he wished to enter.   Rogers was still sitting on the cot, looking so crushed and sorrowful that I could not help pitying him.   I began to think that, if he were left to himself a day or two longer, he would tell all we wished to know without any grilling.

I confided this idea to Godfrey as we went down the front steps.

" Perhaps you're right," he agreed.   " I don't believe the fellow is really crooked.   Something has happened to him — something in connection with that woman — and he has never got over it. Well, we shall have to find out what it was. Hello, here are Simmonds's men," he added, as two policemen stopped before the house.

" Is this Mr. Godfrey? " one of them asked.

" Yes," said Godfrey.

" Mr. Simmonds told us to report to you, sir, if you were here."

" What we want you to do," said Godfrey, " is to watch the house — watch it from all sides — patrol clear around it, and see that no one approaches it."

" Very well, sir," and the men touched their

caps, and one of them went around to the back of the house, while the other remained in front.

" Perhaps if they concealed themselves," I suggested, " the fellow might venture back and be nabbed."

But Godfrey shook his head.

" I don't want him to venture back," he said. " I want to scare him off. I want him to see we're thoroughly on guard." He hailed a passing taxi, and paused with one foot on the step. " I've already told you, Lester," he added, over his shoulder, " that I'm afraid of him. Perhaps you thought I was joking, but I wasn't. I was never more serious in my life. The *Record* office," he added to the chauffeur, and rattled away, leaving me staring after him.

As I turned homeward, I could not but ponder over this remarkable and mysterious being with whom Godfrey was so impressed. Never before had I known him to hesitate to match himself with any adversary; but now, it seemed to me, he shunned the contest, or at least feared it — feared that he might be outwitted and outplayed! How great a compliment that was to the mysterious unknown only I could guess!

And then I shivered a little as I recalled that mocking and ironic laughter. And I quickened my step, with a glance over my shoulder; for if Godfrey was afraid, how much more reason had I to be! It was with a sense of relief, of which I was a little ashamed, that I reached my apartment at the Marathon and locked the door.

Just before I turned in for the night, I heard from Godfrey again, for my telephone rang and it was his voice that answered.

"I just wanted to tell you, Lester," he said, "that your guess was right. The mysterious Frenchman came over on the *France*, landing at noon yesterday. He came in the steerage, and the stewards know nothing about him. What time was it he got to Vantine's?"

"About two, I should say."

"So he probably went directly there from the boat, as you thought. That accounts for nobody knowing him. The steamship company is holding a bag belonging to him. I'll get them to open it to-morrow, and perhaps we shall find out who he was."

"But, Godfrey," I broke in, "how about this other fellow — the man with the burning eyes? He gives me the shivers!"

" Don't let him do that, Lester! " he laughed. " We're in no danger so long as we are not around that cabinet! That's the storm centre! I can't tell you more than that. Good-night! " and he hung up without waiting for me to answer.

CHAPTER XIII

A DISTINGUISHED CALLER

IT was shortly after I reached the office next morning, that the office-boy came in and handed me a card with an awed and reverent air so at variance with his usual demeanour that I glanced at it in some astonishment. Then, I confess, an awed and reverent feeling crept over me also, for the card bore the name of Sereno Hornblower.

That name is quite unknown outside the legal profession of the three great cities of the east, New York, Boston and Philadelphia; for Sereno Hornblower has never held a public office, has never made a public speech, has never responded to a toast, has never served on a public committee, has never, so far as I know, conducted a case in court or addressed a jury — has never, in a word, figured in the newspapers in any way; and yet his income must outrank that of any other lawyer in the country two or three times over.

For Sereno Hornblower is the confidential attorney of most of our "best families." He has held that position for years, and it is said that no case placed unreservedly in his hands ever resulted in a public scandal. He accepts clients with great care; he has steadfastly refused the business of Pittsburgh millionaires, remunerative as it was certain to be; but he seems to take a sort of personal pride in keeping intact the reputations of the old families, even when their scions engage in the most outrageous escapades. If you are descended from the Pilgrims or the Patroons, Mr. Hornblower will ask no further recommendation.

His reputation for tact and delicacy is tremendous; and yet those who have found themselves opposed to him have never been long in realising that there was a most redoubtable mailed fist under the velvet glove. Altogether a remarkable man, whose memoirs would make absorbing reading, could he be persuaded to write them — which is quite beyond the bounds of possibility. I had never met him either professionally or personally, and it was with some eagerness that I told the office-boy to show him in at once.

Sereno Hornblower did not look the part. His reputation led one to expect a sort of cross between Uriah Heep and Sherlock Holmes, but there was nothing secretive or insinuating about his appearance. He was a bluff and hearty man of middle age, rather heavy-set, fresh-faced and clean-shaven, and with very bright blue eyes — evidently a man with a good digestion and a comfortable conscience. Had I met him on Broadway, I should have taken him for a ripe and finished comedian, with a livelier sense of humour than most comedians have. It may have been this very appearance of bluff sincerity and honest downrightness which accounted for his success; at least it could not fail to be a very valuable asset.

We shook hands, and he sat down and plunged at once, without an instant's hesitation, into the business which had brought him. Looking back at it, understanding as I do now the delicate nature of that business, I admire more and more that bluff readiness; though the more I think of it, the more I am convinced that he had thought out definitely beforehand precisely what he was going to say. The man who can carry through a carefully premeditated scene with an air of complete unpremeditation has an immense advantage.

"Mr. Lester," he began, "I understand that you are the administrator of the estate of the late Philip Vantine?"

" Our firm is," I corrected.

" But you, personally, have been attending to his business? "

" Yes."

" He was a collector of old furniture, I believe? "

" Yes."

" And on his last trip to Europe, from which he returned only a few days ago, he purchased of Armand & Son, of Paris, a Boule cabinet? "

I could not repress a start of astonishment.

" Are you acting for Armand & Son? " I queried.

" Not at all. I am acting for a lady whom, for the present, we will call Madame X."

The thought flashed through my mind that Madame X. and the mysterious Frenchwoman might be one and the same person. Then I put aside the idea as absurd. Sereno Hornblower would never accept such a client.

" Mr. Vantine did buy such a cabinet," I said.

" And it is in your possession? "

" There is at his residence a Boule cabinet which was shipped him from Paris, but only a few hours before his death, Mr. Vantine assured me that it was not the one he had purchased."

" You mean that a mistake had been made in the shipment ? "

" That is what we supposed, and a cablegram from Armand & Son has since confirmed it."

Mr. Hornblower pondered this for a moment.

" Where is the cabinet which Mr. Vantine did buy ? " he asked at last.

" I have no idea. Perhaps it is still in Paris. But I am expecting a representative of the Armands to call very soon to straighten things out."

Again my companion fell silent and sat rubbing his chin absently.

" It is very strange," he said, finally. " If the cabinet was still in Paris, one would think it would have been discovered before my client made inquiry about it."

" There are a good many things which are strange about this whole matter," I supplemented.

" Would you have any objection to my client seeing this cabinet, Mr. Lester ? "

It was my turn to hesitate.

" Mr. Hornblower," I said finally, " I will be frank with you. There is a certain mystery surrounding this cabinet which we have not been able to solve. I suppose you have read of the mysteri-

ous deaths of Mr. Vantine and of an unknown
Frenchman, both in the same room at the Vantine
house, and both apparently from the same cause?"

He nodded.

"Do you mean that this cabinet is connected
with them in any way?" he asked quickly.

"We believe so; though as yet we have been
able to prove absolutely nothing. But we are
guarding the cabinet very closely. I should not
object to your client seeing it, but I could not permit her to touch it — not, at least, without knowing why she wished to do so. You will remember
that you have told me nothing of why she is interested in it."

"I am quite ready to tell you the story, Mr.
Lester," he said. "It is only fair that I should do
so. After you have heard it, if you agree, we will
take Madame X. to see the cabinet."

"Very well," I assented.

He settled back in his chair, and his face became more grave.

"My client," he began, "is a member of a
prominent American family — a most prominent
family. Some years ago, she married a French
nobleman. You can, perhaps, guess her name, but
I should prefer that neither of us utter it."

I nodded my agreement.

" This nobleman has been both prodigal and unfaithful. He has scattered my client's fortune with both hands. He has flaunted his mistresses in her face. He has even tried to compel her to receive one of them. I am free to confess that I consider her a fool not to have left him long ago. At last her trustees interfered, for her father had been wise enough to place a portion of her fortune in trust. They paid her husband's debts, placed him on an allowance, and notified his creditors that his debts would not be paid again."

I had by this time, of course, guessed the name of his client, since these details had long been a matter of public notoriety, and, I need hardly say, listened to the story with a heightened interest.

" The allowance is a princely one," Mr. Hornblower continued, " but it does not suffice Monsieur X. No allowance would suffice him — the more money he had, the more ways he would find of spending it. So he has become a thief. He has taken to selling the objects of art with which his residences are filled, and which are really the property of my client, since they were purchased with her money. About two weeks ago, my client returned to Paris from a stay at her château in Normandy to find that he had almost denuded the town house. Tapestries, pictures, sculptures — everything had been sold. Among other things which he had taken was a Boule cabinet, in which my client had been accustomed to keep her private papers. The cabinet was a most valuable one, but it is not its monetary value which makes my client so anxious to recover it."

He paused an instant and cleared his throat, and I realised that he was coming to the really delicate part of the story.

"Monsieur X. had had the decency," he went on, more slowly, "to, as he thought, retain his wife's private papers. He had caused the contents of the various drawers to be dumped out upon a chair. But there was one drawer of which he knew nothing — a secret drawer, known only to my client. That drawer contained a packet of letters which my client is most anxious to regain. Of their nature, I will say nothing — indeed, I know very little about them, for, after all, that is none of my business. But she has given me to understand that their recovery is essential to her peace of mind"

I nodded again; there was really no need that

he should say more. Only, I reflected, a faith-
less husband has no reason to complain if his wife
repays him in the same coin!

"My client went to work at once to regain
the cabinet," continued Mr. Hornblower, plainly
relieved that the thinnest ice had been crossed.
"She found that it had been sold to Armand &
Son. Hastening to their offices, she learned that
it had been resold by them to Mr. Vantine and
sent forward to him here. So she came over on
the first boat, ostensibly to visit her family, but
really to ask Mr. Vantine's permission to open
the drawer and take out the letters. His death
interfered with this, and, in despair, she came
to me. I need hardly add that no member of
her family knows anything about this matter, and
it is especially important that her husband should
never even suspect it. On her behalf, I apply to
you, as Mr. Vantine's executor, to restore these
letters to their owner."

I sat for a moment turning this extraordinary
story over in my mind and trying to make it fit
in with the occurrences of the past two days.
But it would not fit — at least, it would not fit with
my theory as to the cause of those occurrences.
For, surely, Madame X. would scarcely guard the
secret of that drawer with poison!

"Does any one besides your client know of the existence of these letters?" I asked at last.

"I think not," answered Mr. Hornblower, smiling drily. "They are not of a nature which my client would care to communicate to any one. In short, Mr. Lester, as you have doubtless suspected, they are compromising letters. We must get them back at any cost."

"As a matter of fact," I pointed out, "there are always at least two people who know of the existence of every letter — the person who writes it and the person who receives it."

"I had thought of that, but the person who wrote these letters is dead."

"Dead?" I repeated.

"He was killed in a duel," explained Mr. Hornblower gravely.

"By Monsieur X.?" I asked quickly.

"By Monsieur X.," said Mr. Hornblower, and sat regarding me, his lips pursed, as an indication, perhaps, that he would say no more.

But there was no necessity that he should. I knew enough of French law and of French habits of thought to realise that if those letters ever came into possession of Monsieur X., the game would be entirely in his hands. His wife would be absolutely at his mercy. And the thought flashed through my mind that perhaps in some way he had learned of the existence of the letters and was trying desperately to get them. That thought was enough to swing the balance in his wife's favour.

"I am sure," I said, "that Mr. Vantine would instantly have consented to your client opening the drawer and taking out the letters. And as his executor, I also consent, for whoever may own the cabinet, the letters are the property of Madame X. All this providing, of course, that this should prove to be the right cabinet. But I must warn you, Mr. Hornblower, that I believe two men have already been killed trying to open that drawer," and I told him, while he sat there staring in profound amazement, of my theory in regard to the death of Philip Vantine and of the unknown Frenchman. "I am inclined to think," I concluded, "that Vantine blundered upon the drawer while examining the cabinet; but there is no doubt that the other man knew of the drawer, and also, presumably, of its contents."

"Well!" exclaimed my companion. "I have listened to many astonishing stories in my life, but never one to equal this. And you know nothing of this Frenchman?"

"Nothing except that he came from Havre on the *France* last Thursday, and drove from the dock direct to Vantine's house."

"My client also came on the *France* — but that, no doubt, was a mere coincidence."

"That may be," I agreed, "but it is scarcely a coincidence that both he and your client were after the contents of that drawer."

"You mean . . ."

"I mean that the mysterious Frenchman may very possibly have been an emissary of Monsieur X.. Madame may have betrayed the secret to him in an unguarded moment."

Mr. Hornblower rose abruptly. He was evidently much disturbed.

"You may be right," he agreed. "I will communicate with my client at once. I take it that she has your permission to see the cabinet, and if it proves to be the right one, that she may open the drawer and remove the letters."

"If she cares to take the risk," I assented.

"Very well; I will call you as soon as I have seen her," he said. "In any event, I thank you for your courtesy," and he left the office.

He must have driven straight to her family residence on the Avenue; or perhaps she was awaiting him at his office; at any rate, he called me up inside the half hour.

"My client would like to see the cabinet at once," he said. "She is in a very nervous condition, especially since she learned that some one else has tried to open the drawer. When will it be convenient for you to go with us?"

"I can go at once," I said.

"Then we will drive around for you. We should be there in fifteen or twenty minutes."

"Very well," I said, "I'll be ready. I shall, of course, wish to take a witness with me."

"That is quite proper," assented Mr. Hornblower. "We can have no objection to that. In twenty minutes, then."

I got the *Record* office as soon as I could, but Godfrey was not there. He did not come on usually, some one said, until the middle of the afternoon. I rang his rooms, but there was no reply. Finally I called up the Vantine house.

"Parks," I said, "I am bringing up some people to look at that cabinet. It might be just as well to get that cot out of the way and have all the lights going."

"The lights are already going, sir," he said.

"Already going? What do you mean?"

"Mr. Godfrey has been here for quite a while, sir, fooling with that cabinet thing."

"He has!" and then I reflected that I ought to have guessed his whereabouts. "Tell him, Parks, that I am bringing some people up to see the cabinet, and that I should like him to stay there and be a witness of the proceedings."

"Very well, sir," assented Parks.

"Everything quiet?"

"Oh yes, sir; there were two policemen outside all night, and Rogers and me inside."

"Mr. Hornblower's car is below, sir," announced the office-boy, opening the door.

"All right," I said. "We are coming right up, Parks. Good-bye," and I hung up and slipped into my coat.

Then, as I took down my hat, a sudden thought struck me.

If the unknown Frenchman was indeed an emissary of Monsieur X., Madame might be acquainted with him. It was a long shot, but worth trying! I stepped to my desk, took out the photograph which Godfrey had given me, and slipped it into my pocket. Then I hurried out to the elevator.

CHAPTER XIV

THE VEILED LADY

THERE were three persons in the car. Mr.
Hornblower sat on one of the strapontins at the
front, and two women were on the rear seat.
Both were dressed in black and heavily veiled, but
there was about them the indefinable distinction
of mistress and maid. It would be difficult to tell
precisely in what the distinction consisted, but it
was there.

Mr. Hornblower glanced behind me as I entered.

"You spoke of a witness," he said.

"He is at the Vantine house," I explained, and
took the other strapontin.

"This is Mr. Lester," he said, and the veiled
lady whom I had known at once to be the mistress
inclined her head a little.

Those were the only words spoken. The car
rolled out to Broadway and then turned northward, making such progress as was possible
along that crowded thoroughfare. I glanced
from time to time at the two women and was
struck by the contrast in their behaviour. One sat

quite still, her hands in her lap, her head bent, admirably self-contained; the other was restless and uneasy, unable to control a nervous twitching of the fingers. I wondered why the maid should seem more upset than her mistress, and decided finally that her uneasiness was merely lack of breeding. But the contrast interested me.

At Tenth Street, the car turned westward again, skirted Washington Square, turned into the Avenue, and stopped before the Vantine house. Mr. Hornblower assisted the women to alight, and I led the way up the steps. But as we reached the top and came upon the funeral wreath on the door, the veiled lady stopped with a little exclamation.

"I did not know," she said quickly. "Perhaps, after all, we would better wait. I did not realise . . ."

"There are no relatives to be hurt, madame," I interrupted. "As for the dead man, what can it matter to him?" and I rang the bell.

Parks opened the door, and nodding to him, I led the way along the hall and into the ante-room. Godfrey was awaiting us there, and I saw the flame of interest which leaped into his eyes as Mr. Hornblower and the two veiled women entered.

"This is my witness," I said to the former. "Mr. Godfrey — Mr. Hornblower."

Godfrey bowed, and Hornblower regarded him with a good-humoured smile.

"If I were not sure of Mr. Godfrey's discretion," he said, "I should object. But I have tested it before this, and know that it can be relied upon."

"There is only one person to whom I yield precedence in the matter of discretion," rejoined Godfrey, smiling back at him, "and that is Mr. Hornblower.   He is in a class quite by himself."

"Thank you," said the lawyer, and bowed gravely.

During this interchange of compliments, the woman I had decided was the maid had sat down, as though her legs were unable to sustain her, and was nervously clasping and unclasping her hands; even her mistress showed signs of impatience.

"The cabinet is in here," I said, and led the way into the inner room, the two men and the veiled lady at my heels.

It stood in the middle of the floor, just as it had stood since the night of the tragedy, and all the lights were going.   As I entered, I noticed Godfrey's gauntlet lying on a chair.

"Is it the right one, madame?" I asked.

She gazed at it a moment, her hands pressed against her breast.

"Yes!" she answered, with a gasp that was almost a sob.

I confess I was astonished. I had never thought it could be the right one; even now I did not see how it could possibly be the right one.

"You are sure?" I queried incredulously.

"Do you think I could be mistaken in such a matter, sir? I assure you that this cabinet at one time belonged to me. You permit me?" she added, and took a step toward it.

"One moment, madame," I interposed. "I must warn you that in touching that cabinet you are running a great risk."

"A great risk?" she echoed, looking at me.

"A very great risk, as I have pointed out to Mr. Hornblower. I have reason to believe that two men met death while trying to open that secret drawer."

"I believe Mr. Hornblower did tell me something of the sort," she murmured; "but of course that is all a mistake."

"Then the drawer is not guarded by poison?" I questioned.

" By poison? " she repeated blankly, and carried her handkerchief to her lips. " I do not understand."

I knew that my theory was collapsing, utterly, hopelessly. I dared not look at Godfrey.

" Is there not, connected with the drawer," I asked, " a mechanism which, as the drawer is opened, plunges two poisoned fangs into the hand which opens it? "

" No, Mr. Lester," she answered, astonishment in her voice, " I assure you there is no such mechanism."

I clutched at a last straw, and a sorry one it was!

" The mechanism may have been placed there since the cabinet passed from your possession," I suggested.

" That is, perhaps, possible," she agreed, though I saw that she was unconvinced.

" At any rate, madame," I said, " I would ask that, in opening the drawer, you wear this gauntlet," and I picked up Godfrey's gauntlet from the chair on which it lay. " It is needless that you should take any risk, however slight. Permit me," and I slipped the gauntlet over her right hand.

THE BOULE CABINET 171

As I did so, I glanced at Godfrey. He was staring at the veiled lady with such a look of stupefaction that I nearly choked with delight. It had not often been my luck to see Jim Godfrey mystified, but he was certainly mystified now!

The veiled lady regarded the steel glove with a little laugh.

" I am now free to open the drawer? " she asked.

" Yes, madame."

She moved toward the cabinet, Godfrey and I close behind her. At last the secret which had defied us was to be revealed. And with its revelation would come the end of the picturesque and romantic theory we had been building up so laboriously.

Instinctively, I glanced toward the shuttered window, but the semi-circle of light was unobscured.

The veiled lady stepped close to the cabinet and disposed the fingers of her right hand to fit the metal inlay midway of the left side.

" It is a little awkward," she said. " I have always been accustomed to using the left hand. You will notice that I am pressing on three points; but to open the drawer, one must press these points in a certain order — first this one, then this one, and then this one."

There was a sharp click, and, at the side of the cabinet a piece of the metal inlay fell forward.

"That is the handle," said the veiled lady, and without an instant's hesitation, while my heart stood still, she grasped it and drew out a shallow drawer. "Ah!" and casting aside the ridiculous gauntlet, she caught up the packet of papers which lay within. Then, with an effort, she controlled herself, slipped off the ribbon which held the packet together, and spread out before my eyes ten or twelve envelopes. "You will see that they are only letters, Mr. Lester," she said in a low voice, "and I assure you that they belong to me."

"I believe you, madame," I said, and with a sigh of relief that was almost a sob, she rebound the packet and slipped it into her bag. "There is one thing," I added, "which madame can, perhaps, do for me."

"I shall be most happy!" she breathed.

"As I have told Mr. Hornblower," I continued, "two men died in this room the day before yesterday. Or rather, it was in the room beyond that they died; but we believed it was here they received the wounds which caused death. It seems that we were wrong in this."

"Undoubtedly," she agreed. "There has never been any such weird mechanism as you described connected with that drawer, Mr. Lester. At least, not since I have had it. There is a legend, you know, that the cabinet was made for Madame de Montespan."

She was talking more freely now; evidently a great load had been lifted from her — perhaps I did not guess how great!

"Mr. Vantine suspected as much," I said. "He was a connoisseur of furniture and there was something about this cabinet which told him it had belonged to the Montespan. He was examining it at the time he died. What the other man was doing we do not know, but if we could identify him, it might help us."

"You have not identified him?"

"We know nothing whatever about him except that he was presumably a Frenchman, and that he arrived on the *France* two days ago."

"That is the boat upon which I came over."

"It has occurred to me, madame, that you may have seen him — that he may even be known to you."

" What was his name? "

" The card he sent in to Mr. Vantine bore the name of Théophile d'Aurelle."

She shook her head.

" I have never before heard that name, Mr. Lester."

" We believe it to have been an assumed name," I said; " but perhaps you will recognise this photograph," and I drew it from my pocket and handed it to her.

She took it, looked at it, and again shook her head.   Then she looked at it again, turning aside and raising her veil in order to see it better.

" There seems to be something familiar about the face," she said at last, " as though I might have seen the man somewhere."

" On the boat, perhaps," I suggested, but I knew very well it was not on the boat, since the man had crossed in the steerage.

" No; it was not on the boat.   I did not leave my stateroom on the boat.   But I am quite sure that I have seen him — and yet I can't say where."

" Perhaps," I said, in a low voice, " he may have been one of the friends of your husband."

I saw her hand tremble under the blow, but it had to be struck.   And she was brave.

"The same thought occurred to me, Mr. Lester," she answered; "but I know very few of my husband's friends; certainly not this one.   And yet . . . . Perhaps my maid can help us."

Photograph in hand, she stepped through the doorway into the outer room.   The maid was sitting on the chair where we had left her, her hands clenched tightly together in her lap, as though it was only by some violent effort she could maintain her self-control.

"Julie," said the veiled lady in rapid French, "I have here the photograph of a man who was killed in this room most mysteriously a few days ago.   These gentlemen wish to identify him.   The face seems to me somehow familiar, but I cannot place it.   Look at it."

Julie put forth a shaking hand, took the photograph, and glanced at it; then with a long sigh, slid limply to the floor, before either Godfrey or I could catch her.

As she fell, her veil, catching on the chair-back, was torn away; and looking down at her, a great emotion burst within me, for I recognised the mysterious woman whose photograph d'Aurelle had carried in his watch-case.

CHAPTER XV

THE SECRET OF THE UNKNOWN FRENCHMAN

FOR a moment I stood spell-bound, staring down at that jaded and passion-stained countenance; then Godfrey sprang forward and lifted the unconscious woman to the couch.

" Bring some water," he said, and as he turned and looked at me, I saw that his face was glowing with excitement.

I rushed to the door and snatched it open. Rogers was standing in the hall outside, and I sent him hurrying for the water and turned back into the room.

Godfrey was chafing the girl's hands, and the veiled lady was bending over her, fumbling at the fastenings of her collar. Evidently she could not see them, for with a sudden movement, she put back her veil. My heart warmed to her at that act of sacrifice, and after a single glance at her, I turned away my eyes.

I saw Godfrey's start of recognition as he looked down at her; then he, too, looked aside.

"Here's the water, sir," said Rogers, and handed me glass and carafe.

The next instant his eyes fell upon the woman on the couch. He stood staring, his face turning slowly purple; then, clutching at his throat, he half-turned and fell, just as I had seen him do once before.

Hornblower, who was staring at the unconscious woman and mopping his face feverishly, spun around at the crash.

"Well, I'll be damned!" he said, in a hoarse voice, as he saw Rogers extended on the floor at his feet. "What's the matter with this house, anyway?"

So great was the tension on my nerves that I could scarcely restrain a shout of laughter. I turned it into a shout for Parks; but his face, when he appeared on the threshold, was too much for me and I sank into a chair, laughing hysterically.

"For God's sake!" Parks began   .   .   .

"It's all right," Godfrey broke in sharply "Rogers has had another fit. Get the ammonia!"

Parks staggered away, and Mr. Hornblower sat down weakly.

" I don't see the joke ! " he growled, glaring at me, his face crimson.

" Get a grip of yourself, Lester," said Godfrey savagely, seized the carafe from my hand, and hurried with it to madame.

I *did* get a grip of myself, and when Parks came back a moment later with the ammonia, was able to hold up Rogers's head, while Parks applied the phial to his nostrils.

" Give me a whiff of it, too, Parks," I said unsteadily, and in an instant my eyes were streaming; but I had escaped hysteria. " Straighten Rogers out and let him lie there," I gasped, and sat dizzily down upon the floor. But I dared not look at Hornblower. I felt that another glance at his dazed countenance would send me off again.

Madame, meanwhile, had dashed some water into the face of the unconscious Julie — much to the detriment of her complexion ! — watched her a moment, then stood erect and lowered her veil.

" She will soon be all right again," she said; and truly enough, at the end of a few seconds the girl opened her eyes and looked dazedly about her. Then a violent trembling seized her.

" What is it, Julie ? " asked her mistress, taking her hand. " You knew this man ? "

A hoarse sob was the only answer.

"You must tell me," went on madame, quietly but firmly. "Perhaps a crime has been committed. You must tell me everything. You may rely upon the discretion of these gentlemen. You knew this man?"

The girl nodded, and closed her eyes; but the hot tears brimmed from them and ran down over her cheeks.

"In Paris?"

The girl nodded again.

"He was your lover?"

A third nod, and a fresh flood of tears.

"I remember, now," said madame suddenly. "I saw him with her once. What was he doing in this house?" she went on; more sternly. "Tell us!"

"Madame will never forgive me!" sobbed the girl, and I began to think that she was more concerned for herself than for her lover. The same thought occurred to her mistress too, no doubt, for her voice hardened.

"Try me," she said. "Understand well, you must tell — if not here, then before an officer of the police."

"Oh, no, no!" screamed Julie, sitting suddenly

erect. "Never that! I could not bear that!
Madame would not be so cruel!"

"Then tell us now!" said the veiled lady inexorably.

"Very well, madame!" cried the girl, dabbing
at her eyes with her handkerchief, and speaking
in a mixture of French and English which I shall
not attempt to transcribe. "I will tell; I
will tell everything. After all, I was not to
blame. It was that creature. I did not love him
— but I feared him. He possessed a power over
me. He could make me do anything. He even
beat me! And still I went back to him!"

"What was his name?" asked the veiled lady.

"Georges Drouet — he lived in the Rue de
la Huchette, just off the Rue Saint Jacques — on
the top floor, under the gutters. He was bad —
bad; — he lived off women. I met him six
months ago. He knew how to fascinate one; I
thought he loved me. Then he began to borrow
money from me, until he had taken all that I had
saved; then my rings — every one!" She
held up her hands to show their bareness.
"Then . . ."

She stopped and glanced at her mistress.

"Continue!" said the latter. "Tell what you
have to tell."

"I knew that madame also . . ."

She stopped again. I walked over to the window and stood staring at the wooden shutter, strangely moved.

"Well, why not?" she demanded fiercely, and I felt that she was addressing my turned back. "Why not? Shall a woman not be loved? Shall a woman endure what madame endured . . ."

"That will do, Julie," broke in the veiled lady, her voice cold as ice. "Tell your story."

"I knew of the secret drawer; I had seen madame open it; I knew what it contained. But I was faithful to madame; I loved her; I was glad that she had found some one. . . . Madame will remember her despair, her horror, when she entered her room to find the cabinet gone, taken away, sold by that . . . I, too, was in despair — I desired with my whole soul to help madame. That night I had a rendezvous with him," and she nodded toward the photograph which lay upon the floor. "I told him."

Her mistress stood as though turned to stone. I could guess her anguish and humiliation.

"He questioned me — he learned everything — the drawer, how it was opened — all. But I did not suspect what was in his mind — not for an instant did I suspect. But on the boat I saw him,

and then I knew.   Well, he has got what he deserved!"

She shivered and pressed her hands against her
eyes.

"I think that is all, madame," she added
hoarsely.

"It is all of that story," said Godfrey, in a crisp
voice; "but there is another."

"Another?" echoed the veiled lady, looking at
him.

"Ask her, madame, for what purpose she called
at this house, night before last, and saw Philip
Vantine in this room."

"I did not!" shrieked the girl, her face ablaze.
"It is a lie!"

"She does not need to tell!" went on Godfrey
inexorably.   "Any fool could guess.   She came
for the letters!   She had resolved to blackmail
you herself, madame!"

"It is a lie!" shrieked the girl again.   "I
came hoping to save her — to . . ."

A storm of angry sobbing choked her.

I could see how the veiled lady was trembling.
I placed a chair for her, and she sank into it with
a murmur of thanks.

"Besides, we have a witness to her visit,"

added Godfrey. " Shall I call the police, madame? "

" No, no! " and the girl sat upright again, her face ghastly. " I will tell. I will tell all. Give me but a moment! "

She sat there struggling for self-control, her streaked and grotesque countenance contorted with emotion. Then I saw her eyes widen, and glancing around, I saw that Rogers had dragged himself to a sitting posture and was staring at her, his face livid.

The sight of him seemed to madden her.

" It was you! " she shrieked, and shook her clenched fist at him. " It was you who told! Coward! Coward! "

But Godfrey, his face very grim, laid a heavy hand upon her arm.

" Be still! " he cried. " He told us nothing! He tried to shield you — though why he should wish to do so . . ."

Rogers broke in with a hollow and ghastly laugh.

" It was natural enough, sir," he said hoarsely. " She's my wife! "

CHAPTER XVI

PHILIP VANTINE'S CALLER

It was a sordid story that Rogers gasped out to us; and as it concerns this tale only incidentally, I shall pass over it as briefly as may be.

Eight or ten years before, the fair Julie — at least, she was fairer then than now! — had come to New York to enter the employ of a family whose mistress had decided that life without a French maid was unendurable. Rogers had met her, had been fascinated by her black eyes and red lips, had, in the end, proposed honourable marriage — quite unnecessarily, no doubt! — had been accepted, and for some months had led an eventful existence as the husband of the siren. Then, one morning, he awakened to find her gone.

He had, of course, entrusted his savings to her — that had been one condition of the marriage! — and the savings were gone, also. Julie, it seems, had been overcome with longing for the Paris asphalt; no doubt, too, she had found herself ennuied by the lack of romance in married life with Rogers; and she had flown back to

France. Rogers had thought of following, but, appalled at the difficulty of finding her in Paris, not knowing what he should do if he did find her, he had finally given it up and had settled gloomily down to live upon his memories. Some sort of affection for her had kept alive within him, and when he opened the door of Vantine's house and found her standing on the steps, he was as wax in her hands.

Julie had listened to all this indifferently, even disdainfully, without denying anything nor seeking to excuse herself. Perhaps the idea that she needed excuse did not occur to her. And when the story was finished, she was quite herself again; even a little proud, I think, of holding the centre of the stage in the rôle of siren. It was almost a rejuvenescence, and there was gratitude in the gaze she turned on Rogers.

"This is all true, I suppose?" asked the veiled lady.

"All quite true, madame," answered Julie, with a shrug. "I was younger then and the love of excitement was too strong for me. I am older now and have more sense — besides, I am no longer sought after as I was."

"And so," said madame, with irony, "you are

now, no doubt, willing to return to your husband."

"I have been considering it, madame," replied
Julie, with astounding simplicity, "ever since I
saw him here the other evening and learned that
he still cared for me. One must have a harbour
in one's old age."

I glanced at Rogers and was astonished to see
that he was regarding the woman with affectionate
admiration. Evidently the harbour was waiting,
should Julie choose to anchor there.

"I have hesitated," she added, "only because
of madame. Where would madame get another
maid such as I? No one but I can arrange her
hair — no one but I can prepare her bath . . ."

"We will discuss it," said the veiled lady,
"when we are alone. And now, perhaps, you will
be so good as to tell us of your previous visit
here."

"Very well, madame," and Julie settled into a
more comfortable posture. "It was one day on
the boat as I was looking down at the passengers
of the third class that I perceived Georges —
Monsieur Drouet — strolling about. I was
bouleversée — what you call upset with amazement, and then he looked up and our eyes met,

and he came beneath me and commanded that I
meet him that evening. It was then that I learned
his plan. It was to secure those letters for himself and to dispose of them."

"To whom?" asked Godfrey.

"To the person who would pay the greatest
price for them, most certainly," answered Julie,
surprised that it should have been thought necessary to ask such a question. "They were to be
offered first to madame at ten thousand francs
each; should she refuse, they were then to be
offered to Monsieur le Duc — he would surely
desire to possess them!"

The veiled lady shivered a little, and her hand
instinctively sought her bag to assure herself
that the precious packet was safe.

"That night," continued Julie, "in my cabin, I
tossed and tossed, trying to discover a way to
prevent this, for I had seen long since that
Georges no longer cared for me — I knew that it
was upon some other woman that money would be
spent. I decided that, at the first moment, I
would hasten to this house, I would explain the
matter to Monsieur Vantine, I would persuade him
to restore to me the letters, with which I would fly
to madame. I knew, also, that I could rely upon

her gratitude," added the girl. "After all, one must provide for oneself."

She paused and glanced around the room, smiling at the interest in our faces.

"You have at least one virtue — that of frankness," said the veiled lady. "Continue."

"It was not until evening that I found an opportunity to leave madame," Julie went on. "I hastened here; I rang the bell; but I confess I should have failed, I should not have secured an entrance, if it had not been that it was my husband who opened the door to me. Even after I was inside the door, he refused to permit me to see his master, but as we were debating together, Monsieur Vantine himself came into the hall, and I ran to him and begged that he hear me. It was then that he invited me to enter this room."

She paused again, and a little shiver of expectancy ran through me. At last we were to learn how Philip Vantine had met his death!

"I sat down," continued Julie. "I told him the story from the very beginning. He listened with much interest, but when I proposed that he should restore to me the letters, he hesitated. He walked up and down the room, trying to decide; then he took me through that door into the room

beyond.   The cabinet was standing in the centre
of the floor, and all the lights were blazing.

" ' Is that the cabinet? ' he asked me, and when
I said that most assuredly it was, he seemed surprised.

" ' It is an easy thing to prove,' I said, and
I went to the cabinet and pressed on the three
springs, as I had seen madame do.   The little
handle at the side fell out, but suddenly he stopped
me.

" ' Yes, it is the cabinet,' he said.   ' I see that.
And no doubt the drawer contains the letters, as
you say.   But those letters do not belong to you.
They belong to your mistress.   I cannot permit
that you take them away, for, after all, I do not
know you.   You may intend to make some bad
use of them.'

" I protested that such a suspicion was most unjust, that my character was of the best, that I
was devoted to my mistress and desired to pro-
tect her.   He listened, but he was not convinced.
In the end, he brought me back into this room.
I could have cried with rage!

" ' Return to your mistress,' he said, ' and inform her that I shall be most happy to return the
letters to her.   But it must be in her own hands

that I place them. The letters are here, whenever it pleases her to claim them.'

"I saw that it was of no use to argue further; he was of adamant. So I left the house, he himself opening the door for me. And that is all that I know, madame."

There was a moment's silence; then I heard Godfrey draw a deep breath. I could see that, like myself, he was convinced that the girl was telling the truth.

"Of course," he suggested gently, "as soon as you reached home you related to your mistress what had occurred?"

Julie grew a little crimson.

"No, monsieur," she said, "I told her nothing."

"I should have thought you would have wished to prove your devotion," went on Godfrey, in his sweetest tone.

"I feared that, without the letters, she would misunderstand my motives," said Julie, sullenly.

"And then, of course, without the letters, there would be no reward," Godfrey supplemented.

Julie did not reply, but she looked very uncomfortable.

The veiled lady rose.

"Have you any further questions to ask her?"
she said.

"No, madame," said Godfrey. "The story
is complete."

Julie resumed her veil, shooting at Godfrey a
glance anything but friendly. The veiled lady
turned to me and held out her hand.

"I thank you, Mr. Lester, for your kindness,"
she said. "Come, Julie," and she moved toward
the door, which Rogers hastened to open.

Mr. Hornblower nodded and passed out after
them, and Godfrey and I were left alone together.

We both sat down and for a moment neither
of us spoke.

"Well!" said Godfrey, at last. "Well!
what a story it would make! And I can't use it!
It's a bitter reflection, Lester!"

"It would certainly shake the pillars of society," I agreed. "I'm rather shaken myself."

"So am I! I was all at sea for a while — I
was dumb with astonishment when I heard you and
the veiled lady talking about the secret drawer
— I could see you laughing at me! I don't know
the whole story yet. How did she happen to
come to you?"

I told him of Hornblower's visit, of the story

he told me, and of the arrangement we had made.
Godfrey nodded thoughtfully when I had finished.

"The story is straight, of course," he said.
"Hornblower would not be engaged in anything
tricky. Besides, I recognised the lady. I suppose you did, too."

"Yes, I have seen pictures of her. And I admired her for putting back her veil."

"So did I. She has changed since the day of
her wedding, Lester — she was a smooth-faced
girl, then! Those years of life with her duke
have left their mark on her!"

He fell silent, staring thoughtfully at the carpet. Then he shook himself.

"And the maid's story was most interesting,"
he added. "Nevertheless, there are still a number of things which are not quite clear to me."

"There is one thing I don't understand myself," I said. "I hadn't any idea this was the
right cabinet. I didn't see how it could be."

"That's it exactly. How did it happen, when
the veiled lady went to Armand & Son in Paris,
that she was directed to Philip Vantine? According to his own story, he did not purchase this
cabinet; he had never seen it before; it was presumably shipped him by mistake; Armand & Son

cable you that it was a mistake; and yet they cite
Vantine as the purchaser.   There is something
twisted somewhere, Lester; just where I'll try to
find out."

"Which reminds me that Armand's representative hasn't been around yet.   No doubt he can
straighten the matter out."

"It won't do any harm to hear his story, anyway," Godfrey agreed.   "Now let's have a look
at that drawer."

It was standing open as we had left it, and Godfrey pushed it back into place, calling my attention to the cunning way in which its outline was
concealed by the inlay about it.   Then he worked
the spring, the handle fell into place, and he drew
the drawer out again as far as it would come,
and examined it carefully.

"The fellow who devised that was a genius,"
he said admiringly, pushing it back into place.
"I wonder what its contents have been from the
days of Madame de Montespan down to the present?   Love letters mostly, I suppose, since they
are the things which need concealment most.
Don't you wish this drawer could tell its secrets,
Lester?"

"There is one I wish it would tell, if it knows

it," I said. "I wish it would tell who killed Philip Vantine. I suppose you will agree with me that our pretty theory has got a knock-out blow this time."

"It looks that way, doesn't it?"

"There is no poisoned mechanism about that drawer — that's sure," I added.

"No, and never has been," Godfrey agreed.

"And that leaves us all at sea, doesn't it? It leaves the whole affair more mysterious than ever. I can't understand it," and I sat down in my bewilderment and rubbed my head. I really felt for an instant as though I had gone mentally blind. "There is one thing sure," I added. "The killing, whatever its cause, was done out there in the ante-room, not in here."

"What makes you think that?"

"We believe that Drouet came here to get Vantine's permission to open this drawer and get the letters, no doubt representing himself as the agent of their owner."

"I think it's a pretty good guess," said Godfrey pensively.

"Our theory was that after being shown into the ante-room, he discovered the cabinet, tried to open the drawer, and was killed in the attempt.

But it is evident enough now that there is nothing about that drawer to hurt any one."

" Yes, that's evident, I think," Godfrey agreed.

" If he had opened the drawer, then, he would have taken the letters, since there was nothing to prevent him. Since they were not taken, it follows, doesn't it, that he was killed before he had a chance at the drawer? Perhaps he never saw the cabinet. He must have been killed out there in the ante-room, a few minutes after Parks left."

" And how about Vantine? " Godfrey asked.

" I don't know," I said helplessly. " He didn't want the letters — if he opened the drawer at all, it was merely out of curiosity to see how it worked. Only, of course, the same agency that killed Drouet, killed him. Yes — and now that I think of it, it's certain he didn't open the drawer either."

" How do you know it's certain? "

" If he had opened the drawer," I pointed out, " and been killed in the act of opening it, it would have been found open. I had thought that perhaps it closed of itself, but you see that it does not. You have to push it shut and then snap the handle up into place."

" That's true," Godfrey assented, " and it

sounds pretty conclusive.   If it is true of Vantine,
it is also true of Drouet.   The inference is, then,
that neither of them opened the drawer.   Well,
what follows? "

" I don't know," I said helplessly.   " Nothing
seems to follow."

" There is an alternative," Godfrey suggested.

" What is it? " I demanded.

" The hand that killed Drouet and Vantine
may also have closed the drawer," said Godfrey,
and looked at me.

" And left the letters in it? " I questioned.
" Surely not! "

He glanced at the shuttered window, and I
understood to whom he thought that hand belonged.

" Besides," I protested, " how would he get
in?   How would he get away?   What was he
after, if he left the letters behind? "   Then I
rose wearily.   " I must be getting back to
the office," I said.   " This is Saturday, and we
close at noon.   Are you coming? "

" No," he answered; " if you don't mind, I'll
sit here a while longer and think things over,
Lester.   Perhaps I'll blunder on to the truth
yet! "

CHAPTER XVII

ENTER MONSIEUR ARMAND

I GOT back to the office to find that M. Félix Armand, of Armand et Fils, had called, and finding me out, had left his card with the pencilled memorandum that he would call again Monday morning. There was another caller who had awaited my return — a tall, angular man, with a long moustache, who introduced himself as Simon W. Morgan, of Osage City, Iowa.

"Poor Philip Vantine's nearest living relative, sir," he added. "I came as soon as possible."

"It was very good of you," I said. "The funeral will be at ten o'clock to-morrow morning, from the house."

"You had a telegram from me?"

"Yes," I answered.

He hitched about in his chair uneasily for a moment. I knew what he wanted to say, but saw no reason to help him.

"He left a will, I suppose?" he asked, at last.

"Oh, yes; we have arranged to probate it

197

Monday. You can examine it then, if you wish."

"Have you examined it?"

"I am familiar with its provisions. It was drawn here in the office."

He was pulling furiously at his moustache.

"Cousin Philip was a very wealthy man, I understand," he managed to say.

"Comparatively wealthy. He had securities worth about a million and a quarter, besides a number of pieces of real property — and, of course, the house he lived in. He owned a very valuable collection of art objects — pictures, furniture, tapestries, and such things; but what they are worth will probably never be known."

"Why not?" he asked.

"Because he left them all to the Metropolitan Museum of Art. Outside of a few legacies to old servants, he left his whole fortune to the same institution."

I put it rather brutally no doubt, but I was anxious to end the interview.

Mr. Morgan's face grew very red.

"He did!" he ejaculated. "Ha — well, I have heard he was rather crazy."

"He was as sane as any man I ever knew."

I retorted drily. And then I remembered the doubts which had assailed me that last day, when Vantine was fingering the Boule cabinet. But I kept those doubts to myself.

"Ha — we'll have to see about that!" said my visitor, threateningly.

"By all means, Mr. Morgan," I assented heartily. "If you have any doubt about it, you should certainly look into it. And now, if you will pardon me, I have many things to do, and we close early to-day."

He got to his feet and went slowly out; and that was the last I ever saw of him. I suppose he consulted an attorney, learned the hopeless nature of his case, and took the first train back to Osage City. He did not even wait for the funeral.

Few people, indeed, put themselves out for it. There was a sprinkling of old family friends, representatives of the museum and of various charities in which Vantine had been interested, a few friends of his own, and that was all. He had dropped out of the world with scarcely a ripple; of all who had known him, I dare say Parks felt his departure most. For Vantine had been, in a sense, a solitary man; not many men nodded oftener during a walk up the Avenue, and yet not many dined oftener alone; for there was about him a certain self-detachment which discouraged intimacy. He was a man, like many another, with acquaintances in every country on the globe, and friends in none.

All this I thought over a little sadly, as I sat at home that night; and not without some self-questioning as to my own place in the world. Most of us, I think, are a little saddened when we realise our unimportance; most of us, no doubt, would be a little shocked could we return a day or two after our death and see how merrily the world wags on! I would be missed, I knew, scarcely more than Vantine. It was not a pleasant thought, for it seemed to argue some deficiency in myself.

Then, too, the mystery of Vantine's death had a depressing effect upon me. So long as there seemed some theory to build on, so long as there was a ray of light ahead, I had hoped that the tragedy would be explained and expiated; but now my theory had crumbled to pieces; I was left in utter darkness, from which there seemed no way out. Never before, in the face of any mystery, had I felt so blind and helpless, and the feeling took such a grip upon me that it kept me awake for a long time after I got to bed. It seemed, in some mysterious way, that I was contending with a power greater than myself, a power threatening and awful, which could crush me with a turn of the wrist.

Vantine's will was probated next morning. He had directed that his collection of art objects be removed to the museum, and that the house and such portion of its contents as the museum did not care for be sold for the museum's benefit. I had already notified the director of the museum of the terms of the will, and the museum's attorney was present when it was read. He stated that he had been requested to ask me to remain in charge of things for a week or two, until arrangements for the removal could be made. It would be necessary to make an inventory of Vantine's collection, and Mr. Breck, the assistant director, would get this under way at once.

I acquiesced in all these arrangements, but I was feeling decidedly blue when I started back to the office. Vantine's collection had always seemed to me somehow a part of himself; more especially a part of the house in which it had been assembled. It would lose much of its beauty

and significance ticketed and arranged stiffly
along the walls of the museum, and the thought
came to me that it would be a splendid thing for
New York if this old house and its contents could
be kept intact as an object lesson to the nervous
and hurrying younger generation of the easier
and more finished manner of life of the older one;
something after the fashion that the beautiful old
Plantin-Moretus mansion at Antwerp is a rebuke
to those present-day publishers who reckon litera-
ture a commodity, along with soap and cheese.

That, of course, it would be impossible to do;
the last barrier to the commercial invasion of the
Avenue would be removed; that heroic rear-guard
of the old order of things would be destroyed;
in a year or two, a monster of steel and stone
would rise on the spot where three generations
of Vantines had lived their lives; and the collection, so unified and coherent, to which the last
Vantine had devoted his life, would be merged
and lost in the vast collections of the museum.
It was a sad ending.

"Gentleman to see you, sir," said the office-
boy, as I sat down at my desk, and a moment
later, Félix Armand was shown in to me.

I have only to close my eyes to call again before

me that striking personality, for Félix Armand
was one of the most extraordinary men I ever had
the pleasure of meeting. Ruddy-faced, bright-
eyed, with full red lips, and waving hair almost
jet black — hair that crinkled about his ears in
a way that I can describe by no other word than
fascinating — he gave the impression of tremendous strength and virility. There was about him,
too, an air of culture not to be mistaken; the air
of a man who had travelled much, seen much,
and mixed with many people, high and low; the
air of a man at home anywhere, in any society.
It is impossible for me, by mere words, to con-
vey any adequate idea of his vivid personality;
but I confess that, from the first moment, I was
both impressed and charmed by him. And I am
still impressed; more, perhaps, than at first, now
that I know the whole story.

"I speak English very badly, sir," he said, as
he sat down. "If you speak French . . ."

"Not half so well as you speak English," I
laughed. "I can tell that from your first sentence."

"In that event, I will do the best that I can,"
he said, smiling, "and you must pardon my
blunders. First, Monsieur, on behalf of Ar-

mand et Fils, I must ask your pardon for this mistake, so inexcusable."

" It *was* a mistake, then? " I asked.

" One most embarrassing to us. We can not find for it an explanation. Believe me, Monsieur, it is not our habit to make mistakes; we have a reputation of which we are very proud; but the cabinet which was purchased by Monsieur Vantine remained in our warehouse, and this other one was boxed and shipped to him. We are investigating most rigidly."

" Then Mr. Vantine's cabinet is still in Paris? "

" No, Monsieur, the error was discovered some days ago and the cabinet belonging to Monsieur Vantine was shipped to me here. It should arrive next Wednesday on the *Ile de France*. I shall myself receive it and deliver it to Monsieur Vantine."

" Mr. Vantine is dead," I said. " You did not know? "

He sat staring at me for a moment, as though unable to comprehend.

" Did I understand that you said Monsieur Vantine is dead? " he stammered.

I told him briefly as much as I knew of the tragedy, while he sat regarding me with an air of stupefaction.

"It is curious you saw nothing of it in the papers," I added. "They were full of it."

"I have been visiting friends at Quebec," he explained. "It was there that the message from our house found me, commanding me to hasten here. I started at once, and reached this city Saturday. I drove here directly from the station, but was so unfortunate as to miss you."

"I am sorry to have caused you so much trouble," I said.

"But my dear Monsieur Lester," he protested, "it is for us to take trouble. A blunder of this sort we feel as a disgrace. My father, who is of the old school, is most upset concerning it. But this death of Monsieur Vantine — it is a great blow to me. I have met him many times. He was a real connoisseur — we have lost one of our most valued patrons. You say that he was found dead in a room at his house?"

"Yes, and death resulted from a small wound on the hand, into which some very powerful poison had been injected."

"That is most curious. In what manner was such a wound made?"

"That we don't know. I had a theory . . ."

" Yes? " he questioned, his eyes gleaming with interest.

" A few hours previously, another man had been found in the same room, killed in the same way."

" Another man? "

" A stranger who had called to see Mr. Vantine. My theory was that both this stranger and Mr. Vantine had been killed while trying to open a secret drawer in the Boule cabinet. Do you know anything of the history of that cabinet, Monsieur Armand? "

" We believe it to have been made for Madame de Montespan by Monsieur Boule himself," he answered. " It is the original of one now in the Louvre which is known to have belonged to the Grand Louis."

" That was Mr. Vantine's belief," I said. " Why he should have arrived at that conclusion, I don't know —"

" Monsieur Vantine was a connoisseur," said Armand quietly. " There are certain indications which no connoisseur could mistake."

" It was his guess at the history of the cabinet," I explained, " which gave me the basis for my theory. A cabinet belonging to Madame de

Montespan would, of course, have a secret
drawer; and since it was made in the days of de
Brinvilliers and La Voisin, what more natural
than that it should be guarded by a poisoned
mechanism?"

"What more natural, indeed!" breathed my
companion, and I fancied that he looked at me
with a new interest in his eyes. "It is good rea-
soning, Monsieur."

"It seemed to explain a situation for which
no other explanation has been found," I said.
"And it had also the merit of picturesqueness."

"It is unique," he agreed eagerly, his eyes
burning like two coals of fire, so intense was his
interest. "I have been from boyhood," he
added, noticing my glance, "a lover of tales of
mystery. They have for me a fascination I cannot explain; there is in my blood something that
responds to them. I feel sometimes that I would
have made a great detective — or a great criminal. Instead of which, I am merely a dealer in
curios. You can understand how I am fascinated
by a story so outré as this."

"Perhaps you can assist us," I suggested, "for
that theory of mine has been completely disproved."

" Disproved?   In what way? " he demanded.

" The secret drawer has been found   .   .   ."

" *Comment?* " he cried, his voice sharp with surprise.   " Found?   The secret drawer has been found? "

" Yes, and there was no poisoned mechanism guarding it."

He breathed deeply for an instant; then he pulled himself together with a little laugh.

" Really," he said, " I must not indulge myself in this way.   It is a kind of intoxication. But you say that the drawer was found and that there was no poison?   Was the drawer empty? "

" No, there was a packet of letters in it."

" Delicious!   Love letters, of a certainty! *Billets-doux* from the great Louis to the Montespan, perhaps? "

" No, unfortunately they were of a much more recent date.   They have been restored to their owner.   I hope that you agree with me that that was the right thing to do? "

He sat for a moment regarding me narrowly, and I had an uneasy feeling that, since he undoubtedly knew of whom the cabinet had been purchased, he was reconstructing the story more completely than I would have wished him to do.

"Since the letters have been returned," he said at last, a little drily, "it is useless to discuss the matter. But no doubt I should approve if all the circumstances were known to me. Especially if it was to assist a lady."

"It was," I said, and I saw from his face that he understood.

"Then you did well," he said. "Has no other explanation been found for the death of Monsieur Vantine and of this stranger?"

"I think not. The coroner will hold his inquest to-morrow. He has deferred it in the hope that some new evidence would be discovered."

"And none has been discovered?"

"I have heard of none."

"You do not even know who this stranger was?"

"Oh yes, we have discovered that. He was a worthless fellow named Drouet."

"A Frenchman?"

"Yes, living in an attic in the Rue de la Huchette, at Paris."

Monsieur Armand had been gazing at me intently but now his look relaxed and I fancied that he drew a deep breath as a man might do when re-

lieved of a burden. At the back of my brain a
vague and shadowy suspicion began to form — a
suspicion that perhaps my visitor knew more of
this affair than he had as yet acknowledged.

"You did not, by any chance, know him?" I
asked carelessly.

"No, I think not. But there is one thing I
do not understand, Monsieur Lester, and you will
pardon me if I am indiscreet. But I do not understand what this Drouet, as you call him, was
doing in the house of Monsieur Vantine."

"He was trying to get possession of the letters," I said.

"Oh, so it was that!" and my companion
nodded. "And in trying to get those letters,
he was killed?"

"Yes, but what none of us understands, Mon-
sier Armand, is how he was killed. Who or what
killed him? How was that poison administered?
Can you suggest an explanation?"

He sat for a moment staring thoughtfully out
of the window.

"It is a nice problem," he said, "a most interesting problem. I will think it over. Perhaps
I may be able to make a suggestion. I do not
know. But in any event, I shall see you again

Wednesday. If it is agreeable to you, we can meet at the house of Monsieur Vantine and exchange the cabinets."

" At what time? "

" I do not know with exactness. There may be some delay in getting the cabinet from the ship. Perhaps it would be better if I called for you? "

" Very well," I assented.

" Permit me to express again my apologies that such a mistake should have been made by us. Really, we are most careful; but even we sometimes suffer from careless servants. It desolates me to think that I cannot offer these apologies to Monsieur Vantine in person. Till Wednesday, then, Monsieur Lester."

" Till Wednesday," I echoed, and watched his erect and perfectly-garbed figure until it vanished through the doorway. A fascinating man I told myself as I turned back to my desk, and one whom I should like to know more intimately; a man with a hobby for the mysteries of crime, with which I could fully sympathise; and I smiled as I thought of the burning interest with which he had listened to the story of the double tragedy. How naïvely he had confessed his thought that he would have

made a great detective — or a great criminal;
instead of which he was only a dealer in curios.
Well, I had had the same thought more than
once — and here was I, merely a not-too-success-
ful lawyer. Decidedly, Monsieur Armand and
myself had much in common!

CHAPTER XVIII

THE coroner's inquest was held next day, and my surmise proved to be correct. The police had discovered practically no new evidence; none, certainly, which shed any light on the way in which Drouet and Philip Vantine had met death. Each of the witnesses told his story much as I have told it here, and it was evident that the jury was bewildered by the seemingly inextricable tangle of circumstances.

To my relief, Drouet's identity was established without any help from me. The bag which he had left on the pier had been opened at the request of the police and a card-case found with his address on it. Why he had sent in to Vantine a card not his own, and what his business with Vantine had been, were details concerning which the police could offer no theory, and which I did not feel called upon to explain, since neither in any way made clearer the mystery of his death.

An amusing incident of the inquest was the attempt made by Goldberger to heckle Godfrey, evidently at Grady's suggestion.

"On the morning after the tragedy," Goldberger began sweetly, "you printed in the *Record* a photograph which you claimed to be that of the woman who had called upon Mr. Vantine the night before, and who was, presumably, the last person to see him alive. Where did you get that photograph?"

"It was a copy of one which Drouet carried in his watch-case," answered Godfrey.

"Since then," pursued Goldberger, "you have made no further reference to that feature of the case. I presume you found out that you were mistaken?"

"On the contrary, I proved that I was correct."

Goldberger's face reddened, and his look was not pleasant.

"'Prove' is rather a strong word, isn't it?" he asked.

"It is the right word."

"What was the woman's connection with the man Drouet?"

"She had been his mistress."

"You say that very confidently," said Goldberger, his lips curling. "After all, it is merely a guess, isn't it?"

"I have reason to say it confidently," retorted Godfrey quietly, "since the woman confessed as much in my presence."

Again Goldberger reddened.

"I suppose she also confessed that it was really she who called upon Mr. Vantine?" he sneered.

"She not only confessed that," said Godfrey, still more quietly, "but she told in detail what occurred during that visit."

"The confession was made to yourself alone, of course?" queried Goldberger, in a tone deliberately insulting.

Godfrey flushed a little at the words, but answered calmly enough.

"Not at all," he said. "It was made in the presence of Mr. Lester and of another distinguished lawyer whose name I am not at liberty to reveal."

Goldberger swallowed hard, as though he had received a slap in the face. I dare say he felt as though he had!

"This woman is in New York?" he asked.

"I believe so."

"What is her name and address?"

"I am not at liberty to answer."

Goldberger glared at him.

"You *will* answer," he thundered, "or I'll commit you for contempt!"

Godfrey was quite himself again.

"Very well," he said smiling. "I have not the slightest objection. But I would think it over, if I were you. Mr. Lester will assure you that the woman was in no way connected with the death either of Drouet or of Mr. Vantine."

Goldberger did think it over; he realised the danger of trying to punish a paper so powerful as the *Record,* and he finally decided to accept Godfrey's statement as a mitigation of his refusal to answer.

"That is only one of the details which Commissioner Grady has missed," Godfrey added pleasantly.

"That will do," Goldberger broke in, and Godfrey left the stand.

I was recalled to confirm his story. I also, of course, refused to give the woman's name, explaining to Goldberger that I had learned it professionally, that I was certain she had been guilty of no crime, and that to reveal it would seriously

embarrass an entirely innocent woman. With
that statement, the coroner was compelled to appear satisfied.

Grady did not go on the stand; he was not even
at the inquest. In fact, since the first day, he had
not appeared publicly in connection with the case
at all; and I had surmised that he did not care
to be identified with a mystery which there seemed
to be no prospect of solving, and from which no
glory was to be won. The case had been placed
in Simmonds's hands, and it was he who testified
on behalf of the police, admitting candidly that
they were all at sea. He had made a careful examination of the Vantine house, he said, particularly of the room in which the bodies had been
found, and had discovered absolutely nothing in
the shape of a clue to the solution of the mystery.
There was something diabolical about it; something almost supernatural. He had not aban-
doned hope, and was still working on the case;
but he was inclined to think that, if the mystery
was ever solved, it would be only by some lucky
accident or through the confession of the guilty
man.

Goldberger was annoyed; that was evident
enough from the nervous way in which he gnawed

his moustache; but he had no theory any more than the police; there was not a scintilla of evidence to fasten the crime upon any one; and the end of the hearing was that the jury brought in a verdict that Philip Vantine and Georges Drouet had died from the effects of a poison administered by a person or persons unknown.

Godfrey joined me at the door as I was leaving, and we went down the steps together.

"I was glad to hear Simmonds confess that the police are up a tree," he said. "Of course, Grady is trying to sneak out of it, and blame some one else for the failure — but I'll see that he doesn't succeed. I'll see, anyway, that Simmonds gets a square deal — he's an old friend of mine, you know."

"Yes," I said, "I know; but we're all up a tree, aren't we?"

"For the present," laughed Godfrey, "we do occupy that undignified position. But you don't expect to stay there forever, do you, Lester?"

"Since my theory about the Boule cabinet exploded," I said, "I have given up hope. By the way, I'm going to turn the cabinet over to its owner to-morrow."

"To its owner?" he repeated, his eyes narrowing. "Yes, I thought he'd be around for it, though I hardly thought he'd come so soon. Who does it happen to be, Lester?"

"Why," I said, a little impatiently, "you know as well as I do that it belongs to Armand & Son."

"You've seen their representative, then?" he queried, a little flush of excitement which I could not understand spreading over his face.

"He came to see me yesterday. I'd like you to meet him, Godfrey. He is Félix Armand, the 'son' of the firm, and one of the most finished gentlemen I ever met."

"I'd like to meet him," said Godfrey, smiling queerly. "Perhaps I shall, some day; I hope so, anyway. But how did he explain the blunder, Lester?"

"In some way, they shipped the wrong cabinet to Vantine. The right one will get here on the *Ile de France* to-morrow," and I told him in detail the story which Félix Armand had told me. "He was quite upset over it," I added. "His apologies were almost abject."

Godfrey listened intently to all this, and he nodded with satisfaction when I had finished.

"It is all most interesting," he commented.

"Did Monsieur Armand happen to mention where he is staying?"

"No, but he won't be hard to find, if you want to see him. He's at one of the big hotels, of course — probably the Plaza or the Ritz. He's too great a swell for any minor hostelry."

"What time do you expect him to-morrow?"

"Sometime in the afternoon. He's to call for me as soon as he gets Vantine's cabinet off the boat. Godfrey," I added, "I felt yesterday when I was talking with him that perhaps he knew more about this affair than he would admit. I could see that he guessed in an instant who the owner of the letters was, and what they contained. Do you think I ought to hold on to the cabinet a while longer? I could invent some pretext for delay, easily enough."

"Why, no; let him have his cabinet," said Godfrey, with an alacrity that surprised me. "If your theory about it has been exploded, what's the use of hanging on to it?"

"I don't see any use in doing so," I admitted, "but I thought perhaps you might want more time to examine it."

"I've examined it all I'm going to," Godfrey answered, and I told myself that this was the

first time I had ever known him to admit himself
defeated.

" I have a sort of feeling," I explained, " that
when we let go of the cabinet, we give up the only
clue we have to this whole affair. It is like a confession of defeat."

" Oh no, it isn't," Godfrey objected. " If
there is nothing more to be learned from the cabinet, there is no reason to retain it. I should
certainly let Armand have it. Perhaps I'll
see you to-morrow," he added, and we parted at
the corner.

But I did not see him on the morrow. I was
rather expecting a call from him during the morning, and when none came, I was certain I should
find him awaiting me when I arrived at the Vantine house, in company with Armand. But he
was not there, and when I asked for him, Parks
told me that he had not seen him since the day
before.

I confess that Godfrey's indifference to the fate
of the cabinet surprised me greatly; besides, I was
hoping that he would wish to meet the fascinating
Frenchman. More fascinating, if possible, than
he had been on Monday, and I soon found myself
completely under his spell. There had been less

delay than he had anticipated in getting the cabinet off the boat and through the customs, and it was not yet three o'clock when we reached the Vantine house.

"I haven't seen Mr. Godfrey," Parks repeated, "but there's others here as it fair breaks my heart to see."

He motioned toward the door of the music-room, and stepping to it, I saw that the inventory was already in progress. The man in charge of it nodded to me, but I did not go in, for the sight was anything but a pleasant one.

"The cabinet is in the room across the hall," I said to Monsieur Armand, and led the way through the ante-room into the room beyond.

Parks switched on the lights for us, and my companion glanced with surprise at the heavy shutters covering the windows.

"We put those up for a protection," I explained. "We had an idea that some one would try to enter. In fact, one evening we *did* find a wire connecting with the burglar-alarm cut, and later on, saw some one peering in through the hole in that shutter yonder."

"You did?" Armand queried quickly.

"Would you recognise the man, if you were to meet him again?"

"Oh, no; you see the hole is quite small. There was nothing visible except a pair of eyes. Yet I might know them again, for I never before saw such eyes — so bright, so burning. It was the night that Godfrey and I were trying to find the secret drawer, and those eyes gleamed like fire as they watched us."

Armand was gazing at the cabinet, apparently only half listening.

"Ah yes, the secret drawer," he said. "Will you show me how it is operated, Monsieur Lester? I am most curious about it."

I placed my hand upon the side of the cabinet and pressed the three points which the veiled lady had shown us. The first time I got the order wrong, but at the second trial the little handle fell forward with a click and I pulled the drawer open.

"There it is," I said. "You see how cleverly it is constructed. And how well it is concealed. No one would suspect its existence."

He examined it with much interest; pushed it back into place, and then opened it himself.

"Very clever indeed," he agreed. "I have

never seen another so well concealed. And the
idea of opening it only by a certain combination
is most happy and original. Most secret drawers
are secret only in name; a slight search reveals
them; but this one . . ."

He pushed it shut again, and examined the
inlay around it.

" My friend and I went over the cabinet very
carefully and could not find it," I said.

" Your friend — I think you mentioned his
name? "

" Yes — his name is Godfrey."

" A man of the law, like yourself? "

" Oh no, a newspaper man. But he had been
a member of the detective force before that. He
is extraordinarily keen, and if anybody could have
found that drawer, he could. But that combination was too much for him."

Armand snapped the drawer back into place
with a little crash.

" I am glad, at any rate, that it *was* discovered," he said. " I will not conceal from you,
Monsieur, that it adds not a little to the value
of the cabinet."

" What is its value? " I asked. " Mr. Vantine wanted me to buy it for him and named a

most extravagant figure as the limit he was willing to pay."

" Really," Armand answered, after an instant's hesitation, " I would not care to name a figure without further consultation with my father. The cabinet is quite unique — the most beautiful, perhaps, that Boule ever produced. Did you discover Madame de Montespan's monogram? "

" No. Mr. Vantine said he was sure it existed; but Godfrey and I did not look for it."

Monsieur Armand opened the doors which concealed the central drawers.

" *Voilà!* " he said, and traced with his finger the arabesque just under the pediment. " See how cunningly it has been blended with the other figures. And here is the emblem of the giver." He pointed to a tiny golden sun with radiating rays on the base of the pediment, just above the monogram. " *Le roi soleil!* "

" *Le roi soleil!* " I repeated. " Of course. We were stupid not to have discerned it. That tells the whole story, doesn't it? What is it, Parks? " I added, as that worthy appeared at the door.

" There's a van outside, sir," he said, " and

a couple of men are unloading a piece of furniture. Is it all right, sir?"

"Yes," I answered. "Have them bring it in here. And ask the man in charge of the inventory to step over here a minute. Mr. Vantine left his collection of art objects to the Metropolitan Museum," I explained to Armand, "and I should like the representative of the museum to be present when the exchange is made."

"Certainly," he assented. "That is very just."

Parks was back in a moment, piloting two men who carried between them an object swathed in burlap, and the Metropolitan man followed them in.

"I am Mr. Lester," I said to him, "Mr. Vantine's executor; and this is Monsieur Félix Armand, of Armand & Son, of Paris. We are correcting an error which was made just before Mr. Vantine died. That cabinet yonder was shipped him by mistake in place of one which he had bought. Monsieur Armand has caused the right one to be sent over, and will take away the one which belongs to him. I have spoken to the museum's attorney about the matter, but I wished you to be present when the exchange was made."

"I have no doubt it is all right, sir," the museum man hastened to assure me. "You, of course, have personal knowledge of all this?"

"Certainly. Mr. Vantine himself told me the story."

"Very well, sir," but his eyes dwelt lovingly upon the Boule cabinet. "That is a very handsome piece," he added. "I am sorry the museum is not to get it."

"Perhaps you can buy it from Monsieur Armand," I suggested, but the curator laughed and shook his head.

"No," he said, "we couldn't afford it. But Mr. Robinson might persuade Mr. Blumenthal to buy it for us — I'll mention it to him."

The two men, meanwhile, under Armand's direction, had been stripping the wrappings from the other cabinet, and it finally stood revealed. It, too, was a beautiful piece of furniture, but even my untrained eye could see how greatly it fell below the other.

"We shall be very pleased to have Mr. Blumenthal see it," said Armand, with a smile. "I will not conceal from you that we had already thought of him — as what dealer does not when he acquires something rare and beautiful? I shall endeavour to secure an appointment with him. Meanwhile . . ."

"Meanwhile the cabinet is yours," I said.

He made a little deprecating gesture, and then proceeded to have the cabinet very carefully wrapped in the burlap which had been around the other one. I watched it disappear under the rough covering with something like regret, for already my eyes were being opened to its beauty. Besides, I told myself again, with it would disappear the last hope of solving the mystery of Philip Vantine's death. However my reason might protest, some instinct told me that, in some way, the Boule cabinet was connected with that tragedy.

But at last the packing was done, and Armand turned to me and held out his hand.

"I shall hope to see you again, Monsieur Lester," he said, with a cordiality which flattered me, "and to renew our very pleasant acquaintance. Whenever you are in Paris, I trust you will not fail to honour my by letting me know. I shall count it a very great privilege to display for you some of the beauties of our city not known to every one."

"Thank you," I said. "I shall certainly remember that invitation. And meanwhile, since you are here in New York . . ."

" You are most kind," he broke in, " and I was myself hoping that we might at least dine together. But I am compelled to proceed to Boston this evening, and from there I shall go on to Quebec. Whether I shall get back to New York I do not know — it will depend somewhat upon Mr. Blumenthal's attitude; we would scarcely entrust a business so delicate to our dealer. If I do get back, I shall let you know."

" Please do," I urged. " It will be a very great pleasure to me. And I am still hoping that some solution of this mystery may occur to you."

He shook his head with a little smile.

" I fear it is too difficult for a novice like myself," he said. " It is impenetrable to me. If a solution is discovered, I trust you will inform me. It is certain to be most interesting."

" I will," I promised, and we shook hands again.

Then he signed to the two men to take up the cabinet, and himself laid a protecting hand upon it as it was carried through the door and down the steps to the van which was backed up to the curb.

It was lifted carefully inside, the two men clambered in beside it, the driver started his engine, and the van rolled away up the Avenue.

Armand watched it for a moment, then mounted into the car which was waiting, waved a last farewell to me, and followed after the van. We watched it until it turned westward at the first cross-street.

"Mr. Godfrey's occupation will be gone," said Parks, with a little laugh. "He has fairly lived with that cabinet for the past three or four days. He was here last night for quite a while."

"Last night?" I echoed, surprised. "I was sure he would be here to-day," I added, reflecting that Godfrey might have decided to have a final look at the cabinet. "He half-promised to be here, but I suppose something more important detained him."

The next instant, I was jumping down the steps two at a time, for a taxi in which two men were sitting came up the Avenue, and rolled slowly around the corner in the direction taken by the van.

And just as it disappeared, one of its occupants turned toward me and waved his hand — and I recognised Jim Godfrey.

CHAPTER XIX

" LA MORT ! "

THAT my legs, without conscious effort of my own, should carry me up the Avenue and around the corner after the taxi in which I had seen Godfrey was a foregone conclusion, and yet it was with a certain vexation of spirit that I found myself racing along, for I realised that Godfrey had not been entirely frank with me. Certainly he had dropped no hint of his intention to follow Armand; but, I told myself, that might very well have been because he deemed such a hint unnecessary. I might have guessed, in spite of his seeming unconcern, that he would not allow the cabinet to pass from his sight; if he had been willing for me to turn it over to Armand, it was only because he expected developments of some sort to follow that transfer.

And it suddenly dawned upon me that even I did not know the cabinet's destination! It had not occurred to me to inquire where Armand proposed to take it, and he had volunteered no information.

So after a moment, I took up the chase more contentedly, telling myself that Godfrey would not have waved to me if he had not wanted me along, and I reached the corner in time to see the van turn northward into Sixth Avenue. As soon as it and the cars which followed it were out of sight, I sprinted along the sidewalk at top speed, and on arriving at the corner, had the satisfaction of seeing them only a little way ahead. Here the congestion of traffic was such that the van could proceed but slowly, and I had no difficulty in keeping pace with it, without the necessity of making myself conspicuous by running. Indeed I rather hung back, burying myself in the crowds on the sidewalk, for fear that Armand might chance to glance around and see me in pursuit.

I saw that Godfrey evidently had the same fear, for the taxi in which he was drew up at the curb and waited there until the van had got some distance ahead. At Sixteenth Street, it turned westward again, and then northward into Seventh Avenue.

What could Armand be doing in this part of the town, I asked myself? Did he propose to leave that priceless cabinet in this dingy quarter? And then I halted abruptly and slipped into an areaway, for the van had stopped some distance ahead and was backing up to the curb.

Looking out discreetly, I saw the car containing Armand stop also, and that gentleman alighted and paid the driver. The other car rattled on at a good pace and disappeared up the Avenue. Then the two porters lifted out the cabinet, and, with Armand showing them the way, carried it into the building before which the van had stopped.

They were gone perhaps ten minutes, from which I argued that they were carrying it upstairs; then they reappeared, with Armand accompanying them. He tipped them and went out also to tip the driver of the van. Then the porters climbed aboard and it rattled away out of sight. Armand stood for a moment on the step, looking up and down the Avenue, then disappeared indoors.

An instant later, I saw Godfrey and another man whom I recognised as Simmonds, come out of a shop across the street and dash over to the house into which the cabinet had been taken. They were standing on the door-step when I joined them.

It was a dingy building, entirely typical of the

dingy neighbourhood. The ground floor was oc-
cupied by a laundry which the sign on the front
window declared to be French; and the room
which the window lighted extended the whole
width of the building except for a door which
opened presumably on the stairway leading to
the upper stories.

Godfrey's face was flaming with excitement as
he turned the knob of this door gently — gently.
The door was locked. He stooped and applied
an eye to the key-hole.

" The key is in the lock," he whispered.

Simmonds took from his pocket a pair of slender
pliers and passed them over.

Godfrey looked up and down the street, saw
that for the moment there was no one near, inserted the pliers in the keyhole, grasped the end
of the key, and turned it slowly.

" Now ! " he said, softly opened the door and
slipped inside. I followed, and Simmonds came
after me like a shadow, closing the door carefully
behind him.

Then we all stopped, and my heart was in my
mouth, for from somewhere overhead came the
sound of a man's voice talking excitedly.

Even in the semi-darkness, I could see the look

of astonishment and alarm on Godfrey's face as he stood for a moment motionless, listening to that voice. I also stood with ears a-strain, but I could make nothing of what it was saying; then suddenly I realised that it was speaking in French. And yet it was not Armand's voice — of that I was certain.

Fronting us was a narrow stair mounting steeply to the story overhead, and after that moment's amazed hesitation, Godfrey sat down on the bottom step and removed his shoes, motioning us to do the same. Simmonds obeyed phlegmatically, but my hands were trembling so with excitement that I was in mortal terror lest I drop one of my shoes; but I managed to get them both off without mishap and to set them softly on the floor at the stair-foot.

When at last I looked up with a sigh of relief, Godfrey and Simmonds were stealing slowly up the stair, revolver in hand. I followed them, but I confess my knees were knocking together, for there was something weird and chilling in that voice going on and on. It sounded like the voice of a madman; there was something about it at once ferocious and triumphant . . .

Godfrey paused an instant at the stairhead, lis-

tening intently, then he moved cautiously forward
toward an open door from which the voice seemed
to come, motioning us at the same time to stay
where we were.   And as I knelt, bathed in perspiration, I caught one word, repeated over and
over:

"*Revanche! — Revanche! — Revanche!*"

Then the voice fell to a sort of low growling, as
of a dog which worries its prey, and I caught a
sound as of ripping cloth.

Godfrey, on hands and knees, was peering into
the room.   Then he drew back and motioned us
forward.

I shall never forget the sight which met my
eyes as I peered cautiously around the corner of
the door.

The room into which I was looking was lighted
only by the rays which filtered between the slats
of a closed shutter.   In the middle of the floor
stood the Boule cabinet, and before it, with his
back to the door, stood a man ripping savagely
away the strips of burlap in which it had been
wrapped, talking to himself the while in a sort
of savage sing-song, and pausing from moment to
moment to glance at a huddled bundle lying on the
floor against the opposite wall.   For a time, I

could not make out what this bundle was, then, straining my eyes, I saw that it was the body of a man, wrapped round and round in some web-like fabric.

And as I stared at him, I caught the glitter of his eyes as he watched the man working at the cabinet — a glitter not to be mistaken — the same glitter which had so frightened me once before . . .

Godfrey drew me back with a firm hand and took my place. As for me, I retreated to the stair and sat there feverishly mopping my face and trying to understand. Who was this man? What was he doing there against the wall? What was the meaning of this ferocious scene . . .

Then my heart leaped into my throat, for Godfrey, with a sharp cry of *"Halte-là!"* sprang erect and dashed into the room, Simmonds at his heels.

I suppose two seconds elapsed before I reached the threshold, and I stopped there staring, clutching at the wall to steady myself.

That scene is so photographed upon my brain that I have only to close my eyes to see it again in every detail.

There was the cabinet with its wrappings torn away, but the figure on the floor had disappeared, and before an open doorway into another room stood a man, a giant of a man, his hands above his head, his face working with fear and rage, while Godfrey, his lips curling into a mocking smile, pressed a pistol against his breast.

Then, as I stood there staring, it seemed to me that there was a sort of flicker in the air above the man's head, and he screamed shrilly.

"*La mort!*" he shrieked. "*La mort!*"

For one dreadful instant longer he stood there motionless, his hands still held aloft, his eyes staring horribly; then, with a strangled cry, he pitched forward heavily at Godfrey's feet.

CHAPTER XX

I HAVE a confused remembrance of Godfrey
stooping for an instant above the body, staring
at it, and then, with a sharp cry, hurling himself
through that open doorway. A door slammed
somewhere, there was a sound of running feet,
and before either Simmonds or myself understood
what was happening, Godfrey was back in the
room, crossed it at a bound, and dashed to the
door opening into the hall, just as it was slammed
in his face.

I saw him tear desperately at the knob, then retreat two steps and hurl himself against it. But
it held firm, and from the hall outside came a
burst of mocking laughter that fairly froze my
blood.

" Come here, you fools! " cried Godfrey between clenched teeth. " Don't you see he's getting away! "

Simmonds was quicker than I, and together
they threw themselves at the door. It cracked
ominously, but still held; again they tried, and this

time it split from top to bottom.   Godfrey kicked
the pieces to either side and slipped between them,
Simmonds after him.

Then, in a sort of trance, I staggered to it,
and after a moment's aimless fumbling, was out
in the hall again.   I reached the stairhead in
time to see Godfrey try the front door, and then
turn along the lower hall leading to the back of
the house.   An instant later, a chorus of frenzied
women's shrieks made my hair stand on end.

How I got down the stair I do not know; but
I, too, turned back along the lower hall, expecting
any instant to come upon I knew not what horror;
I reached an open door, passed through it, and
found myself in the laundry, in the midst of a
group of excited and indignant women, who
greeted my appearance with a fresh series of
screams.

Unable to go farther, I sat limply down upon
a box and looked at them.

I dare say the figure I made was ridiculous
enough, for the screams gave place to subdued
giggles; but I was far from thinking of my appearance, or of caring what impression I produced.   And I was still sitting there when Godfrey came back, breathing heavily, chagrin and

anger in his eyes. The employes of the laundry, conscious that something extraordinary was occurring, crowded about him, but he elbowed his way through them to the desk where the manager sat.

"A crime has been committed upstairs," he said. "This gentleman with me is Mr. Simmonds, of the detective bureau," and at the words Simmonds showed his shield. "We shall have to notify headquarters," Godfrey went on, "and I would advise that you keep your girls at their work. I don't suppose you want to be mixed up in it."

"Sure not," agreed the manager promptly, and while Simmonds went to the 'phone and called police headquarters, the manager dismounted from his throne, went down among the girls, and had them back at their work in short order.

Godfrey came over to me and laid his hand on my shoulder.

"Why, Lester," he said, "you look as though you were at your last gasp."

"I am," I said. "I'm going to have nervous prostration if this thing keeps up. You're not looking particularly happy yourself."

"I'm not happy. I've let that fellow kill a

man right under my nose — literally, under my nose! — and then get away!"

"Kill a man?" I repeated. "Do you mean . . ."

"Go upstairs and look at the right hand of the man lying there," said Godfrey curtly, "and you'll see what I mean!"

I sat staring at him, unable to believe that I had heard aright, unable to believe that Godfrey had really uttered those words . . . the right hand of the man lying there . . . that could mean only one thing . . .

Simmonds joined us with a twisted smile on his lips, and I saw that even he was considerably shaken.

"I got Grady," he said, "and told him what had happened. He says he's too busy to come up, and that I'm to take charge of things."

Godfrey laughed a little mocking laugh.

"Grady foresees his Waterloo!" he said. "Well, it's not far distant. But I'm glad for your sake, Simmonds — you're going to get some glory out of this thing, yet!"

"I hope so," and Simmonds's eyes gleamed an instant. "The ambulance will be around at once," he added. "We'd better get our shoes

on, and go back upstairs and see if anything can
be done for that fellow."

" There can't anything be done for him," said
Godfrey wearily; " but we'd better have a look
at him, I guess," and he led the way out into the
hall.

Not until Simmonds spoke did I remember that
I was shoeless. Now I sat down beside Godfrey,
got fumblingly into my shoes again, and then
followed him and Simmonds slowly up the
stair.

I thought I knew what was passing in Godfrey's mind: he was blaming himself for this latest tragedy; he was telling himself that he should
have foreseen and prevented it; he always blamed
himself in that way when things went wrong —
and then, to have the murderer slip through his
very fingers! I could guess what a mighty shock
that had been to his self-confidence!

The latest victim was lying where he had fallen,
just inside the doorway leading into the inner
room. Simmonds stepped to the window, threw
open the shutters, and let a flood of afternoon
sunshine into the room. Then he knelt beside
the body and held up the limp right hand for us
to see.

Just below the knuckles were two tiny incisions, with a drop or two of blood oozing away from them, and the flesh about them swollen and discoloured.

"I knew what it was the instant he yelled '*la mort!*'" said Godfrey quietly. "And *he* knew what it was the instant he felt the stroke. It is evident enough that he had seen it used before, or heard of it, and knew that it meant instant death."

I sat down, staring at the dead man, and tried to collect my senses. So this fiendish criminal, who slew with poison, had been lurking in Vantine's house and had struck down first Drouet and then the master of the house himself! But why — why! It was incredible, astounding, my brain reeled at the thought. And yet it must be true!

I looked again at the third victim, and saw a man roughly dressed, with bushy black hair and tangled beard; a very giant of a man, whose physical strength must have been enormous — and yet it had availed him nothing against that tiny pin-prick on the hand!

And then a sudden thought brought me bolt upright.

"But Armand!" I cried. "Where is Armand?"

Godfrey looked at me with a half-pitying smile.

"What, Lester!" he said, "don't you understand, even yet? It was your fascinating Monsieur Armand who did that," and he pointed to the dead man.

I felt as though I had been struck a heavy blow upon the head; black circles whirled before my eyes . . .

"Go over to the window," said Godfrey peremptorily, "and get some fresh air."

Mechanically I obeyed, and stood clinging to the window-sill, gazing down at the busy street, where the tide of humanity was flowing up and down, all unconscious of the tragedy which had been enacted so close at hand. And at last, the calmness of all these people, the sight of the world going quietly on as usual, restored me a portion of my self-control. But even yet I did not understand.

"Was it Armand," I asked, turning back into the room, "who lay there in the corner?"

"Certainly it was," Godfrey answered. "Who else could it be?"

"Godfrey!" I cried, remembering suddenly. "Did you see his eyes as he lay there watching the man at the cabinet?"

"Yes; I saw them."

"They were the same eyes . . ."

"The same eyes."

"And the laugh — did you hear that laugh?"

"Certainly I heard it."

"I heard it once before," I said, "and you thought it was a case of nerves!"

I fell silent a moment, shivering a little at the remembrance.

"But why did Armand lie there so quietly?" I asked, at last. "Was he injured?"

Godfrey made a little gesture toward the corner.

"Go see for yourself," he said.

Something lay along the wall on the spot where I had seen that figure, and as I bent over it, I saw that it was a large net, finely meshed but very strong.

"That was dropped over Armand's head as he came up the stairs," said Godfrey, "or flung over him as he came into the room. Then the dead man yonder jumped upon him and trussed him up with those ropes."

Pushing the net aside, I saw upon the floor a little pile of severed cords.

"Yes," I agreed; "he would be able to do that. Have you noticed his size, Godfrey? He was almost a giant!"

"He couldn't have done it if Armand hadn't been willing that he should," retorted Godfrey curtly. "You see he had no difficulty in getting away," and he held up the net and pointed to the great rents in it. "He cut his way out while he was lying there — I ought to have known — I ought to have known he wasn't bound — that he was only waiting — but it was all so sudden . . ."

He threw the net down upon the floor with a gesture of disgust and despair. Then he stopped in front of the Boule cabinet and looked down at it musingly; and after a moment, his face brightened.

The burlap wrappings had been almost wholly torn away, and the cabinet stood, more insolently beautiful than ever, it seemed to me, under the rays of the sun, which sparkled and glittered and shimmered as they fell upon it.

"But we'll get him, Simmonds," said Godfrey, and his lips broke into a smile. "In fact, we've

got him now. We have only to wait, and he'll
walk into our arms. Simmonds, I want you to
lock this cabinet up in the strongest cell your
station possesses, and carry the key yourself."

"Lock it up?" stammered Simmonds, staring
at him.

"Yes," said Godfrey, "lock it up. That's our
one salvation!" His face was glowing; he was
quite himself again, alert, confident of victory.
"You're in charge of this case, aren't you? Well,
lock it up, and give your reasons to nobody."

"That'll be easy," laughed Simmonds. "I
haven't got any reasons."

"Oh yes, you have," and Godfrey bent upon
him a gaze that was positively hypnotic. "You
will do it because I want you to, and because I
tell you that, sooner or later, if you keep this
cabinet safe where no one can get at it, the man
we want will walk into our hands. And I'll tell
you more than that, Simmonds; if we do get him,
I'll have the biggest story I ever had, and you will
be world-famous. France will make you a chev-
alier of the Legion of Honour, Simmonds, mark
my words. Don't you think the ribbon would
look well in your button-hole?"

Simmonds was staring at the speaker as though

he thought he had suddenly gone mad. Indeed, the thought flashed through my own brain that the disappointment, the chagrin of failure, had been too much for Godfrey.

He burst into laughter as he saw our faces.

"No, I'm not mad," he said, more soberly; "and I'm not joking. I'm speaking in deadly earnest, Simmonds, when I say that this fellow is the biggest catch we could make. He's the greatest criminal of modern times — I repeat it, Lester, this time without qualification. And now, perhaps, you'll agree with me."

And with Armand, so finished, so self-poised, so distinguished, in my mind, and the body of his latest victim before my eyes, I nodded gloomily.

"But who is he?" I asked. "Do you know who he is, Godfrey?"

"There's the ambulance," broke in Simmonds, as a knock came at the street door, and he hurried down to open it.

"Come on, Lester," and Godfrey hooked his arm through mine. "There's nothing more we can do here. We'll go down the back way. I've had enough excitement for the time being — haven't you?"

"I certainly have," I agreed, and he led the

way back along the hall to another stair, down it and so out through the laundry.

"But, Godfrey, who is this man?" I repeated. "Why did he kill that poor fellow up there? Why did he kill Drouet and Vantine? How did he get into the Vantine house? What is it all about?"

"Ah!" he said, looking at me with a smile. "That is the important question — what is it all about! But we can't discuss it here in the street. Besides, I want to think it over, Lester; and I want you to think it over. If I can, I'll drop in to-night to see you, and we can thresh it out! Will that suit you?"

"Yes," I said; "and for heaven's sake, don't fail to come!"

CHAPTER XXI

GODFREY WEAVES A ROMANCE

I HAD begun to fear that Godfrey was going to disappoint me, so late it was before his welcome ring came at my door that night. I hastened to let him in, and I could tell by the sigh of relief with which he sank into a chair that he was thoroughly weary.

" It does me good to come in here occasionally and have a talk with you, Lester," he said, filling his pipe mechanically. " I find it restful after a hard day," and he smiled across at me good-humouredly.

" How you keep it up I don't see," I said. " This one case has knocked my nerves all to pieces."

" Well, I don't often strike one as strenuous as this," and he settled back comfortably. " As a matter of fact, I haven't had one for a long time that even touches it. There is nothing really mysterious about most crimes."

" This one is certainly mysterious enough," I remarked.

"What makes it mysterious," Godfrey explained, "is the apparent lack of motive. As soon as one learns the motive for a crime, one learns also who committed it. But where the motive can't be discovered, it is mighty hard to make any progress."

"It isn't only lack of motive which makes it mysterious," I commented; "it's everything about it. I can't understand either why it was done or how it was done. When I get to thinking about it, I feel as though I were wandering around and around in a maze, from which I can never escape."

"Oh yes, you'll escape, Lester," said Godfrey quietly, "and that before very long."

"If you have an explanation, Godfrey," I protested, "for heaven's sake tell me! Don't keep me in the maze an instant longer than is necessary. I've been thinking about it till my brain feels like a snarl of tangled thread. Do you mean to say you know what it is all about?"

"'Know' is perhaps a little strong. There isn't much in this world that we really know. Suppose we say that I strongly suspect." He paused a moment, his eyes on the ceiling. "You know you've accused me of romancing sometimes, Lester — the other evening, for instance; yet that romance has come true."

"I take it all back," I said meekly.

"There's another thing these talks do," continued Godfrey, going off rather at a tangent, "and that is to clarify my ideas. You don't know how it helps me to state my case to you and to try to answer your objections. Your being a lawyer makes you unusually quick to see objections, and a lawyer is always harder to convince of a thing than the ordinary man. You are accustomed to weighing evidence; and so I never allow myself to be convinced of a theory until I have convinced you. Not always, even then," he added, with a smile.

"Well, I'm glad I'm of some use," I said, "if only as a whetstone for you to sharpen your wits on. So please go ahead and romance some more. Tell me first how you and Simmonds came to be following Armand."

"Simply because I had found out he wasn't Armand. Félix Armand is in Paris at this moment. You were too credulous, Lester."

"Why, I never had any doubt of his being Armand," I stammered. "He knew about my cablegram — he knew about the firm's answer . . ."

"Of course he did, because your cable was never received by the Armands, but by a confederate in this fellow's employ; and it was that confederate who answered it. Our friend, the unknown, foresaw, of course, that a cable would be sent the Armands as soon as the mistake was discovered, and he took his precautions accordingly."

"Then you still believe that the cabinet was sent to Vantine by design and not by accident?"

"Absolutely. It was sent by the Armands in good faith, because they believed that it had been purchased by Vantine — all of which had been arranged very carefully by the Great Unknown."

"Tell me how you know all this, Godfrey," I said.

"Why, it was easy enough. When you told me yesterday of Armand, I knew, or thought I knew, that it was a plant of some kind. But in order to be sure, I cabled our man at Paris to investigate. Our man went at once to Armand *père,* and he learned a number of very interesting things. One was that the son, Félix Armand, was in Paris; another was that no member of the firm knew anything about your cable or the an-

swer to it; a third was that, had the cable been
received, it would not have been understood, because the Armands' books show that this cabinet
was bought by Philip Vantine for the sum of
eighty thousand francs."

"Not this one!" I protested.

"Yes, this one. And it was cheap at the price.
Of course, the Armands knew nothing about the
Montespan story — they were simply selling at a
profit."

"But I don't understand!" I stammered.
"Vantine told me himself that he did not buy that
cabinet."

"Nor did he. But somebody bought it in his
name and directed that it be sent forward to him."

"And paid eighty thousand francs for it?"

"Certainly — and paid eighty thousand francs
to the Armands."

"Rather an expensive present," I said feebly,
for my brain was beginning to whirl again.

"Oh, it wasn't intended as a present. The
purchaser planned to reclaim it — but Vantine's
death threw him out. If it hadn't been for that
— for an accident which no one could foresee —
everything would have gone along smoothly and
no one would ever have been the wiser."

' " But what was his object? Was he trying to evade the duty? "

" Oh, nothing so small as that! Besides, he would have had to refund the duty to Vantine. Did he refund it to you? "

" No," I said, " I didn't think there was any to refund. Vantine really paid the duty only on the cabinet he purchased, since that was the one shown on his manifest. The other fellow must have paid the duty on the cabinet he brought in; so I didn't see that there was anything coming to Vantine's estate. There is probably something due the government, for the cabinet Vantine brought in was, of course, much more valuable than his manifest showed."

" No doubt of that; and the other cabinet is the one which Vantine really purchased. It was, of course, sent forward to this other fellow's address, here in New York. His plan is evident enough — to call upon Vantine as the representative of the Armands, or perhaps as the owner of the Montespan cabinet, and make the exchange. Vantine's death spoiled that, and he had to make the exchange through you. Even then, he would have been able to pull it off but for the fact that Vantine's death and that of Drouet had called our attention to the cabinet; we followed him, and the incidents of this afternoon ensued."

"And he accomplished all this by means of a confederate in the employ of the Armands?"

"No doubt of it. The clerk who made the supposed sale to Vantine and got a commission on it, resigned suddenly two days ago — just as soon as he had intercepted your cable and answered it. The Paris police are looking for him, but I doubt if they'll find him." ·

I paused to think this over, and then a sudden impatience seized me.

"That's all clear enough," I said. "The cabinets might have been exchanged just as you say they were — no doubt you are right — but all that doesn't lead us anywhere. Why were they exchanged? What is there about that Boule cabinet which makes this unknown willing to do murder for it? Does he think those letters are still in it?"

"He knows they are not in it now — you told him. Before that, he knew nothing about the letters. If he had known of them, he would have had them out before the cabinet was shipped."

"What is it, then?" I demanded. "And

above all, Godfrey, why should this fellow hide himself in Vantine's house and kill two men? Did they surprise him while he was working over the cabinet?"

" I see no reason to believe that he was ever inside the Vantine house," said Godfrey quietly; "that is, until you took him there yourself this afternoon."

"But look here, Godfrey," I protested, "that's nonsense. He must have been in the house, or he couldn't have killed Vantine and Drouet."

"Who said he killed them?"

"If he didn't kill them, who did?"

Godfrey took two or three contemplative puffs, while I sat there staring at him.

"Well," Godfrey answered, at last, "now I'm going to romance a little. We will return to your fascinating friend, Armand, as we may as well call him for the present. He is an extraordinary man."

"No doubt of it," I agreed.

"I can only repeat what I have said before—in my opinion, he is the greatest criminal of modern times."

"If he is a criminal at all, he is undoubtedly a

great one," I conceded. "But it is hard for me to believe that he is a criminal. He's the most cultured man I ever met."

"Of course he is. That's why he's so dangerous. An ignorant criminal is never dangerous—it's the ignorant criminals who fill the prisons. But look out for the educated, accomplished ones. It takes brains to be a great criminal, Lester, and brains of a high order."

"But why should a man with brains be a criminal?" I queried. "If he can earn an honest living, why should he steal?"

"In the first place, most criminals are criminals from choice, not from necessity, and with a cultured man the incentive is usually the excitement of it. Have you ever thought what an exciting game it is, Lester, to defy society, to break the law, to know that the odds against you are a thousand to one, and yet to come out triumphant? And then, I suppose, every great criminal is a little insane."

"No doubt of it," I agreed.

"Just as every absolutely honest man is a little insane," went on Godfrey quickly. "Just as every great reformer and enthusiast is a little insane. The sane men are the average ones, who

are fairly honest and yet who lie on occasion, who succumb to temptation now and then,
who temporise and compromise, and try to lead
a comfortable and quiet life. I repeat, Lester,
that this fellow is a great criminal, and that he
finds life infinitely more engrossing than either
you or I. I hope I shall meet him some time—
not in a little skirmish like this, but in an out-and-
out battle. Of course I'd be routed, horse, foot
and dragoons—but it certainly would be interesting!" and he looked at me, his eyes glowing.

"It certainly would!" I agreed. "Go ahead
with your romance."

" Here it is. Monsieur Armand is a great criminal and has, of course, various followers upon
whom he must rely for the performance of certain details, since he can be in but one place at a
time. Abject and absolute obedience is necessary to his success, and he compels obedience in
the only way in which it can be compelled among
criminals—by fear. For disobedience, there is
but one punishment—death. And the manner
of the death is so certain and so mysterious as to
be almost supernatural. For deserters and traitors are found to have died, inevitably and invari-

ably, from the effects of an insignificant wound
on the right hand, just below the knuckles."

I was listening intently now, as you may well
believe, for I began to see whither the romance
was tending.

"It is by this secret," Godfrey continued, "that
Armand preserves his absolute supremacy. But
occasionally the temptation is too great, and one
of his men deserts. Armand sends this cabinet
to America. He knows that in this case the temptation is very great indeed; he fears treachery,
and he arranges in the cabinet a mechanism which
will inflict death upon the traitor in precisely the
same way in which he himself inflicts it—by
means of a poisoned stab in the right hand. Imagine the effect upon his gang. He is nowhere
near when the act of treachery is performed, and
yet the traitor dies instantly and surely! Why, it
was a tremendous idea! And it was carried out
with absolute genius."

"But," I questioned, "what act of treachery
was it that Armand feared?"

"The opening of the secret drawer."

"Then you still believe in the poisoned mechanism?"

"I certainly do. The tragedy of this afternoon proves the truth of the theory."

"I don't see it," I said helplessly.

"Why, Lester," protested Godfrey, "it's as plain as day. Who was that bearded giant who was killed? The traitor, of course. We will find that he was a member of Armand's gang. He followed Armand to America, lay in wait for him, caught him in the net and bound him hand and foot. Do you suppose for an instant that Armand was ignorant of his presence in that house? Do you suppose he would have been able to take Armand prisoner if Armand had not been willing that he should?"

"I don't see how Armand could help himself after that fellow got his hands on him."

"You don't? And yet you saw yourself that he was not really bound—that he had cut himself loose!"

"That is true," I said thoughtfully.

"Let us reconstruct the story," Godfrey went on rapidly. "The traitor discovers the secret of the cabinet; he follows Armand to New York, shadows him to the house on Seventh Avenue, waits for him there, and seizes and binds him. He is half mad with triumph—he chants a crazy sing-song about revenge, revenge, revenge! And in order that the triumph may be complete, he does not kill his prisoner at once. He rolls him into a corner and proceeds to rip away the burlap. His triumph will be to open the secret drawer before Armand's eyes. And Armand lies there in the corner, his eyes gleaming, because it is really the moment of *his* triumph which is at hand!"

"The moment of his triumph?" I repeated. "What do you mean by that, Godfrey?"

"I mean that, the instant the traitor opened the drawer, he would be stabbed by the poisoned mechanism! It was for that that Armand waited!"

I lay back in my chair with a gasp of amazement and admiration. I had been blind not to see it! Armand had merely to lie still and permit the traitor to walk into the trap prepared for him. No wonder his eyes had glowed as he lay there watching that frenzied figure at the cabinet!

"It was not until the last moment," Godfrey went on, "when the traitor was bending above the cabinet feeling for the spring, that I realised what was about to happen. There was no time for hesitation—I sprang into the room. Armand vanished in an instant, and the giant also tried to escape; but I caught him at the door. I had no idea of his danger; I had no thought that Armand would dare linger. And yet he did. Now that it is too late, I understand. He *had* to kill that man; there were no two ways about it. Whatever the risk, he had to kill him."

"But why? "I asked. "Why?"

"To seal his lips. If we had captured him, do you suppose Armand's secret would have been safe for an instant? So he had to kill him—he had to kill him with the poisoned barb—and he *did* kill him, and got away into the bargain! Never in my life have I felt so like a fool as when that door was slammed in my face!"

"Perhaps he had that prepared, too," I suggested timidly, ready to believe anything of this extraordinary man. "Perhaps he knew that we were there, all the time."

"Of course he did," assented Godfrey grimly. "Why else would there be a snap-lock on the outside of the door? And to think I didn't see it! To think that I was fool enough to suppose that I could follow him about the streets of New York without his knowing it! He knew from the first that he might be followed, and prepared for it!"

"But it's incredible!" I protested feebly. "It's incredible!"

"Nothing is incredible in connection with that man!"

"But the risk—think of the risk he ran!"

"What does he care for risks? He despises them—and rightly. He got away, didn't he?"

"Yes," I said, "he got away; there's no question of that, I guess."

"Well, that is the story of this afternoon's tragedy, as I understand it," proceeded Godfrey, more calmly. "And now I'm going to leave you. I want you to think it over. If it doesn't hold together, show me where it doesn't. But it *will* hold together—it *has* to—because it's true!"

"But how about Armand?" I protested. "Aren't you going to try to capture him? Are you going to let him get away?"

"He won't get away!" and Godfrey's eyes were gleaming again. "We don't have to search for him, for we've got our trap, Lester, and it's baited with a bait he can't resist—the Boule cabinet!"

"But he knows it's a trap."

"Of course he knows it!"

"And you really think he will walk into it?"
I asked incredulously.

"I know he will! One of these days, he will
try to get that cabinet out of the steel cell at the
Twenty-third Street station, in which we have it
locked!"

I shook my head.

"He's no such fool," I said. "No man is such
a fool as that. He'll give it up and go quietly
back to Paris."

"Not if he's the man I think he is," said Godfrey, his hand on the door. "He will never give
up! Just wait, Lester; we shall know in a day or
two which of us is a true prophet. The only thing
I am afraid of," he added, his face clouding, "is
that he'll get away with the cabinet, in spite of
us!"

And he went away down the hall, leaving me
staring after him.

CHAPTER XXII

"CROCHARD, L'INVINCIBLE!"

IT seemed for once that Godfrey was destined to be wrong, for the days passed and nothing happened—nothing, that is, in so far as the cabinet was concerned. There was an inquest, of course, over the victim of the latest tragedy, and once again I was forced to give my evidence before a coroner's jury. I must confess that, this time, it made me appear considerable of a fool, and the papers poked sly fun at the attorney who had walked blindly into a trap which, now that it was sprung, seemed so apparent.

The Bertillon measurements of the victim had been cabled to Paris, and he had been instantly identified as a· fellow named Morel, well-known to the police as a daring and desperate criminal; in fact, Monsieur Chiappe considered the matter so important that he cabled next day that he was sending Inspector Pigot to New York to investigate the affair further, and to confer with our bureau as to the best methods to be taken to apprehend the murderer. Inspector Pigot, it was added, would sail at once from Havre on the *Paris*.

Meanwhile, Grady's men with Simmonds at their head strained every nerve to discover the whereabouts of the fugitive; a net was thrown over the entire city, but, while a number of fish were captured, the one which the police particularly wished for was not among them. Not a single trace of the fugitive was discovered; he had vanished absolutely, and after a day or two, Grady asserted confidently that he had left New York.

For Grady had come back into the case again, goaded by the papers, particularly by the *Record,* to efforts which he must have considered superhuman. The remarkable nature of the mystery, its picturesque and unique features, the fact that three men had been killed within a few days in precisely the same manner, and the absence of any reasonable hypothesis to explain these deaths— all this served to rivet public attention. Every amateur detective in the country had a theory to exploit—and far-fetched enough most of them were!

Grady did a lot of talking in those days, explaining in detail the remarkable measures he was taking to capture the criminal; but the fact remained that three men had been killed and that no one had been punished; that a series of crimes had been committed and that the criminal was still at large and seemed likely to remain so; and, naturally enough, the papers, having exhausted every other phase of the case, were soon echoing public sentiment that something was wrong somewhere, and that the detective bureau needed an overhauling, beginning at the top.

The Boule cabinet remained locked up in a cell at the Twenty-third Street station, and Simmonds kept the key in his pocket. I know now that he was as much in the dark concerning the cabinet as the general public was, and the general public was very much in the dark indeed, for the cabinet had not figured in the accounts of the first two tragedies at all, and only incidentally in the reports of the latest one. So far as it was concerned, the affair seemed clear enough to most of the reporters, as an attempt to smuggle into the country an art object of great value. Such cases were too common to attract especial attention.

But Simmonds had come to see that Grady was tottering on his throne; he realised, perhaps, that

his own head was not safe, and he had made up
his mind to pin his faith to Godfrey as the only
one at all likely to lead him out of the maze. And
Godfrey laid the greatest stress upon the necessity of keeping the cabinet under lock and key, so
under lock and key it was kept. As for Grady,
I do not believe that, even at the last, he realised
the important part the cabinet had played in the
drama.

But while the Boule cabinet failed to focus the
attention of the public, and while most of the
reporters promptly forgot all about it, I was
amused at the pains which Godfrey took to inform the fugitive as to its whereabouts and as to
how it was guarded. Over and over again, while
the other papers wondered at his imbecility, he
told how it had been placed in the strongest cell
at the Twenty-third Street station; a cell whose
bars were made of chrome-nickel steel which no
saw could bite into; a cell whose lock was worked
not only by a key but by a combination, known to
one man only; a cell isolated from the others,
standing alone in the middle of the third corridor,
in full view of the officer on guard, so that no one
could approach it, day or night, without being instantly discovered; a cell whose door was con-

nected with an automatic alarm over the sergeant's desk in the front room; a cell, in short, from which no man could possibly escape, and which no man could possibly enter unobserved.

Of the Boule cabinet itself Godfrey said little, saving his story for the dénouement which he seemed so sure would come; but the details which I have given above were dwelt upon in the *Record*, until, happening to meet Godfrey on the street one day, I protested that he would only succeed in frightening the fugitive away altogether, even if he still had any designs on the cabinet, which I very much doubted. But Godfrey only laughed.

"There's not the slightest danger of frightening him away," he said. "This fellow isn't that kind. If I am right in sizing him up, he's the sort of dare-devil whom an insuperable difficulty only attracts. The harder the job, the more he is drawn to it. That's the reason I am making this one just as hard as I can."

"But a man would be a fool to attempt to get to that cabinet," I protested. "It's simply impossible.

"It looks impossible, I'm free to admit," he agreed. "But, just the same, I wake every morning cold with fear, and run to the 'phone to make sure the cabinet's safe. If I could think of any further safeguards, I would certainly employ them."

I looked at Godfrey searchingly, for it seemed to me that he must be jesting. He smiled as he caught my glance.

"I was never more in earnest in my life, Lester," he said. "You don't appreciate this fellow as I do. He's a genius; nothing is impossible to him. He disdains easy jobs; when he thinks a job is too easy, he makes it harder, just as a sporting chance. He has been known to warn people that they kept their jewels too carelessly, and then, after they had put them in a safer place, he would go and take them."

"That seems rather foolish, doesn't it?" I queried.

"Not from his point of view. He doesn't steal because he needs money, but because he needs excitement."

"You know who he is, then? "I demanded.

"I think I do—I hope I do; but I am not going to tell even you till I'm sure. I'll say this —if he is who I think he is, it would be a delight to match one's brains with his. We haven't got any one like him over here—which is a pity!"

I was inclined to doubt this, for I have no romantic admiration for gentlemen burglars, even in fiction. However picturesque and chivalric, a thief is, after all, a thief. Perhaps it is my training as a lawyer, or perhaps I am simply narrow, but crime, however brilliantly carried out, seems to me a sordid and unlovely thing. I know quite well that there are many people who look at these things from a different angle. Godfrey is one of them.

I pointed out to him now that, if his intuitions were correct, he would soon have a chance to match his wits with those of the Great Unknown.

"Yes," he agreed, "and I'm scared to death —I have been ever since I began to suspect his identity. I feel like a tyro going up against a master in a game of chess—mate in six moves!"

"I shouldn't consider you exactly a tyro," I said drily.

"It's long odds that the Great Unknown will," Godfrey retorted, and bade me good-bye.

Except for that chance meeting, I saw nothing of him, and in this I was disappointed, for there were many things about the whole affair which

I did not understand. In fact, when I sat down of an evening and lit my pipe and began to think it over, I found that I understood nothing at all. Godfrey's theory held together perfectly, so far as I could see, but it led nowhere. How had Drouet and Vantine been killed? Why had they been killed? What was the secret of the cabinet? In a word, what was all this mystery about? Not one of these questions could I answer; and the solutions I guessed at seemed so absurd that I dismissed them in disgust. In the end, I found that the affair was interfering with my work, and I banished it from my mind, turning my face resolutely away from it whenever it tried to break into my thoughts.

But though I could shut it out of my waking hours successfully enough, I could not control my sleeping ones, and my dreams became more and more horrible. Always there was the serpent with dripping fangs, sometimes with Armand's head, sometimes with a face unknown to me, but hideous beyond description. Its slimy body glittered with inlay and arabesque; its scaly legs were curved like those of the Boule cabinet; sometimes the golden sun glittered on its forehead like a great eye. Over and over again I saw this monster slay its three victims; and always, when that was done, it raised its head and glared at me, as though selecting me for the fourth. . . . But I shall not try to describe those dreams; even yet I cannot recall them without a shudder.

It was while I was sitting moodily in my room one night, debating whether or not to go to bed, weary to exhaustion and yet reluctant to resign myself to a sleep from which I knew I should wake shivering, that a ring came at the door — a short, sharp ring I somehow recognized; and I arose joyfully to admit Godfrey.

I could see by the way his eyes were shining that he had something unusual to tell me, and then, as he looked at me, his face changed.

"What's the matter, Lester?" he demanded. "You're looking fagged out. Working too hard?"

"It's not that," I said. "I can't sleep. This thing has upset me completely, Godfrey. I dream about it — have regular nightmares."

He sat down opposite me, concern and anxiety in his face.

"That won't do," he protested. "You must go away somewhere — take a rest, and a good long one."

"A rest wouldn't do me any good as long as this mystery is unsolved," I said. "It's only by working that I can keep my mind off of it."

"Well," he smiled, "just to oblige you, we will solve it first, then."

"Do you mean you know . . ."

"I know who the Great Unknown is, and I'm going to tell you presently. Day after to-morrow —Wednesday—I'll know all the rest. The whole story will be in Thursday morning's paper. Suppose you arrange to start Thursday afternoon."

I could only stare at him.

" You're looking better already," he said, " as though you were taking a little more interest in life," and he proceeded to help himself to a pipeful of tobacco.

"Godfrey," I protested, "I wish you would pick out somebody else to practise on. You come up here and explode a bomb just to see how high I'll jump. It's amusing to you, no doubt, and perhaps a little instructive; but my nerves won't stand it."

"My dear Lester," he broke in, "that wasn't a bomb; that was a simple statement of fact,"

"Are you serious?"

"Perfectly so."

"But how do you know . . ."

"Before I answer any questions, I want to ask you one. Did you, by any chance, mention me to the gentleman known to you as Monsieur Félix Armand? "

"Yes," I answered, after a moment's thought, "I believe I did. I was telling him about our trying to find the secret drawer—I mentioned your name—and he asked who you were. I told him you were a genius at solving mysteries."

Godfrey nodded.

"That," he said, "explains the one thing I didn't understand. Now go ahead with your questions."

"You said a while ago that you would know all about this affair day after to-morrow."

"Yes."

"How do you know you will?"

"Because I have received a letter which sets the date," and he took from his pocket a sheet of paper and handed it over to me. "Read it!"

The letter was written in pencil, in a delicate and somewhat feminine hand, on a sheet of plain, unruled paper. With an astonishment which increased with every word, I read this extraordinary epistle :—

"My Dear Mr. Godfrey:

"I have been highly flattered by your interest in the affaire of the cabinet Boule, and admire most deeply your penetration in arriving at a conclusion so nearly correct regarding it. I must thank you, also, for your kindness in keeping me informed of the measures which have been taken to guard the cabinet, and which seem to me very complete and well thought out. I have myself visited the station and inspected the cell, and I find that in every detail you were correct.

"It is because I so esteem you as an adversary that I tell you, in confidence, that it is my intention to regain possession of my property on Wednesday next, and that, having done so, I shall beg you to accept a small souvenir of the occasion.

"I am, my dear sir,

"Most cordially yours,
"JACQUES CROCHARD,
"L'Invincible!"

I looked up to find Godfrey regarding me with a quizzical smile.

"Of course it's a joke," I said. Then I looked

at him again. "Surely, Godfrey, you don't believe this is genuine!"

"Perhaps we can prove it," he said quietly.
"That is one reason I came up. Didn't Armand
leave a note for you the day he failed to see you?"

"Yes; on his card; I have it here!" and with
trembling fingers, I got out my pocket-book and
drew the card from the compartment in which
I had carefully preserved it.

One glance at it was enough. The pencilled
line on the back was unquestionably written by
the same hand which wrote the letter.

"And now you know his name," Godfrey
added, tapping the signature with his finger.
"I have been certain from the first that it was
he!"

I gazed at the signature without answering.
I had, of course, read in the papers many times
of the Brobdingnagian exploits of Crochard —
" The Invincible," as he loved to call himself, and
with good reason. But his achievements, at least as
the papers described them, seemed too fantastic to
be true. I had suspected more than once that he
was merely an invention of the Parisian space-
writers, a sort of reserve for the dull season; or
else that he was a kind of scape-goat saddled by

the French police with every crime which proved too much for them. Now, however, it seemed that Crochard really existed; I held his letter in my hand; I had even talked with him — and as I remembered the fascination, the finish, the distinguished culture of Félix Armand, I understood something of the reason for his extraordinary reputation.

"There can be no two opinions about him," said Godfrey, reaching out his hand for the letter and sinking back in his chair to contemplate it. "Crochard is one of the greatest criminals who ever lived, full of imagination and resource, and with a sense of humour most acute. I have followed his career for years—it was this fact that gave me my first clue. He killed a man once before, just as he killed this last one. The man had betrayed him to the police. He was never betrayed again."

"What a fiend he must be!" I said, with a shudder.

But Godfrey shook his head quickly.

"Don't get that idea of him," he protested earnestly. "Up to the time of his arrival in New York, he had never killed any man except that traitor. Him he had a certain right to kill

—according to thieves' ethics, anyway. His own life has been in peril scores of times, but he has never killed a man to save himself. Put that down to his credit."

"But Drouet and Vantine," I objected.

"An accident for which he was in no way responsible," said Godfrey promptly.

"You mean he didn't kill them?"

"Most certainly not. This last man he did kill was a traitor like the first. Crochard, I think, reasons like this: to kill an adversary is too easy; it is too brutal; it lacks finesse. Besides, it removes the adversary. And without adversaries Crochard's life would be of no interest to him. After he had killed his last adversary, he would have to kill himself.

"I can't understand a man like that," I said.

"Well, look at this," said Godfrey, and tapped the letter again. "He honours me by considering me an adversary. Does he seek to remove me? On the contrary, he gives me a handicap. He takes off his queen in order that it may be a little more difficult to mate me!"

"But surely, Godfrey," I protested, "you don't take that letter seriously! If he wrote it at all, he wrote it merely to throw you off the track. If he says Wednesday, he really intends to try for the cabinet to-morrow."

"I don't think so. I told you he would think me only a tyro. And beside him, that is all I am. Do you know where he wrote that letter, Lester? Right in the *Record* office. That is a sheet of our copy paper. He sat down there, right under my nose, wrote that letter, dropped it into my box, and walked out. And all that sometime this evening, when the office was crowded."

"But it's absurd for him to write a letter like that, if he really means it. You have only to warn the police . . ."

"You'll notice he says it is in confidence."

" And you intend to keep it so? "

" Certainly I do; I consider that he has paid me a high compliment. I have shown it to no one but you—also in confidence."

"It is not the sort of confidence the law recognises," I pointed out. "To keep a confidence like that is practically to abet a felony."

"And yet you will keep it," said Godfrey cheerfully. "You see I am going to do everything I can to prevent that felony. And we will see if Crochard is really invincible!"

" I'll keep it," I agreed, " because I think the

letter is just a blind. And by the way," I added, " I have a letter from Armand & Son confirming the fact that their books show that the Boule cabinet was bought by Philip Vantine. Under the circumstances, I shall have to claim it and hand it over to the Metropolitan."

"I hope you won't disturb it until after Wednesday," said Godfrey quickly. "I won't have any interest in it after that."

"You really think Crochard will try for it Wednesday?"

"I really do."

I shrugged my shoulders. What was the use of arguing with a man like that?

"Till after Wednesday, then," I agreed; and Godfrey, having verified his letter and secured from me the two promises he was after, bade me good-night.

CHAPTER XXIII

WE MEET MONSIEUR PIGOT

I WAS just getting ready to leave the office the next afternoon when Godfrey called me up.

"How are you feeling to-day, Lester?" he asked.

"Not as fit as I might," I said.

"Have you arranged to start on that vacation Thursday?"

"I don't think that's a good joke, Godfrey."

"It isn't a joke at all. I want you to arrange it. But meanwhile, how would you like a whiff of salt air this evening?"

"First rate. How will I get it?"

"The *Paris* will get to quarantine about six o'clock. I'm going down on our boat to meet her. I want to have a talk with Inspector Pigot — the French detective. Will you come along?"

"Will I!" I said. "Where shall I meet you?"

"At the foot of Liberty Street, at five o'clock."

"I'll be there," I promised. And I was.

The boat was cast loose as soon as we got

aboard, backed out into the busy river, her whistle shrieking shrilly, then swung about and headed down stream. It was a fast boat—the *Record,* which prided itself on outdistancing its contemporaries in other directions, would of course try to do so in this—and when she got fairly into her stride, with her engines throbbing rhythmically, the shore on either hand slipped past us rapidly.

The New York sky-line, as seen from the river, is one of the wonders of the world, and I stood looking at it until we swung out into the bay. There were two other men on board—the regular ship reporters, I suppose—and Godfrey had gone into the cabin with them to talk over some detail of the evening's work; so I went forward to the bow, where I would get the full benefit of the salt breeze, with the taste of it on my lips. The Statue of Liberty was just ahead, and already the great light in her torch was streaming across the water. Craft innumerable crossed and recrossed, their lights reflected in the waves, and far ahead, a little to the left, I could see the white glow against the sky which marked the position of Coney Island.

Godfrey joined me presently, and we stood

for some time looking at this scene in silence.

"It's a great sight, isn't it?" he said at last. "Hello! look at that boat!" he added, as a yacht coming down the bay drew abreast of us and then slowly forged ahead. "She can go some, can't she? This boat of ours is no slouch, you know; but just look how that one walks away from us. I wonder who she is? What boat is that, captain?" he called to the man on the bridge.

"Don't know, sir," answered the captain, after a look through his glasses. "Private yacht—can't make out her name—there's a flag or something hanging over the stern. She's flying the French flag. There come the other press boats behind us, sir," he added. "And there's the *Paris* just slowing down at quarantine."

Far ahead we could see the great hull of the liner, dark against the horizon, and crowned with row upon row of glowing lights.

"One doesn't appreciate how big those boats are until one sees them from the water," I remarked. "Isn't she immense?"

"And yet she's not one of the biggest ones either," said Godfrey. "To swing in under the real giants—like the *Leviathan*—is an experience to remember."

The *Paris* had by this time slowed down until she was just holding her own against the tide, and one of her lower ports swung open. A moment later a boat puffed up beside her, made fast, and three or four men clambered aboard and disappeared through the port.

"There go the doctors," said Godfrey. "And there is that French boat going alongside."

The tug from quarantine dropped astern and the French yacht took her place. After a short colloquy, one man from her was helped aboard the *Paris*. Then it was our turn, and after what seemed to me a tremendous swishing and swirling at imminent risk of collision, we swung up to the open port, a line was flung out and made fast, and a moment later Godfrey and I and the other two men were aboard the liner.

My companions exchanged greetings with the officer in charge of the open port, and then we hurried forward along a narrow corridor, smelling of rubber and heated metal, then up stair after stair, until at last we came to the main companionway. Here the two men left us to seek certain distinguished passengers, I suppose, whose views upon the questions of the day were (presumably) anxiously awaited by an expectant public. Godfrey stopped in front of the purser's office and passed his card through the little window to the man inside the cage.

"I should like to see Monsieur Pigot, of the Paris *Service du Sûreté,*" he said. "Perhaps you will be so kind as to have a steward take my card to him?"

"That is unnecessary, sir," replied the purser, courteously. "That is Monsieur Pigot yonder—the gentleman with the white hair, with his back to us. You will have to wait for a moment, however; the gentleman speaking with him is from the French consulate, and has but this moment come aboard."

I could not see Inspector Pigot's face, but I could see that he held himself very erect, in a manner bespeaking military training. The messenger from the legation was a youngish man, with waxed moustache and wearing an eyeglass. He was greeting Monsieur Pigot at the moment, and after a word or two, produced from an inside pocket an official-looking envelope, tied with red tape and secured with an immense red seal.

Pigot looked at it an instant, while his companion added a sentence in his ear; then, with a nod of assent, the detective turned down one of the passage-ways, the other man at his heels.

"Official business, no doubt," commented the
purser, who had also been watching this little
scene. "Monsieur Pigot is one of the best of our
officers and you will find it a pleasure to talk with
him. He will no doubt soon be disengaged."

"Yes, but meanwhile my esteemed contemporaries will arrive," said Godfrey with a grimace. "They are on my heels—here they are
now!"

In fact, for the next twenty minutes, reporters
from the other papers kept arriving, till there was
quite a crowd before the purser's office. And
from nearly every paper a special man had been
detailed to interview Pigot. Evidently all the
papers were alive to the importance of the subject. There was some good-natured chaffing, and
then one of the stewards was bribed to carry the
cards of the assembled multitude to Pigot's
stateroom, with the request for an audience.

The steward went away laughing and came
back presently to say that Monsieur Pigot would
be pleased to see us in a few minutes. But when
five minutes more passed and he did not appear,
impatience broke out anew. The lords of the
press were not accustomed to being kept waiting.

"I move we storm his castle," suggested the *World* man.

And just then Monsieur Pigot himself stepped out into the companionway. In an instant he was surrounded.

"My good friends of the press," he said, speaking slowly but with only the faintest accent, and he smiled around at the faces bent upon him. "You will pardon me for keeping you in waiting, but I had some affairs of the first importance to attend to; and also my bag to pack. Steward," he added, "you will find my bag outside my door. Please bring it here, so that I may be ready to go ashore at once." The steward hurried away and Pigot turned back to us. "Now, gentlemen," he went on, "what is it that I can do for you?"

It was to Godfrey that the position of spokesman naturally fell.

"We wish first to welcome you to America, Monsieur Pigot," he said, "and to hope that you will have a pleasant and interesting stay in our country."

"You are most kind," responded the Frenchman, with a charming smile. "I am sure that I shall find it most interesting—especially your

wonderful city, of which I have heard many marvellous things."

"And in the next place," continued Godfrey,
"we hope that, with your assistance, our police
may be able to solve the mystery surrounding the
death of the three men recently killed here, and
to arrest the murderer. Of themselves, they
seem able to do nothing."

Monsieur Pigot spread out his hands with a
little deprecating gesture.

"I also hope we may be successful," he said;
"but if your police have not been, my poor help
will be of little account. I have a profound admiration for your police; the results which they
accomplish are wonderful, when one considers the
difficulties under which they labour."

He spoke with an accent so sincere that I was
almost convinced he meant every word of it; but
Godfrey only smiled.

"It is a proverb," he said, "that the French
police are the best in the world. You, no doubt,
have a theory in regard to the death of these
men?"

"I fear it is impossible, sir," said Monsieur
Pigot regretfully, "to answer that question at
present or to discuss this case with you. I have my

report first to make to the chief of your detective bureau. To-morrow I shall be most happy to tell you all that I can. But for to-night my lips are closed, sad as it makes me to seem discourteous."

I could hear behind me the little indrawn breath of disappointment at the failure of the direct attack. Pigot's position was, of course, absolutely correct, but nevertheless Godfrey prepared to attack it on the flank.

" You are going ashore to-night ? " he inquired.

" I was expecting a representative of your bureau to meet me here," Pigot explained. " I was hoping to return with him to the city. I have no time to lose. In addition, the more quickly we get to work, the more likely we shall be to succeed. Ah! perhaps that is he," he added, as a voice was heard inquiring loudly for Moosseer Piggott.

I recognised that voice and so did Godfrey, and I saw the cloud of disappointment which fell upon his face.

An instant later, Grady, with Simmonds in his wake, elbowed his way through the group.

" Moosseer Piggott! " he cried, and enveloped the Frenchman's slender hand in his great paw and gave it a squeeze which was no doubt painful.

"Glad to see you, sir. Welcome to our city, as we say over here in America. I certainly hope you can speak English, for I don't know a word of your lingo. I'm Commissioner Grady, in charge of the detective bureau; and this is Simmonds, one of my men."

Monsieur Pigot's perfect suavity was not even ruffled.

"I am most pleased to meet you, sir; and you Monsieur Simmòn," he said. "Yes — I speak English — though, as you see, with some difficulty."

"These reporters bothering your life out, I see," and Grady glanced about the group, scowling as his eyes met Godfrey's. "Now you boys might as well fade away. You won't get anything out of either of us to-night — eh, Moosseer Piggott?"

"I have but just told them that my first report must be made to you, sir," assented Pigot.

"Then let's go somewhere and have a drink," suggested Grady.

"I was hoping," said Pigot, gently, "that we might go ashore at once. I have my papers ready for you . . ."

"All right," agreed Grady. "And after I've

looked over your papers, I'll show you Broadway, and I'll bet you agree with me that it beats anything in gay Paree. Our boat's waiting, and we can start right away. This your bag? Yes? Bring it along, Simmonds," and Grady started for the stair.

But the attentive steward got ahead of Simmonds.

Monsieur Pigot turned to us with a little smile.

" Till to-morrow, gentlemen," he said. " I shall be at the Hotel Brevoort, and shall be glad to see you — shall we say at eleven o'clock? I am truly sorry that I can tell you nothing to-night."

He shook hands with the purser, waved his hand to us and joined Grady, who was watching these amenities with evident impatience. Together they disappeared down the stair.

" A contrast in manners, was it not, gentlemen?" asked Godfrey, blandly looking about him.

The men laughed, for they knew he was after Grady, and yet it was evident enough that they agreed with him.

" Come on, Lester," he added; " we might as well be getting back. I can send the boat down again after the other boys," and he turned down the stair.

CHAPTER XXIV

THE SECRET OF THE CABINET

GODFREY bade me good-bye at the dock and hastened away to the office to write his story, and I smiled to myself at thought of the biting fashion in which he would contrast the manners of the detective chiefs of Paris and New York. Yet I did not altogether sympathise with Godfrey's point of view. There could be no question that in manners Grady fell woefully short, but he had some saving qualities. For example, I hadn't the slightest doubt that his hand would plunge' into his pocket to assist someone in need far more readily than would Pigot's. The Frenchman's manners seemed absurd to Grady, and Grady's open-handedness would seem ridiculous to the Frenchman. Of the two, I preferred the open-handedness.

Then I turned my thoughts to dinner, for I was conscious that the trip down the harbor had put an unaccustomed edge to my appetite, and I called a taxi and drove uptown to Pierre's. I know no better place for a hungry man than Pierre's, where the food has a certain robustness of flavor reminiscent of the Midi—the onion soup, for instance, is beyond compare!—and I ambled through the meal in a fashion so leisurely and trifled so long over coffee and cigarette that it was far past ten o'clock when I came out again into Forty-second Street. After an instant's hesitation, I decided to walk home, and turned back toward Broadway, already filling with the after-theatre crowd.

Often as I have seen it, Broadway at night is still a fascinating place to me, with its blazing signs, its changing crowds, its clanging street traffic, its bright shop-windows. But how it has changed during the years that I have known it! Its centre has shifted from Union Square to Madison Square to Times Square. What, ten years ago, was a drab wilderness is now a blaze of light; what, ten years ago, was a blaze of light is now a drab wilderness. It astounds one to think of the fortunes which have been wiped out and the fortunes which have been made by this steady and relentless transformation.

Reaching Madison Square, at last, I walked out under the trees, as I almost always do, to have a look at the Flatiron Building, white against the sky. Then I glanced up at the Metropolitan tower, higher but far less romantic in appearance, and saw by the big illuminated clock that it was nearly half-past eleven.

I crossed back over Broadway, at last, and turned down Twenty-third Street in the direction of the Marathon, when, just at the corner, I came face to face with three men as they swung around the corner in the same direction, and with a little start, I recognised Grady and Simmonds, with Pigot between them. Evidently Grady had felt it incumbent upon himself to make good his promise in the most liberal manner and to display the wonders of the Great White Way from end to end — the ceremony no doubt involving a thorough demonstration of New York's complete contempt for the Volstead act—the result of which was that Grady's legs wobbled perceptibly. As a matter of racial comparison, I glanced at Pigot's, but they seemed in every way normal.

"Hello, Lester," said Simmonds, in a voice which showed that he had not wholly escaped the influences of the evening's celebration; and even Grady condescended to nod, from which I inferred that he was feeling very unusually happy.

"Hello, Simmonds," I answered, and as I turned westward with them, he dropped back and fell into step beside me.

" Piggott is surely a wonder," he said. " A regular sport — wanted to see everything and taste everything. We've certainly shown him that prohibition doesn't prohibit — not in little old New York! "

" Where are you going now? " I asked.

" We're going round to the station. Piggott says he's got a sensation up his sleeve for us — it's got something to do with that cabinet."

" With the cabinet? "

" Yes — that shiny thing Godfrey got me to lock up in a cell."

" Simmonds," I said seriously, " does Godfrey know about this? "

" No," said Simmonds, looking a little uncomfortable. " I told Grady we ought to 'phone him to come up, but the chief got mad and told me to mind my own business. Godfrey's been after him, you know, for a long time."

" Suppose I 'phone him," I suggested. " There'd be no objection to that, would there? "

" *I* won't object," said Simmonds, " and I don't know who else will, since nobody else will know about it."

" All right. And drag out the preliminaries as long as you can, to give him a chance to get up here."

Simmonds nodded.

" I'll do what I can," he agreed, " but I don't
see what good it will do. The chief won't let
him in, even if he does come up."

" We'll have to leave that to Godfrey. But he
ought to be told. He's responsible for the cabinet being where it is."

" I know he is, and Piggott says it was a mighty
wise thing to put it there, though I'm blessed if I
know why. Hurry Godfrey along as much as
you can. Good-night," and he followed his companions into the station.

There was a drugstore at the corner with a
public telephone station, and two minutes later
I was asking to be connected with the city-room at
the *Record* office.

No, said a supercilious voice, Mr. Godfrey was
not there; he had left some time before; no, the
speaker did not know where he was going, nor
when he would be back.

" Look here," I said, " this is important. I
want to talk to the city editor — and be quick
about it."

There was an instant's astonished silence.

" What name? " asked the voice.

" Lester, of Royce and Lester — and you

might tell your city editor that Godfrey is a close friend of mine."

The city editor seemed to understand, for I was switched on to him a moment later. But he was scarcely more satisfactory.

"We sent Godfrey up into Westchester to see a man," he said, "on a tip that looked pretty good. He started just as soon as he got his Pigot story written, and he ought to be back almost any time. Is there a message I can give him?"

"Yes — tell him Pigot is at the Twenty-third Street station, and that he'd better come up as soon as he can."

"Very good. I'll give him the message the moment he comes in."

"Thank you," I said, but the disappointment was a bitter one.

In the street again, I paused hesitatingly at the curb, my eyes on the red light of the police station. What was about to happen there? What was the sensation Pigot had up his sleeve? Had I any excuse for being present?

And then, remembering Grady's nod and his wobbly legs — remembering, too, that at the worst he could only put me out! — I turned toward the light, pushed open the door and entered.

There was no one in sight except the sergeant at the desk.

"My name is Lester," I said. "You have a cabinet here belonging to the estate of the late Philip Vantine."

"We've got a cabinet, all right; but I don't know who it belongs to."

"It belongs to Mr. Vantine's estate."

"Well, what about it?" he asked, looking at me to see if I was drunk. "You haven't come in here at midnight to tell me that, I hope?"

"No; but I'd like to see the cabinet a minute."

"You can't see it to-night. Come around to-morrow. Besides, I don't know you."

"Here's my card. Either Mr. Simmonds or Mr. Grady would know me. And to-morrow won't do."

The sergeant took the card, looked at it, and looked at me.

"Wait a minute," he said at last, and disappeared through a door at the farther side of the room. He was gone three or four minutes, and the station-clock struck twelve as I stood there. I counted the sonorous, deliberate strokes, and then, in the silence that followed, my hands began to tremble with the suspense. Suppose Grady should refuse to see me? But at last the sergeant came back.

"Come along," he said, opening the gate in the railing and motioning me through. "Straight on through that door," he added, and sat down again at his desk.

With a desperate effort at careless unconcern, I opened the door and passed through. Then, involuntarily, I stopped. For there, in the middle of the floor, was the Boule cabinet with Pigot standing beside it and Grady and Simmonds sitting opposite, flung carelessly back in their chairs and puffing at black cigars.

They all looked at me as I entered, Pigot with an evident contraction of the brows which showed how strongly his urbanity was strained; Simmonds with an affectation of surprise, and Grady with a bland and somewhat vacant smile. My heart rose when I saw that smile.

"Well, Mr. Lester," he said, "so you want to see this cabinet?"

"Yes," I answered; "it really belongs to the Vantine estate, you know; I'm going to put in a claim for it — that is, if you are not willing to surrender it without contest."

"Did you just happen to think of this in the middle of the night?" he inquired quizzically.

"No," I said boldly; "but I saw you and Mr. Simmonds and this gentleman" — with a bow to Pigot — "turn in here a moment ago, and it occurred to me that the cabinet might have something to do with your visit. Of course we don't want the cabinet injured. It is very valuable."

"Don't worry," said Grady easily, "we're not going to injure it. And I think we'll be ready to surrender it to you at any time after to-night. Moosseer Piggott here wants to do a few tricks with it first. I suppose you have a certain right to be present — so, if you like sleight-of-hand, sit down."

I hastily sought a chair, my heart singing within me. Then I attempted to assume a mask of indifference, for Pigot was obviously annoyed at my presence, and I feared for a moment that his Gallic suavity would be strained to breaking. But Grady, if he noticed his guest's annoyance, paid no heed to it and I began to suspect that the Frenchman's impeccable manners had ended by rubbing Grady the wrong way, they were in such violent contrast to his own hob-nailed mentality. Whatever the cause, there was a certain malice in the smile he turned upon the Frenchman.

"And now, Moosseer Piggott," he said, settling back in his chair a little farther, "we're ready for the show."

"What I have to tell you, sir," began Pigot, in a voice as hard as steel and cold as ice, "has, understand well, to be told in confidence. It must remain between ourselves until the criminal is secured."

Grady's smile hardened a little. Perhaps he did not like the imperatives. At any rate, he ignored the hint.

"Understand, Mr. Lester?" he asked, looking at me, and I nodded.

I saw Pigot's eyes flame and his face flush with anger, for Grady's tone was almost insulting. For an instant I thought that he would refuse to proceed; but he controlled himself.

Standing there facing me in the full light, it was possible for me to examine him much more closely than had been possible on board the boat, and I looked at him with interest. He was typically French,— smooth-shaven, with a face seamed with little wrinkles and very white, eyes shadowed by enormously bushy lashes, and close-

cropped hair as white as his face. But what at-
tracted me most was the mouth — a mouth at once
delicate and humourous, a little large and with the
lips full enough to betoken vigour, yet not too full
for fineness. He was about sixty years of age, I
guessed, and there was about him the air of a man
who had passed through a hundred remarkable ex-
periences, without once losing his aplomb. Certainly he was not going to lose it now.

"The story which I have to relate," he began
in his careful English, clipping his words a little
now and then, "has to do with the theft of the
famous Michaelovitch diamonds. You may, perhaps, remember the case."

I remembered it certainly, for the robbery had
been conceived and carried out with such brilliancy
and daring that its details had at once arrested my
attention — to say nothing of the fact that the
diamonds, which formed the celebrated collection
belonging to one of the erstwhile Grand Dukes of
Russia — sojourning in Paris because unappre-
ciated in his native land and also because of the
supreme attraction of the French capital to one
of his temperament — were valued at many
millions of francs.

"That theft," continued Pigot, "was ac-

complished in a manner at once so bold and so
unique that we were certain it could be the work of
but a single man — a rascal named Crochard,
who calls himself also 'The Invincible'— a rascal
who has given us very great trouble, but whom we
have never been able to convict.   In this case, we
had against him no direct evidence; we subjected
him to an interrogation and found that he had
taken care to provide a perfect alibi; so we were
compelled to release him.   We knew that it would
be quite useless to arrest him unless we should
find some of the stolen jewels in his possession.   He appeared as usual upon the boulevards,
at the cafés, everywhere.   He laughed in our
faces.   For us, it was not pleasant; but our law
is strict.   For us to accuse a man, to arrest him,
and then to be compelled to own ourselves mistaken, is a very serious matter.   But we did what
we could.   We kept Crochard under constant sur-
veillance; we searched his rooms and those of his
mistress not once but many times.   On one occasion, when he passed the barrier at Vincennes,
our agents fell upon him and searched him, under
pretence of robbing him.

"He was, understand well, not for an instant
deceived.   He knew thoroughly what we were

doing, for what we were searching. He knew also that nowhere in Europe would he dare to attempt to sell a single one of those jewels. We suspected that he would attempt to bring them to this country, and we warned your department of customs. For we knew that here he could sell all but the very largest not only almost without danger, but at a price far greater than he could obtain for them in Europe. We closed every avenue to him, as we thought — and then, all at once, he disappeared.

" For two weeks we heard nothing — then came the story of this man Drouet, killed by a stab on the hand. At once we recognised the work of Crochard, for he alone of living men possesses the secret of the poison of the Medici. It is a fearful secret, which, in his whole life, he had used but once — and that upon a man who had betrayed him."

Pigot paused and passed his hand across his forehead.

" We were at a loss to understand Crochard's connection with Drouet," he continued. " Drouet, while a worthless hanger-on of the cafés of the boulevards, was not a criminal. Then came the death of that creature Morel, in an effort to gain possession of this cabinet, and we began to understand. We made inquiries concerning the cabinet; we learned its history and the secret of its construction, and we arrived at a certain conclusion. It was to ascertain if that conclusion is correct that I came to America."

"What is the conclusion?" queried Grady, who had listened to all this with a manifest impatience in strong contrast to my own absorbed interest.

For I had already guessed what the conclusion was, and my pulses were bounding with excitement.

"Our theory," replied Pigot, without the slightest acceleration of speech, "is that the Michaelovitch diamonds are concealed in this cabinet. Everything points to it — and we shall soon see."

As he spoke, he drew from his pocket a steel gauntlet marvellously like the one Godfrey had used, and slipped it over his right hand.

"When one attempts to fathom the secrets of *L'Invincible*," he said with a smile, "one must go armoured. Already three men have paid with their lives the penalty of their rashness."

"Three men!" repeated Grady wonderingly.

"Three," and Pigot checked them off upon his fingers. "First the man who gave his name as

d'Aurelle, but who was really a blackmailer named
Drouet; second, Monsieur Vantine, the connoisseur; third, the creature Morel. Of these, the
only one who really matters is Monsieur Vantine;
his death was most unfortunate, and I am sure
that Crochard regrets it exceedingly. He might
also regret my death, but at any rate I have no
wish to be the fourth. Not I," and he adjusted
the gauntlet carefully.

"One moment, monsieur," I said, bursting in,
unable to remain longer silent. "This is all so
wonderful — so thrilling — will you not tell us
more? For what were these three men searching?
For the jewels?"

"Monsieur is as familiar with the facts as I,"
he answered, in a sarcastic tone. "He knows that
Drouet was killed while searching for a packet of
letters which would have compromised most seriously a great lady; he knows that Monsieur
Vantine was killed while endeavouring to open
the drawer after its secret had been revealed to
him by the maid of that same great lady, who was
hoping to get a reward for them; Morel met
death directly at the hands of Crochard because
he was a traitor and deserved it."

More and more fascinated, I stared at him.

What secret was safe, I asked myself, from this
astonishing man? Or was he merely piecing together the whole story from such fragments as
he knew?

"But even yet," I stammered, "I do not understand. We have opened the secret drawer of the
cabinet — there was no poison. How could it
have killed Drouet and Mr. Vantine?"

"Very simply," said Pigot, coldly. "Death
came to Drouet and Monsieur Vantine because
the maid of Madame la Duchesse mistook her
left hand for her right. The drawer which contained the letters is at the left of the cabinet —
see," and he pressed the series of springs, caught
the little handle, and pulled the drawer open.
"You will notice that the letters are gone, for the
drawer was opened by Madame la Duchesse herself, in the presence of Monsieur Lestaire, who
gallantly permitted her to resume possession of
them. The drawer which Drouet and Monsieur
Vantine opened," and here his voice grew a little
strident under the stress of great emotion, "is on
the right side of the cabinet, exactly opposite the
other, and opened by a similar combination. But
there is one great difference. About the first
drawer there is nothing to harm any one; the

other is guarded by the deadliest poison the world has ever known. Observe me, gentlemen! "

Impelled by an excitement so intense as to be almost painful, I had risen from my chair and drawn near to him. As he spoke, he moved around the cabinet and pressed three fingers along the right side. There was a sharp click, and a section of the inlay fell outward, forming a handle, just as I had seen it do on the other side of the cabinet.

Pigot hesitated an instant — any man would have hesitated before that awful risk! — then, catching the handle firmly with his armoured hand, he drew it quickly out.

There was a sharp clash, as of steel on steel, and the drawer stood open.

CHAPTER XXV

THE MICHAELOVITCH DIAMONDS

MONSIEUR PIGOT, cool and imperturbable, held out to us with a little smile, a hand which showed not a quiver of emotion — his gauntleted hand; and I saw that, on the back of it, were two tiny depressions. At the bottom of each depression lay a drop of bright red liquid — blood-red, I told myself, as I stared at it fascinated. And what nerves of steel this man possessed! A sudden warmth of admiration for him glowed within me.

"That liquid, gentlemen," he said in his smooth voice, "is the most powerful poison ever distilled by man. Those two tiny drops would kill a score of people, and kill them instantly. Its odour betrays its origin "— and, indeed, the air was heavy with the scent of bitter almonds —"but the poison ordinarily derived from that source is as nothing compared with this. This poison is said to have been discovered by Rémy, the remarkable man who brought about the death of the Duc d'Anjou. Its distillation was supposed to be one of the lost arts, but the secret was rediscovered by this man Crochard. No secret, indeed, is safe from him; criminal history, criminal memoirs — the mysteries and achievements of the great confederacy of crime which has existed for many centuries, and whose existence few persons even suspect — all this is to him an open book. It is this which renders him so formidable. No man can stand against him. Even the secret of this drawer was known to him, and he availed himself of it when need arose."

Monsieur Pigot paused, his head bent in thought, and I seemed to be gazing with him down long avenues of crime, extending far into the past — dismal avenues like those of Père Lachaise, where tombs elbowed each other; where, at every step, one came face to face with a mystery, a secret, or a tragedy. Only, here, the mysteries were all solved, the secrets all uncovered, the tragedies all understood. But only to the elect, to criminals really great, were these avenues open; to all others they were forbidden. Alone of living men, perhaps, Crochard was free to wander there unchallenged.

Some such vision as this, I say, passed before my eyes, and I had a feeling that Monsieur Pigot

shared in it; but after an instant, he turned back
to the cabinet.

" Now, Monsieur Simmón," he said briskly, in
another tone, " if you will have the kindness to
hold the drawer for a moment in this position, I
will draw the serpent's fangs. There is not the
slightest danger," he added, seeing that Simmonds
very naturally hesitated.

Thus assured, Simmonds grasped the handle of
the drawer and held it open, while the Frenchman
took from his pocket a tiny flask of crystal.

" A little farther," he said; and as Simmonds,
with evident effort, drew the drawer out to its
full length, a tiny, two-tined prong pushed itself
forward from underneath the cabinet. " There
are the fangs," said Pigot. He held the
mouth of the flask under first one and then the
other, passing his other hand carefully behind and
above them. " The poison is held in place by
what we in French call *attraction capillaire* — I
do not know the English; but I drive it out by introducing the air behind it — ah, you see ! "

He stood erect and held the flask up to the
light. It was half full of the red liquid.

" Enough to decimate France," he said, screwed
the stopper carefully into place, and put the flask

in his pocket. "Release the drawer, if you please, monsieur," he added to Simmonds.

It sprang back into place on the instant, the arabesqued handle snapping up with a little click.

"You will observe its ingenuity," said Pigot. "It is really most clever. For whenever the hand, struck by the poisoned fangs, loosened its hold on the drawer, the drawer sprang shut as you see, and everything was as before — except that one man more had tasted death. Now I open it. The fangs fall again; they strike the gauntlet; but for that, they would pierce the hand, but death no longer follows. By turning this button, I lock the spring, and the drawer remains open. The man who devised this mechanism was so proud of it that he described it in a secret memoir for the entertainment of the Grand Louis. There is a copy of that memoir among the archives of the Bibliothéque Nationale; the original is owned by Crochard. It was he who connected that memoir with this cabinet, who rediscovered the mechanism, rewound the spring, and renewed the poison. No doubt the stroke with the poisoned fangs, which he used to punish traitors, was the result of reading that memoir."

"This Croshar — or whatever his name is,

— seems to be a 'strordinary feller," observed Grady, relighting his cigar.

"He is," agreed Pigot quietly; "a most extraordinary man. But even he is not infallible; for, since the memoir made no mention of the other secret drawer — the one in which Madame la Duchesse concealed her love letters — Crochard knew nothing of it. It was that fact which defeated his combinations — a pure accident which he could not foresee. And now, gentlemen, it shall be my pleasure to display before you some very beautiful brilliants."

Not until that instant had I thought of what the drawer contained; I had been too fascinated by the poisoned fangs and by the story told so quietly but so effectively by the French detective; but now I perceived that the drawer was filled with little rolls of cotton, which had been pressed into it quite tightly.

Pigot removed the first of these, unrolled it and spread it out upon the desk, and instantly we caught the glitter of diamonds — diamonds so large, so brilliant, so faultlessly white that I drew a deep breath of admiration. Even Pigot, evidently as he prided himself upon his imperturbability, could not look upon those gems

wholly unmoved; a slow colour crept into his
cheeks as he gazed down at them, and he picked up
one or two of the larger ones to admire them more
closely. Then he unfolded roll after roll, stopping from time to time for a look at the larger
brilliants.

"These are from the famous necklace which
the Grand Duke inherited from his grandmother,"
he said, calling our attention to a little pile of
marvellous gems in one of the last packets.
"Crochard, of course, removed them from their
settings — that was inevitable. He could melt
down the settings and sell the gold; but not one
of these brilliants would be marketable in Europe
for many years. Each of them is a marked gem.
Here in America, your police regulations are not
so complete; but I fancy that, even here, he would
have had difficulty in marketing this one," and he
unfolded the last packet, and held up to the light a
rose-diamond which seemed to me as large as a
walnut, and a-glow with lovely colour.

"Perhaps you have stopped to admire the Mazarin diamond in the *galérie d'Apollon* at the
Louvre," said Pigot. "There is always a
crowd about that case, and a special attendant is
installed there to guard it, for it contains some

articles of great value. But the Mazarin is not one of them; for it is not a diamond at all; it is paste — a paste facsimile of which this is the original. Oh, it is all quite honest," he added, as Grady snorted derisively. " Twenty years ago, the directors of the Louvre needed a fund for the purchase of new paintings; needed also to clean and restore the old ones. They decided that it was folly to keep ten millions of francs imprisoned in a single gem, when their Michael Angelos and da Vincis and Murillos were encrusted with dirt and fading daily. So they sought a purchaser for the Mazarin; they found one in the empress of Russia, who had a craze for precious stones, and who, at her death, left this remarkable collection to her favourite son, who had inherited her passion. A paste replica of the Mazarin was placed in the Louvre for the crowds to admire, and every one soon forgot that it was not really the diamond. For myself, I think the directors acted most wisely. And now," he added, with a gesture toward the glittering heap, "what shall we do with all this? "

" There's only one thing to do," said Grady, awaking suddenly as from a trance, " and that's to get them in a safe-deposit box as quick as possible. There's no police-safe I'd trust with 'em!

Why, they'd tempt the angel Gabriel!" and he
drew a deep breath.

"Can we find a box of safe-deposit at this hour
of the night?" asked Pigot, glancing at his
watch. "It is almost one o'clock and a half."

"That's easy in New York," said Grady.
"We'll take 'em over to the Day and Night Bank
on Fifth Avenue. It never closes. Wait till I
get something to put 'em in."

He went out and came back presently with a
small valise.

"This will do," he said. "Stow 'em away, and
I'll call up the bank and arrange for the box."

Simmonds and Pigot rolled up the packets carefully and placed them in the valise, while I sat
watching them in a kind of daze. And I understood the temptation which would assail a man in
the presence of so much beauty. It was not the
value of the jewels which shook and dazzled me
— I scarcely thought of that; it was their seduc-
tive brilliance, it was the thought that, if I possessed them, I might take them out at any hour of
the day or night and run my fingers through them
and watch them shimmer and quiver in the light.

"The Grand Duke must have been quite
considerably upset," remarked Simmonds, who,

throughout all this scene, had lost no whit of his serenity of demeanour.

"He has been like a madman," said Pigot, smiling a little at Simmonds's unemotional tone. "These jewels are a passion with him; he worships them; he never has parted with them, even for a day; where he goes, they have gone. In his most desperate need of money — and he has had such need many times — he has never sold one of his brilliants. On the contrary, whenever he has money or credit, and the opportunity comes to purchase a stone of unusual beauty, he cannot resist, even though his debts go unpaid. Since the loss of these stones, he has raved, he has cursed, he has beat his servants — one of them has died in consequence. We are all a little mad on some one subject, I have heard it said; well, the Grand Duke is very mad on the subject of diamonds."

"Why didn't he offer a reward for their return?" queried Simmonds.

"Oh, he did," said Pigot. "He offered immediately his whole fortune for their return. But his fortune was not large enough to tempt Crochard, for the Grand Duke has nothing left except such investments as he was wise enough to

make outside of Russia. It will be a great joy
to him that we have found them."

The thought flashed through my mind that
doubtless Monsieur Pigot was in the way of re-
ceiving a handsome present.

" There they are," said Simmonds, and closed
the bag with a snap, as Grady came in again.

" I've arranged for the box," said Grady, "and
one of our cars is at the door. I thought we'd
better not trust a taxi — might turn over or run
into something, and we can't afford to take any
chances — not this trip. Simmonds, you go along
with Moosseer Piggott, and put an extra man on
the seat with the driver. Maybe that Croshar
might try to hold you up."

The same thought was in my own mind, for
Crochard must have learned of Pigot's arrival;
and I could scarcely imagine that he would sit
quietly by and permit the jewels to be taken away
from him — to say nothing of his chagrin over
his unfulfilled boast to Godfrey. So I was
relieved that Grady was wise enough to take no
risk.

" You'd better get a receipt," Grady went on,
" and arrange that the valise is to be delivered
only when you and Moosseer Piggott appear to-

gether. That will be satisfactory, moosseer?"
he added, turning to the Frenchman.

"Entirely so, sir."

"Very well, then; I'll see you in the morning.
I congratulate you on the find. It was certainly
great work."

" I thank you, sir," replied Pigot, gravely.
"Au revoir, monsieur," and with a bow to me, he
followed Simmonds into the outer room.

Grady sat down and got out a fresh cigar.

"Well, Mr. Lester," he said, as he struck a
match, "what do you think of these Frenchmen,
anyway?"

"They're marvellous," I said. "Even yet I
can't understand how he knew so much."

"Maybe he was just guessing at some of it,"
Grady suggested.

"I thought of that, but I don't believe anybody could guess so accurately. For instance, how
did he know about those letters?"

"Fact is," broke in Grady, "that's the first
I'd heard of 'em. What *is* that story?"

I told him the story briefly, carefully suppress-
ing everything which would give him a clue to the
identity of the veiled lady.

"There are certain details." I added, "which

I supposed were known to no one except myself and two other persons — and yet Pigot knew them. Then again, how did he know so certainly just how the mechanism worked? How did he know which roll of cotton contained that Mazarin diamond? You will remember he told us what was in that roll before he opened it."

Grady smiled good-naturedly and a little patronisingly.

"That was the last roll, wasn't it?" he demanded. "Since that big diamond hadn't shown up in any of the others, he knew it had to be in that roll. It was just one of the little plays for effect them Frenchies are so fond of."

"Perhaps you are right," I agreed. "But it seemed to me that he handled that mechanism as though he was familiar with it. Of course he may have prepared himself by studying the drawings which no doubt accompany the secret memoir. He may even have had a working model made."

Grady nodded tolerantly.

"Them fellers go to a lot of trouble over little things like that," he said. "They like to slam their cards down on the table with a big hurrah, even when the cards ain't worth a damn."

"He certainly held trumps this time, anyway,"

I commented. "And he played his hand superbly. He is an extraordinary man."

"And a great actor," Grady supplemented. "Them fellers always behave like they was on the stage, right in the spot-light. It makes me a little tired sometimes. Hello! Who's that?"

The front door had been flung open; there was an instant's colloquy with the desk-sergeant, then a rapid step crossed the outer room, and Godfrey burst in upon us.

He cast a rapid glance at the Boule cabinet, at the secret drawer standing open, empty; and then his eyes rested upon Grady.

"So he got away with it, did he?" he inquired.

"Who in hell do you think you are?" shouted Grady, his face purple, "coming in here like this? Get out, or I'll have you thrown out!"

"Oh, I'll go," retorted Godfrey coolly. "I've seen all I care to see. Only I'll tell you one thing, Grady—you've signed your own death-warrant to-night!"

"What do you mean by that?" Grady demanded, in a lower tone.

"I mean that you won't last an hour after the story of this night's work gets out."

Grady's colour slowly faded as he met the burning and contemptuous gaze Godfrey turned upon him.

"Do you mean to say it wasn't Piggott?" stammered Grady, at last.

Godfrey laughed scornfully.

"No, you blithering idiot!" he said. "It wasn't Pigot. It was Crochard himself!"

And he stalked out, slamming the door behind him.

CHAPTER XXVI

THE FATE OF MONSIEUR PIGOT

WHATEVER may have been Grady's defects of insight and imagination, he was energetic enough when thoroughly aroused. Almost before the echo of that slamming door had died away, he was beside the sergeant's desk.

"Get out the reserves," he ordered, "and have the big car around. 'Phone headquarters to rush every man available up to the Day and Night Bank, and say it's from me!"

He stood chewing his cigar savagely as the sergeant hastened to obey. In a moment, the reserves come tumbling out, struggling into their coats; there was the hoot of a siren in the street as the car dashed up; the reserves piled into it, permitting me to crowd in beside them, Grady jumped to the seat beside the driver, and we were off like the wind, our siren waking the echoes of the silent street.

I clung to the seat as the heavy car swayed back and forth or bounded into the air as it struck the car-tracks, and stared out into the night,

struggling to understand.   Could Godfrey be
right?   But of course he was right!   Some intui-
tion told me that; and yet how had Crochard managed to substitute himself for the French detective?   Where was Pigot?   Was he lying somewhere in a crumpled heap, with a tiny wound upon
his hand?   But that could not be—Grady and
Simmonds had been with him all the evening!
And could that aged Frenchman with the white,
fine, wrinkled skin be also the bronzed and virile
personage whom I had known as Félix Armand?
My reason reeled before the seeming impossibility
of it — and yet somehow I knew that Godfrey
was right!

The car came to a stop so suddenly that I
was thrown violently against the man next to me,
and the reserves, leaping out, swept me before
them.   We were in front of the Day and Night
Bank, and at a word from Grady the men spread
into a close cordon before the building.

Another police car stood at the curb with
the driver still on the seat, but as Grady started
toward it, a figure appeared at the door of the
bank and shouted to us — shouted in inarticulate
words which I could not understand.   But Grady
seemed to understand them and went up the steps

two at a time, with an agility surprising in so large
a man, and which I was hard put to it to match.
A little group stood at one side of the vestibule
looking down at some one extended on a cush-
ioned seat. And an instant later, I saw that it
was Simmonds, lying on his back, his eyes open
and staring apparently at the ceiling.

But at the second glance, I saw that the eyes
were sightless.

Grady elbowed his way savagely through the
group.

"Where's Kelly?" he demanded.

At the words, a white-faced man in uniform
arose from a chair into which he had plainly
dropped exhausted.

"Oh, there you are!" and Grady glowered at
him ferociously. "Now tell me what happened
—and tell it quick!"

"Why, sir," stammered Kelly, "there wasn't
anything happened. Only when we stopped out
there at the curb and I got down and opened
the door, there wasn't nobody in the car but
Mr. Simmonds. I spoke to him and he didn't
answer — and then I touched him and he kind
of fell over — and then I rushed in here and
'phoned the station, but they said you'd already

started for the bank, and then we went out and brought him in here—and that's all I know, sir."

"You didn't hear anything—no sound of a struggle?"

"Not a sound, sir; not a single sound."

"And you haven't any idea where the other man got out?"

"No, sir."

"Mr. Simmonds had a little valise with him—did you notice it?"

"Yes, sir, and I looked for it in the wagon, but it ain't there."

Grady turned away with a curse as four or five men ran in from the street—the men from headquarters, I told myself. I could hear him talking to them in sharp, low tones, and then they departed as suddenly as they had come. The reserves also hurried away, and I concluded that Grady was trying to throw a net about the territory in which the fugitive was probably concealed, but my interest in that manœuvre was overshadowed, for the time being, by my anxiety for Simmonds. I picked up his right hand and looked at it; then I drew a deep breath of relief, for it was uninjured.

"Has anyone sent for a doctor?" I asked.

"Yes, sir," one of. the bank attachés answered, "We telephoned for one at once—here he is now!" he added, as a little black-bearded man entered, carry the inevitably-identifying medicine case.

The newcomer glanced at the body, waved us back, fell on one knee, stripped away the clothing from the breast and applied his ear to the heart. Then he looked into the staring eyes, drew down the lids, watched them snap up again, and then hastily opened his case.

"Let's have some water," he said.

"Then he's not dead?" I questioned, as one of the clerks sprang to obey.

"Dead? No, but he's had a taste or whiff of something that has stopped the heart action."

With a queer, creepy feeling over my scalp, I remembered the little flask, half-full of blood-red liquid which Crochard carried in his pocket.

But he had not meant murder this time; I remembered that Godfrey had said he never killed an adversary. The doctor worked briskly away, and at the end of a few minutes, Simmonds's eyes suddenly closed, he drew a long breath and sat erect. Then his eyes opened, and he sat swaying unsteadily and staring amazedly about him.

"Best lie down again," said the doctor soothingly. "You're a little wobbly yet, you know."

"Where am I?" gasped Simmonds. Then his
eyes encountered mine. "Lester!" he said.
"Where is he—Piggott? Not . . ."

He stopped short, looked once around at the
gleaming marble of the bank, fumbled for
something at his side, and fell senseless on the
seat.

I have no recollection of how I got back to the
Marathon. I suppose I must have walked, but
my first distinct remembrance is of finding myself
sitting in my favourite chair, pipe in hand. The
pipe was lit, so I suppose I must have lighted it
mechanically, and I found that I had also mechanically changed into my lounging-coat. I glanced
at my watch and saw that it was nearly four
o'clock.

The top of my head was burning as though with
fever, and I went into the bathroom and turned
the cold water on it. The shock did me a world
of good, and by the time I had finished a vigorous
toweling I felt immensely better. So I returned
to my chair and sat down to review the events of
the evening; but I found that somehow my brain

refused to work, and black circles began to whirl before my eyes again.

"I told Godfrey I couldn't stand any more of this," I muttered, and stumbled into my bedroom, undressed with difficulty, and turned out the light.

Then as I lay there, staring up into the darkness, a stinging thought brought me upright.

Godfrey—where was Godfrey? Was he on the track of Crochard? Was he daring a contest with him? Perhaps, even at this moment . . .

Scarcely knowing what I did, I groped my way to the telephone and asked for Godfrey's number —hoping against hope absurdly—and at last, to my intense surprise and relief, I heard his voice— not a very amiable voice . . .

"Hello!" he said.

"Godfrey," I began, "it's Lester. He got away."

"Of course he got away. You didn't call me out of bed to tell me that, I hope?"

"Then you knew about it?"

"I knew he'd get away."

"When the wagon got to the bank there was nobody inside but Simmonds. Simmonds went along, you know."

"Was he hurt?"

"He was unconscious, but he came around all right."

"That's good—but Crochard wouldn't hurt him. He got away with the jewels, of course?"

"Of course," I assented, surprised that Godfrey should take it so coolly. "When you rushed out that way," I added, "I thought maybe you were going after him."

"With him twenty minutes in the lead? I'm no such fool! He got away from me the other day with a start of about half a second."

"I tried to get you," I explained, "as soon as Simmonds told me they were going to look at the cabinet. I 'phoned the office. The city editor said he had sent you out into Westchester."

Godfrey laughed shortly.

"It was a wild-goose chase," he said, "cooked up by our friend Crochard. But even then I'd have got back if we hadn't punctured a tire when we were five miles from anywhere. I knew what was up—but there I was. Oh, he's made fools of us all, Lester. I told you he would!"

"Then you didn't get my message?"

"Yes—they gave it to me when I 'phoned in that the Westchester business was a fake. I rushed for the station, though I knew I'd be too late."

"But, Godfrey," I said, "I can't understand, even yet, how he did it. Grady and Simmonds left the boat with Pigot and were with him all evening, showing him the sights. How did Crochard get into it? What did he do with Pigot? Where *is* Pigot?"

" He's on the *Paris*. I rushed a wireless down to her as soon as I left the station. They made a search and found Pigot bound and gagged under the berth in his stateroom."

I could only gasp.

" And to think I didn't suspect! " added Godfrey bitterly. " We stood there and saw that yacht with the French flag walk away from us; we saw her put a man aboard the *Paris*; we saw that man talking to Pigot . . ."

"Yes," I said breathlessly; "yes."

"Well, that man was Crochard. He got Pigot into his stateroom—gave him a whiff of the same stuff he used on Simmonds, no doubt; put him out of the way under the berth; got into his clothes, made up his face, put on a wig—and all that while we were kicking our heels outside waiting for him."

"But it was a tremendous risk," I said. "There were so many people on board who knew Pigot—it would have to be a perfect disguise."

"Crochard wouldn't stop for that. But it wasn't much of a risk. None of us had seen Pigot closely; all we had seen of him was the back of his head, and the passengers were all on deck watching the quarantine men. And yet of course the disguise was a perfect one. Crochard is an artist in that line, and naturally he was thoroughly familiar with Pigot's appearance. He deceived the purser — but the purser wouldn't suspect anything!"

"So it was really Crochard . . ."

"But *we* ought to have suspected. We ought to have suspected everything, questioned everything. I ought to have looked up that visitor and found out what became of him. Instead of which, Crochard put Pigot's papers in his pocket, set his bag outside the stateroom door, and then came out calmly to meet his dear friends of the press; and I stood there talking to him like a little schoolboy—no wonder he thinks I'm a fool!"

"But nobody would have suspected!" I gasped. "Why, that man is—is . . ."

"A genius," said Godfrey. "An absolute and

unquestioned genius. But I knew that all the
time, and I ought to have been on guard. You
remember he said he would come today?"

"Yes."

"And you didn't believe it."

"I can't believe it yet."

"There's one consolation—it will break
Grady."

"But, Godfrey," I said, "if you could have seen
those diamonds—those beautiful diamonds—and
to think he should be able to get away with them
from right under our noses!"

"It's pretty bad, isn't it? But there's no use
crying over spilt milk. Lester," he added, in another tone, "I want you to be in your office at
noon to-morrow—or rather, to-day."

"All right," I promised; "I'll be there."

"Don't fail me. There is one act of the comedy still to be played."

"I'll be there," I said again. "But I'm afraid
the last act will be an anti-climax. Look here,
Godfrey . . ."

"Now go to bed," he broke in; "you're talking
like a somnambulist. Get some sleep. Have you
arranged for that vacation?"

"Godfrey," I said, "tell me . . ."

"I won't tell you anything. Only I've got one more bomb to explode, Lester, and it's a big one. It will make you jump!"

I could hear him chuckling to himself.

"Good-night," he said, and hung up.

CHAPTER XXVII

THE LAST ACT OF THE DRAMA

I OVERSLEPT next morning so outrageously that it was not until I had got a seat in a subway express that I had time to open my paper. My first glance was for the big head that would tell of the diamond robbery, and then I realised that no morning paper would have a word of it. For the robbery was only a few hours old—and yet it seemed to me an age had passed since that moment when Godfrey had rushed in upon Grady and me. So the city moved on, as yet blissfully unconscious of the sensation which would be sprung with the first afternoon editions, and over which reporters and artists and photographers were even now, no doubt, labouring. I promised myself a happy half hour in reading Godfrey's story!

It was then that I remembered the appointment for twelve o'clock. The last act of the drama was yet to be staged, Godfrey had said, and he had also spoken of a bomb—a big one! I wondered what it could be. One thing was certain; if God-

frey had prepared it, its explosion would be startling enough!

There were a number of things at the office de-
manding my attention, and I was so late in getting
there and the morning passed so rapidly that when
the office-boy came in and announced that Mr.
Grady and Mr. Simmonds were outside and
wished to see me, I did not for a moment connect
their visit with Godfrey. Then I looked at my
watch, saw that it was five minutes to twelve, and
realised that the actors were assembling.

"Show them in," I said, and they entered together a minute later.

Grady was evidently much perturbed. His
usually florid face was drawn and haggard, his
cheeks hung in ugly lines, there were dark pouches
under his eyes, and the eyes themselves were blood-
shot. I guessed that he had not been to bed;
that he had spent the night searching for Crochard—and it was easy enough to see that the
search had been unsuccessful. Simmonds, too,
was looking rather shaky, and no doubt still felt
the after-effects of that whiff of poison.

"I'm glad to see you are better, Simmonds," I
said, shaking hands with him. "That was a close
call."

"It certainly was," Simmonds agreed, sinking into a chair. "If I had got a little more of it, I'd never have waked up."

"Do you remember anything about it?"

"Not a thing. One minute we were sitting there talking together as nice as you please—and the next thing I knew was when I woke up in the bank."

"Where's that man Godfrey?" broke in Grady.

"He said he'd be here at noon," I said, and glanced at my watch. "It's noon now. Were you to meet him here?"

Grady glanced at me suspiciously.

"Don't you know nothing about it?" he asked.

"I only know that Godfrey asked me to be here at noon to-day. What's up?"

"Blamed if I know," said Grady sulkily. "I got word from him that I'd better be here, and I thought maybe he might know something. I'm so dizzy over last night's business that I'm running around in circles this morning. But I won't wait for him. He can't make me do that! Come along, Simmonds."

"Wait a minute," I broke in, as the outer door opened. "Perhaps that's Godfrey now."

And so it proved. He came in accompanied by a man whom I knew to be Arthur Shearrow, chief counsel for the *Record*.

Godfrey nodded all around.

"I think you know Mr. Shearrow," he said, placing on my desk a small leather bag he was carrying. "This is Mr. Lester, Mr. Shearrow," he added, and we shook hands. "The object of this conference, Lester," he concluded, "is to straighten out certain matters connected with the Michaelovitch diamonds—and incidentally to give the *Record* the biggest scoop it has had for months."

"I ain't here to fix up no scoop for the *Record*," broke in Grady. "That paper never did treat me right."

"It has treated you as well as you deserved," retorted Godfrey. "I'm going to talk plainly to you, Grady. Your goose is cooked. You can't hold on for an hour after last night's get-away becomes public."

"We'll see about that!" growled Grady, but the fight had evidently been taken out of him.

"I understand you wouldn't let Simmonds telephone for me last night?" queried Godfrey.

"That's right—it wasn't none of your business."

"Perhaps not. And yet if I had been there, the cleverest thief in Paris, if not in the world, would be safe behind those chrome-nickel steel bars at the Twenty-third Street station, instead of at liberty to go ahead and rob somebody else."

"You're mighty cocksure," retorted Grady. "It's easy to be wise after it's all over."

"Well, I'm not going to argue with you," said Godfrey. "I admit it was a good disguise and a clever idea—but just the same you ought to have seen through it. That's your business."

Grady mopped his face.

"Oh, of course!" he sneered. "I ought to have seen through it! I ought to have suspected, even when I found you tryin' to interview him, even when I got him off the boat myself, even when I went through his papers and found them all right—yes, even to the photograph on his passport! That's plain enough now, ain't it! If people only had as good foresight as they have hindsight, how easy it would be!"

"Look here, Grady," said Godfrey, more kindly, "I haven't anything against you personally, and I admit that it was foolish of me to stand there talking to Crochard and never suspect who he was. But that's all beside the mark. You're at the head of the detective bureau, and you're the man who is responsible for all this. You're energetic enough and all that, but you're not fit for your job—it's too big for you and you know it. Take my advice and go to the 'phone there and send in your resignation."

Grady stared at him as though unable to believe his ears.

"'Phone in my resignation!" he echoed. "What kind of a fool do you think I am?"

"I see you're a bigger one than I thought you were! Your pull can't help you any longer, Grady."

"Was it to tell me that you got me over here?"

"No," said Godfrey, "all this is just incidental —you began the discussion yourself, didn't you? I got you here to meet . . ."

The outer door opened again, and Godfrey looked toward it, smiling.

"Moosseer Piggott!" announced the office-boy.

And then I almost bounced from my seat, for I would have sworn that the man who stood on the threshold was the man who had opened the secret drawer.

He came forward, looking from face to face; then his eyes met Godfrey's and he smiled.

"Behold that I am here, monsieur," he said and I started anew at the voice, for it was the voice of Crochard. "I hope that I have not kept you waiting."

"Not at all, Monsieur Pigot," Godfrey assured him, and placed a chair for him.

I could see Grady and Simmonds gripping the arms of their chairs and staring at the newcomer, their mouths open, and I knew the thought that was flashing through their brains. Was this Pigot? Or was the man who had opened the cabinet Pigot? Or was neither Pigot? Was it possible that this could be a different man than the one who had opened the cabinet?

I confess that some such thought flashed through my own mind—a suspicion that Godfrey, in some way, was playing with us.

Godfrey looked about at us, smiling as he saw our expressions.

"I went down the bay this morning and met the *Paris*," he said. "I related to Monsieur Pigot last night's occurrences and begged him to be present at this meeting. He was good enough to agree. I assure you," he added, seeing Grady's look, " that this *is* Monsieur Pigot, of the Paris *Service du Sûreté,* and not Crochard."

"Oh, yes," said Pigot, with a deprecating shrug. "I am myself—and greatly humiliated that I should have fallen so readily into the trap which Crochard set for me. But he is a very clever man."

"It was certainly a marvellous disguise," I said. "It was more than that—it was an impersonation."

"Crochard has had occasion to study me," explained Pigot drily. "And he is an artist in whatever he does. But some day I shall get him—every pitcher to the well goes once too often. There is no hope of finding him here in New York?"

"I am afraid not," said Godfrey.

"Don't be too sure of that!" broke in Grady ponderously. "I ain't done yet—not by no manner of means!"

"Pardon me for not introducing you, Monsieur Pigot," said Godfrey. "This gentlemen is Mr. Grady, who has been the head of our detective bureau; this is Mr. Simmonds, a member of his

staff; this is Mr. Lester, an attorney and friend
of mine; and this is Mr. Shearrow, my personal
counsel. Mr. Grady, Mr. Simmonds and Mr.
Lester were present last night," he added blandly,
"when Crochard opened the secret drawer."

Grady reddened visibly, and even I felt my face
grow hot. Pigot looked at us with a smile of
amusement.

"It must have been a most interesting experience," he said, "to have seen Crochard at work.
I have never had that privilege. But I regret
that he should have made good his escape."

"More especially since he took the Michaelovitch diamonds with him," I added.

"Before we go into that," said Godfrey, with
a little smile, "that are one or two questions I
should like to ask, Monsieur Pigot, in order to
clear up some minor details which are as yet a little
obscure. Is it true that the theft of the Michaelovitch diamonds was planned by Crochard?"

"Undoubtedly. No other thief in France
would be capable of it."

"Is it also true that no direct evidence could
be found against him?"

"That also is true, monsieur. He had arranged the affair so cleverly that we were wholly

unable to convict him, unless we should find him with the stolen brilliants in his possession."

"And you were not able to do that?"

"No; we could discover no trace of the brilliants, though we searched for them everywhere."

"But you did not know of the Boule cabinet and of the secret drawer?"

"No; of that we knew nothing. I must examine that famous cabinet."

"It is worth examining. And it has an interesting history. But you did know, of course, that Crochard would seek a market for the diamonds here in America?"

"We knew that he would try to do so, and we did everything in our power to prevent it. We especially relied upon your customs department to search most thoroughly the belongings of every person with whom they were not personally acquainted."

"The customs people did their part," said Godfrey with a chuckle. "They have quite upset the country! But the diamonds got in, in spite of them. For, of course, a cabinet imported by a man so well known and so above suspicion as Mr. Vantine was passed without question!"

"Yes," agreed Pigot, a little bitterly.

"It was a most clever plan; and now, no doubt, Crochard can sell the brilliants at his leisure."

"Not if you've got a good description of them," protested Grady. "I'll make it a point to warn every dealer in the country; I'll keep my whole force on the job; I'll get Chief Moran to lend me some of his men'. . ."

"Oh, there is no use taking all that trouble," broke in Godfrey negligently. "Crochard won't try to sell them."

"Won't try to sell them?" echoed Grady. "What's the reason he won't?"

"Because he hasn't got them," answered Godfrey, smiling with an evidently deep enjoyment of Grady's dazed countenance.

"Oh, come off!" said that worthy disgustedly. "If he hasn't got 'em I'd like to know who has!"

"I have," said Godfrey, and cleared my desk with a sweep of his arm. "Spread out your handkerchief, Lester," and as I dazedly obeyed, he picked up the little leather bag, opened it, and poured out its contents in a sparkling flood. "There," he added, turning to Grady, "are the Michaelovitch diamonds."

CHAPTER XXVIII

FOR an instant, we gazed at the glittering heap with dazzled eyes, then Grady, with an inarticulate cry, sprang to his feet and picked up a handful of the diamonds, as though to convince himself of their reality.

"But I don't understand!" he gasped. "Have you got Croshar too?"

"No such luck," said Godfrey.

"Do you mean to say he'd give these up without a fight!"

The same thought was in my own mind. If Godfrey had run down Crochard and got the diamonds without a life-and-death struggle, that engaging rascal must be much less formidable than I had supposed.

"My dear Grady," said Godfrey, "I haven't seen Crochard since the minute you took him off the boat. I'd have had him if you had let Simmonds call me. That what I had planned. But he was too clever for us. I knew that he would come to-day . . ."

349

"You knew that he would come to-day?" repeated Grady blankly. "How did you know that — or is it merely hot air?"

"I knew that he would come," said Godfrey curtly, "because he wrote and told me so."

Pigot laughed a dry little laugh.

"That is a favourite device of his," he said; "and he always keeps his word."

"The trouble was," continued Godfrey, "that I didn't look for him so early in the day, and so he was able to send me on a wild-goose chase after a sensation that didn't exist. There's where I was a fool. But I discovered the secret drawer ten days ago — while the cabinet was still at Vantine's — the evening after the veiled lady got her letters. It was easy enough. I am surprised you didn't think of it, Lester."

"Think of what?" I asked.

"Of the key to the mystery. The drawer containing the letters was on the left side of the cabinet, I saw at once that there must be another drawer, opened in the same way, on the right side."

"I didn't see it," I said. "I don't see it yet."

"Think a minute. Why was Drouet killed? Because he opened the wrong drawer. He pressed the combination at the right side of the cabinet, in-

stead of that at the left side.   The fair Julie must
have thought the drawer was on the right side,
instead of the left.   It was a mistake very easy
to make, since her mistress doubtless had her back
turned when Julie saw her open the drawer.   The
suspicion that it was Julie's mistake becomes certainty when she shows the combination to Vantine,
and he is killed too.   Besides, the veiled lady
herself made a remark which revealed the whole
story."

"I didn't notice it," I said resignedly.
"What was it?"

"That she was accustomed to opening the
drawer with her left hand, instead of with her
right.   After that, there could be no further
doubt.   So I discovered the drawer very simply.
It had to be there."

"Yes," I said; "and then?"

"Then I removed the jewels, took them down
to a dealer in false gems and duplicated them as
closely as I could.   I had a hard time getting a
good copy of this big rose-diamond."

He picked it from the heap and held it up between his fingers.

"It's a beauty, isn't it?" he asked.

Pigot smiled a dry smile.

"It is the Mazarin," he said, "and is worth I know not how many million francs. There is a copy of it at the Louvre."

"So that's true, is it?" I asked. "Crochard told us the story."

"It is unquestionably true," said Pigot. "It is not a secret—it is merely something which every one has forgotten."

"Well," continued Godfrey, "after I got the duplicates, I rolled them up in the cotton packets and placed them back in the drawer, being careful to put the Mazarin at the bottom where I had found it."

"It was lucky you thought of that," I said, "or Crochard would have suspected something."

Godfrey looked at me with a smile.

"My dear Lester" he said, "he knew that the game was up the instant he opened the first packet. Do you suppose he would be deceived? Not by the best reproduction ever made!"

And then I remembered the slow flush which had crept into Crochard's cheeks as he opened that first packet!

"I didn't expect to deceive him," Godfrey explained. "I just wanted to give him a little surprise. And to think I wasn't there to see it!"

"But if he knew they were imitations," I protested, "why should he go to all that trouble to steal them?"

"That is what puzzled me last night," said Godfrey; "and for that matter, it puzzles me yet."

"Maybe he's got the real stones, after all," suggested Grady, who had been listening to all this with incredulous countenance. "The story sounds fishy to me. Maybe these are the imitations."

Pigot came forward and picked up the Mazarin and looked at it.

"This one, at least, is real," he said, after a moment. "And I have no doubt the others are," he added, turning them over with his finger.

Grady, still incredulous, picked up one of the brilliants, went to the window and drew it down the pane. It left a deep scratch behind it.

"Yes," he admitted reluctantly, "I guess they're diamonds, all right," and he sat down again.

"And now, gentlemen," continued Godfrey, who had watched Grady's byplay with a tolerant smile, "I am ready to turn these diamonds over to you. I should like you to count them and give me a receipt for them."

"And then, of course, you will write the story," sneered Grady, "and give yourself all the credit."

"Well," asked Godfrey, looking at him, "do you think you deserve any?" And Grady could only crimson and keep silent. "As for the story, it is already written. It will be on the streets in ten minutes—and it will create a sensation. Please count the diamonds. You will find two hundred and ten of them."

"That is the exact number stolen from the Grand Duke," remarked Pigot, and fell to counting. The number was two hundred and ten.

"Mr. Shearrow has the receipt," Godfrey added, and Shearrow took a paper from his pocket, unfolded it, and read the contents.

It proved to be not only a receipt, but a full statement of the facts of the case, without omitting the details of the robbery and the credit due the *Record* for the recovery of the diamonds. Grady's face grew redder and redder as the reading proceeded.

"I won't sign no such testimonial as that," he blustered. "Not on your life I won't!"

"You will sign it, will you not, Monsieur Pigot?" asked Godfrey.

"Certainly," said the Frenchman; "it is a recognition of your services very well deserved," and he stepped forward and signed it with a flourish.

"Now, Simmonds," said Godfrey.

"No you don't!" broke in Grady. "Stay where you are, Simmonds. I forbid you to sign that. Remember I'm your superior officer."

"No he's not, Simmonds," said Godfrey quietly. "He hasn't been an officer at all for an hour and more."

Grady sprang to his feet, his eyes blazing, and strode toward Godfrey.

"What do you mean by that?" he shouted.

"I mean," said Godfrey, looking him squarely in the eye, "that Mr. Shearrow and myself had a talk with the mayor this morning and laid before him certain evidence in our possession—this latest case among others—and that your resignation was accepted at noon to-day."

"My resignation!" snorted Grady. "I never wrote one!"

"Tell the public that, if you want to," retorted Godfrey coldly. "That's your affair. You ought to have 'phoned it in when I told you to. Now, Simmonds."

Grady stood glaring about him an instant like an enraged bull, and I half expected him to hurl himself on Godfrey; instead, he crushed his hat upon his head, strode to the door, jerked it open, and banged it behind him.

"Now, Simmonds," Godfrey repeated as the echo died away, and Simmonds came forward and signed. I witnessed the signatures, and Godfrey, with more eagerness than he had shown in the whole affair, caught up the paper and sprang with it to the door.

"Get that down to the office as quick as you can," he said to a man outside. "I'll 'phone instructions. That," he added, closing the door and turning back to us, "is my reward for all this —or, rather, the *Record's* reward. And now, gentlemen, Mr. Shearrow has his car below, and I think we would better drive around to some safe-deposit box with this plunder."

It was perhaps ten days afterwards that Godfrey dropped in to see me one evening. I was just back from a week on Cape Cod, which had done me a world of good; and I need hardly say, was glad to see him.

"You're looking normal again," he said, surveying me ,as he sat down. "I was worried about you for a while."

"I never felt better. I told you that all I needed was to have that mystery solved."

"And it was solved on schedule time, wasn't it," he smiled; "though not quite in the way I had anticipated. Do you know, Lester," he added, "I am going to claim that cabinet."

"On what grounds?" I demanded.

"Because the man who owned it gave it to me," and he got a paper out of his pocket-book and handed it across to me.

I opened it and recognised the delicate and feminine writing which I had seen once before.

"My dear sir [the letter ran] :

"I find that I made the mistake of underestimating you, and I present you my sincere apologies. I trust that, at some future time, it may be my privilege to be again engaged with you—the result is certain to be most interesting. But at present I find that I must return to Europe on the *Paris,* since, after the trouble I have taken, it is impossible that I should consent to part with the brilliants of His Highness the Grand Duke. As a slight souvenir of my high regard, I trust you will be willing to accept the cabinet Boule, which I am certain that good

M. Lester will surrender to you if you will show to him this letter. The cabinet is not only interesting in itself, but will be doubly so to you because of the part it has played in our little comedy. And I should like to know that it adorns a corner of your home.

"Till we meet again, dear sir, believe me

"Your sincere admirer,

"CROCHARD, L'Invincible!"

"He's a good sport, isn't he?" asked Godfrey, as I silently handed the letter back to him. "What do you say about the cabinet?"

"I suppose there is no doubt that Crochard bought it," I said.

"So that it is mine now?"

"Yes; but I'm going to solicit a bribe."

"Go ahead and solicit it."

"I want a souvenir, too," I said. "I'd like awfully well to have that letter—besides," I added, "it will be a kind of receipt, you know, if anybody ever questions my giving you the cabinet."

Godfrey laughed and threw the letter across the table to me.

"It's yours," he said. "And I'll send for the cabinet to-morrow. I suppose it is still at the station?"

"Yes; I haven't had time to put in a claim for it. But, Godfrey," I added, "when did the *Paris* sail?"

"Last Saturday. She is due at Havre in the morning."

"Did you warn them?"

"Warn them of what?"

"That Crochard is after the diamonds. They went back on the *Paris*, I suppose?"

"Yes—and Pigot went with them. So why should I warn any one? Surely they know that Crochard will get those diamonds if he can. It has become a sort of point of honour with him, I imagine. It is up to them to take care of them."

"That oughtn't to be difficult," I said. "The strong-room of a liner is about the safest place on earth."

"Yes," Godfrey agreed, and blew a meditative ring toward the ceiling.

And presently he went away without saying anything more.

But the more I thought of it, the more the inflection he had given that word seemed an interrogation rather than an affirmation.

And when I opened my paper next morning, I more than half expected to be greeted with a black headline announcing the looting of the strong-room of the *Paris*. But there was no such headline, and with a sigh, half of relief and half of disappointment, I turned to the other news.

But two days later, a black headline *did* catch my eye:

MICHAELOVITCH JEWELS FALSE!

FRENCH DETECTIVE TAKES BACK CLEVER IMITATIONS FROM AMERICA.

Fraud Discovered When the Police Restore Them to Their Owner.

I had no need to read the article which followed, for I saw in a flash what had occurred. I saw, too, why Crochard had retained the paste jewels—he had a use for them! How or where the substitution had been made, I could only guess; but one thing was certain: the two days which had elapsed before the theft was discovered had given him ample opportunity to get away with his plunder. I felt sorry for the Grand Duke; sorrier still for that admirable Monsieur Pigot; but after all, one could not but admire the cleverness of the man who had despoiled them.

Who, I wondered, had bought the Mazarin? Surely there was a diamond most difficult to sell.

It could, of course, be cut up—but that would be sacrilege.

That question was answered, before long, in an unexpected way—a way which filled many columns in the papers, which delighted the comedy-loving French, and which gave Crochard a unique advertisement. One morning, in the personal column of *Le Matin,* appeared a notice of which this is the English;

"To M. the Director of the Museum of the Louvre:

"It has been my good fortune to come into possession of the rose-diamond known as the Mazarin. It is my wish to restore it to your collection, in order that it may no longer be necessary to delude the public with an imitation of coloured glass. It will give me great pleasure to present this brilliant to you, with my compliments, provided His Highness, the Grand Duke, who preceded me in possession of the diamond, will join me in the gift. Should he refuse, it will be my melancholy duty to cleave the diamond into a number of smaller stones, as it is too large for my use. But I hope that he will not refuse.

"CROCHARD, L'Invincible!"

What could the Grand Duke do? To have

refused would have made him the butt of the boulevards. Besides, he was, after all, losing nothing which he had not already lost. So with a better grace than one might have expected, he consented to join in the restoration. Two days later, the director of the Louvre discovered a packet upon his desk. He opened it and found within the Mazarin. When you visit the Louvre, you will see it in the place of honour in the glass case in the centre of the Gallery of Apollo, with an attendant on guard beside it. But already the circumstances of its restoration are fading from the public memory.

And Crochard? I do not know. Each morning, I read first the news from Paris, searching for L'Invincible in some new incarnation. I have his letter framed and hanging above my desk, and every day I read it over. One sentence especially is forever running in my head:

"I trust that, at some future time, it may be my privilege to be again engaged with you—the result is certain to be most interesting."

And I trust that it may be my privilege, also, to be present at that engagement!

www.ingramcontent.com/pod-product-compliance
Lightning Source LLC
Chambersburg PA
CBHW032226010726
47494CB00002B/367